SOMETHING
DEEP
IN MY BONES

SOMETHING DEEP IN MY BONES

Eboni Snoe

sepia

BET☆ BOOKS

BET Publications, LLC
www.bet.com

SEPIA BOOKS are published by

BET Publications, LLC
c/o BET BOOKS
One BET Plaza
1900 W Place NE
Washington, DC 20018-1211

All Kensington Titles, Imprints, and Distributed Lines are available at special quantity discounts for bulk purchases for sales promotions, premiums, fund-raising, and educational or institutional use. Special book excerpts or customized printings can also be created to fit specific needs. For details, write or phone the office of the Kensington Special Sales Manager: Attn. Special Sales Department, Kensington Publishing Corp., 850 Third Avenue, New York, NY 10022, Phone: 1-800-221-2647.

Library of Congress Card Catalogue Number: 2005904513
ISBN: 1-58314-342-4

First Printing: October 2005
10   9   8   7   6   5   4   3   2   1

Printed in the United States of America

With love, to little Brandon,
because you are who you are.

Acknowledgments

Na'imah, during these trying times I could have never completed this book without you. Thank you for your dedication to my cause. Love and happiness always, all ways.

Unexpected

1973

Idella Baxter looked at the clock again. *This makes no sense, no sense at all. When she gets here today I'm going to give her a piece of my—*

The painted metal door opened. Sadie talked as she sashayed in beneath the ADDISON RESTAURANT AND CATERING sign. "I went to the club last night and I met this fine, fine man." She stopped in the middle of the floor. "Turns out"—Sadie's eyes closed slowly—"he was the lo-ove master. Heaven couldn't be that good."

"You need to quit," one worker replied.

"What club wuz-it?" another woman said. "Tonight I'm gonna go there and stand in the exact same spot and see what happens to me."

Laughter erupted all around but Idella didn't find it funny.

"Since Sadie will probably never get to heaven"—she sealed a large tray of deviled eggs with plastic wrap—"I guess she'll never know if that's true or not."

Sadie cut her eyes. "You just jeal—"

"Is this how young folks in Memphis say hello these days?" Helen pushed a sprig of solid gray hair beneath her hair net.

"Hey, Miss Helen." Sadie broke into a too ready smile. "How you doin'? I'm not gonna ask Idella. She's obviously in a bad mood."

"I'm in a bad mood because you're late as usual." Idella glared. "I got permission to leave early today. But because you're an hour late, I've been working like a Hebrew slave to make sure the Breckinridge order will be ready for tonight."

Sadie slowly tied her apron. "You don't look hurt none to me."

Idella put her hand on her hip. "That's not the point, Sadie. We get paid to do a job here. Now, since we both are responsible for this order, if you want to give me your hourly wage for the work I did for you, that'll be fine with me."

"I ain't givin' you nothin'," Sadie said.

"Well, you better start getting here on time or I'm going to report you to Mr. Addison."

Sadie's face hardened. "You would, wouldn't ya?" She turned her head. "Just 'cuz you look like 'em don't mean you have to act like 'em."

"Say what?"

"You heard me." Sadie leaned toward her. "Just 'cuz you're near white don't mean nothin' to me."

Idella just looked at her. "You know what? I'm not taking this from you today." She slammed the refrigerator door. "And before I prove just how black I am, I'm going to leave." She took the plastic bag with her dress in it from the closet.

"I'm not scared of you," Sadie retorted.

"Sadie, why don't you leave Idella alone," Helen said. "I get tired of you messin' with her about how she looks, so I know she's got to."

"Well, you need to tell her to stop gettin' on my nerves. She thinks—"

Idella closed the bathroom door so she wouldn't hear the rest of it.

Later, on her way home from the Urban League, Idella thought about what Sadie had said. She'd had similar conversations throughout her life, and by now Idella was more than tired of the subject. Is she black? Is she white?

My God—Idella turned down East Parkway—*if you must know, I am black. But then that's according to who you talk to. If you talk to folks who know my grandmother, MaMary, then they definitely agree. If you talk to white people who find out that MaMary is my grandmother, then they agree. But if you're talking to some black folks who simply look at my skin color, my hair and even my eyes, they'll tell you and me in a minute, "She ain't black. I don't know what she is, but she ain't black."* She rolled her eyes. *If I had a nickel for every time I had to run the subject of what race I belong to through my mind, at twenty-three years old, I'd be a rich woman today.* She looked down in the plastic bag at the neatly folded Addison Restaurant and Catering uniform she carried. *But right now, me and MaMary are so far in the hole we are about as poor as you can get.*

Idella thought of her grandmother. She shook her head and smiled. That's not how MaMary saw it. MaMary saw things differently from most people. She insisted they were rich in a way many people never could be. MaMary said their wealth was in the love they shared. Deep in her heart Idella felt it was true.

Idella took in the dogwood trees that were in full bloom. They lined both sides of East Parkway and decorated the crystal blue sky with puffy branches of white. The view was a stark contrast to the previous street. Idella couldn't help but admire the flowers and carefully edged lawns that enhanced the expensive houses. *If you can call these houses,* she thought. *My God, I wonder how many people could live in one of these places. MaMary and I make out fine in the shotgun house we live in. When I think about it, these houses look more like hotels than homes. And the funny thing is you never see anyone going in and out of them.* She checked to make sure she was right. *I've never seen one person go in or come out. Not one. Maybe they wait until ordinary folks like me aren't looking. Maybe the splendor of such a human being would burn my ordinary eyes.* She laughed to herself, but stopped when a car door slammed close by.

Idella walked a few more yards past a barrier of tall manicured hedges. She was shocked to see a young black woman about her age, walking from a side driveway toward the front of a huge house.

The woman was dressed impeccably, with shoes that totally matched a pantsuit of an unusual green, and her hair looked as if she had just come from a downtown beauty shop. Her purse hung on her arm as she proceeded up the driveway and then cut across the rich, green grass. Idella stared.

She didn't see Idella and that was fine with her. It gave her an opportunity to study her further. Magnetized, Idella admired how she held her head high as if she knew she was somebody. As if she knew where she was going and what the world thought of her. Idella thought she had never seen anyone her age so. . . .

Suddenly, the woman dropped to the grass as if an unseen force from the sky knocked her down. Her body began to quiver. Then it trembled and quaked as her head thrashed about violently.

Idella was stunned, but that only lasted a moment. MaMary had experienced seizures so Idella knew what to do. She ran toward her. On her way across the lawn, she picked up a sturdy stick to keep the woman from swallowing her tongue.

Oblivious to her new dress, which had taken two months to get out of the layaway, Idella dropped to her knees beside her.

"Hold on," Idella said. "Hold on. I'm going to help you."

She threw the plastic bag with her uniform in it to the side and removed the loose bark from the stick. "Here, I gotta put this in your mouth." It took some effort to hold the woman still enough to place the wood between her clenched teeth, but Idella managed to do it. Out of breath, she looked down at the woman, then up at the house. Idella didn't want to knock on the fancy door and tell the white people inside that there was a black woman on their lawn who needed help. But when Idella looked at the unconscious woman again, she felt she had no choice. She patted her shoulder. "I'm going to get you some help. I'm going to go right up to that house and get you some help."

Idella ran to the door. At first, her knock was hesitant. But when she looked at the woman, who continued to spasm, her knock grew stronger. Then she saw the doorbell and Idella pushed it, hard. Moments later, a maid opened the door.

"I'm sorry, ma'am. I'm so sorry," Idella apologized. "I don't want to cause any trouble for anybody, but there's a woman out here who's having a seizure." Idella pointed. "I didn't know what else to do. Do you think someone here could help her?"

The maid looked at Idella, opened the glass door and stuck her head out. "Oh sweet Jesus, it's Miss Patricia! It's Miss Patricia!" She flung the heavy inner door open. "Miss Rachel! Miss Rachel!"

Through the glass, Idella watched her run up a curved staircase.

"Miss Rachel!" the maid yelled.

"What is it?" Idella heard a faint, cultured reply.

"It's Miss Patricia. She's having one of those seizures out on the front yard."

"Oh no!" A beautiful woman in a cloud of peach material hurried down the stairs. "Don't just stand there, Ruth, go get Sam. Go get him," she ordered the maid as she ran toward the front door.

Idella stepped back as the woman rushed past her, ran across the grass and knelt beside Patricia. "Oh, my baby! Goodness. My Goodness. You're going to be all right, Sweetness. You're going to be all right."

Idella couldn't believe her eyes. She couldn't believe it. A black family lived in this house; a black family with a black maid. She watched Rachel soothe and pat the younger woman's hair as the tremors subsided.

"You're going to be all right." Rachel repeated before she looked up and down the street apprehensively. "Sam, what took you so long?" she demanded as a large black man in overalls came running from the back of the house.

"I was in the back doing some work, Miss Rachel."

"Well, I need you to get Patricia up off this lawn. She doesn't need to be laying out here for everybody to see. Pick her up, Sam, and get her in the house."

"Yes, ma'am. Yes, ma'am." He scooped Patricia up as if she were nothing. Idella watched as Rachel reached the house first. She opened the door so he could carry Patricia inside. Rachel was about to close the door when she noticed Idella for the first time.

"Who are you?"

"Miss Rachel," Ruth said from somewhere inside, "she was the one who told me Patricia was out there."

"Thank you." Rachel softly touched Idella's arm. "Thank you so much." Her gaze swept Idella's face. "You must come in. Please come in and close the door."

Request

Idella stepped inside. Immediately, her feet sank into a thick, tan carpet. It blanketed the entire area, then disappeared into rooms off both sides of the foyer and up the staircase. She didn't know what to say or do, but her hazel eyes had a life of their own. They widened as she looked at the expensive statues, paintings and furniture.

"Ruth," Rachel called as she mounted the stairs, "get this young lady whatever light drink she wants. And put her in the sitting room. I must see after Patricia."

"Yes, ma'am. I will take good care of her," Ruth replied.

"Sam did take Patricia to her room, didn't he? I'm just so upset." Her hand went delicately to her forehead. "I should have instructed him to do so. I know he took her to her room, didn't he?"

"Of course, Miss Rachel," the maid said. "He wouldn't take her anywhere else. He's probably placed her on the bed right now."

"I don't know what else could happen to us in one day." Rachel sounded distressed as she reached the top of the stairs. "I don't know if I could take anything else today, not one more thing."

Idella watched Rachel disappear down the hallway above her.

Ruth watched as well. "Well, you heard what Miss Rachel said."

She tugged at her maid's apron. "So you can come with me to the sitting room."

"Yes, ma'am," Idella replied, acutely aware of everything, including her new dress that now had a grass stain on it. Idella covered the stain with her plastic bag.

She followed Ruth, who walked with an air of confidence. She watched the maid carefully slide open a pair of doors decorated with rectangular panes of frosted glass.

"And, here we are," Ruth announced. "You can have a seat wherever you wish."

Idella picked the chair that was closest to her. It faced a large window that looked out onto the street.

"So, what would you like? Ice tea? Lemonade?"

But Idella didn't hear the question. Her eyes remained focused on the window. She could see East Parkway clearly. Idella thought of the times she had walked down the street wondering what went on in these houses. Now here she sat in one them, having a glimpse of the world that always seemed so far away. "A sitting room," she said, unconsciously.

"Yes, Miss, this is a sitting room," Ruth said. "Have you never been in a sitting room before?"

Idella looked at her. She shook her head. "No, ma'am, I haven't."

Ruth's face relaxed. "Well, before I came to work here, neither had I."

They smiled and Idella felt comfortable enough to share what she was thinking.

"It's just that I always wondered who lived on this street." She sat forward. "Why, I know I've walked past here and wondered who lived in this very house. I never imagined that the people who did, that they were . . ." She looked down.

"That they were black like you and me?"

"Yes." Idella looked at the maid.

"Well, they are, honey. And believe you me, there are many more like them here in Memphis. And as I've come to know, they are everywhere in this country. But it's a closed group, you know. You either have to be born into it or invited in."

"Really?" Idella's eyes widened again.

Ruth laughed. "Don't take me so seriously, even though I am telling the truth." She cleared her throat. "But it's not for me to be telling you about it. My job is to offer you some ice tea or lemonade."

"I'll have some ice tea," Idella said

"All right then. I'll be right back." Ruth walked out of the room.

Idella looked around. She touched the soft, burgundy material of the chair in which she sat.

"How's she doing, Sam?" she heard Ruth ask from somewhere nearby.

"She's doing okay. Coming around. But it's Miss Rachel that I'm more worried about."

Ruth's voice lowered. "That woman's your boss and another man's wife. She don't need you to worry about her. I've seen how you've been looking at her lately."

"And I don't need you to tell me what to do. I'm a grown man."

"Well, you better act like it," Ruth said. "Act like it and think like it. You're just a gardener here. And if you ever start thinking you could be more, you're going to get in trouble. I recommended you for this position because you're my cousin and I care about ya."

There was a pause.

"Does she have these often?" Sam asked.

"No. They started late in her teens from what I've overheard Miss Rachel say. The doctor first called it adolescent epilepsy. But here Miss Patricia is twenty-four years old, so I don't know about that. But this one has Miss Rachel totally upset because she ended up falling out in the front yard."

"What do you mean?"

"She's upset 'cause Miss Patricia fell out on the front lawn where anybody and everybody could see her. You know how concerned with appearances they are around here. And I can understand that. How's it gon' look to the neighbors? How's it gon' look to their friends, that Miss Patricia's got epilepsy?"

"It's a disease," Sam said. "Even I know that. So what can they do 'bout that? Folks should take it for what it is."

"Now you've worked here long enough to know that Miss Agnes

is intent on getting Miss Patricia married, and having her married with the label of an epileptic would not do at all."

"Did you get the young lady something to drink?" Rachel's voice floated in.

"I'm on my way right now, ma'am. I'm gon' get her some ice tea."

"I plan to join her, so make that two," Rachel instructed as she appeared outside the sliding glass doors. "Here you are." Rachel came in and took Idella's hand out of her lap. "I just can't thank you enough for saving Patricia. I don't know what would have happened if she had remained out there all alone and you hadn't come and told us. I can't thank you enough," Rachel repeated.

"It's no problem, ma'am. I was glad to do it," Idella said.

"Here, come let's both sit on the settee. You will be too far away in that chair. I want to know who you are." Rachel descended onto the small couch. Idella sat beside her. "What's your name?"

"Idella Baxter."

"Idella Baxter." Rachel smiled and her eyes beamed sincerity. "Do you live around here?"

"In a way I do. I live several blocks from here. I was on my way home when I saw"—she hesitated—"your daughter."

"I see." Rachel continued her line of questioning. "Are you married?"

"No, ma'am, I'm not married. I live with my grandmother, MaMary. She was sick not too long ago. I was worried about her, but she's doing much better now." Idella looked down. She felt perhaps she'd said too much.

Ruth brought the ice teas and placed them on a table, then slipped out without saying a word.

"That's quite a responsibility to be looking after your grandmother. I know how it is when you have a family member that's getting older. I can really sympathize with you."

"Thank you, ma'am," Idella replied, looking into Rachel's light brown eyes.

"Do you look like your grandmother?" Rachel asked. "You're such a pretty girl."

Idella looked down. "No, ma'am. MaMary and I don't favor at all. I hear that I take after my mother's side of the family."

"You hear?" Rachel looked surprised.

"Yes, ma'am. I've never met my mother." She paused. "It's a long story."

"Well, you don't have to tell me about it if you don't want to. The past is the past and there's nothing we can do about it. Isn't that right?"

"That's what MaMary says. She says we've got to look forward to the future and the best way to do that is by working hard in the present."

"And where do you work?" Rachel asked.

"I work for Addison Restaurant and Catering. It's one of the largest, if not the largest, black catering companies here in Memphis."

Rachel threw back her head and laughed. "Oh really? I know all about Addison Restaurant and Catering. My husband owns it. My name is Rachel Addison."

"My goodness." Idella looked around the room again and then at Rachel.

"This is some coincidence," Rachel said.

"Very much so," Idella replied, more nervous than ever.

"And I pay attention to those kinds of things. I really do," Rachel said. "Because all the while I was up there with Patricia, I was thinking about how in the world can I help the young woman who saved my girl. How would I be able to help you?" she said charmingly. "And here you are already employed by my husband. And I know how much you girls make because for a while I did the books for the company here at home. Now Patricia has taken over that job. So I am more impressed with you, Idella, than ever; impressed that you are taking care of your grandmother on such an income. You must be a very special young lady."

"I don't think so." Idella shrugged. "I love my grandmother and she loves me. So we take care of one another."

"That is so refreshing to hear." Rachel patted Idella's hand. "I've got an idea. We are considering a companion for my mother. She has been ill recently as well, even though she will not admit it. And

I've been concerned about her." Her fair-skinned brow creased. "I want her to have someone who could just be with her during the day, make sure she's not alone when she's doing the things she does around the house. It really wouldn't be a difficult job, and somebody like an older woman would be perfect. Now, just from talking to you, and the kind of woman you've grown to be, I believe your MaMary would fit that description. Do you think she would be interested in the position?"

Idella paused. "I don't know. But I don't see why not."

"I don't see why not either," Rachel replied. "I think it would be the perfect setup. That way you and Patricia could get to know each other a little better as well. And frankly, I'd like to see more of you myself. It's quite obvious you love your grandmother, and I feel it's very special that you're not afraid to express it." Rachel smiled again. "A girl like you, well, I would like to do whatever I can to help her. And believe me, the Addisons have quite a bit of pull in this community."

"Miss Rachel, I don't doubt that at all," Idella replied.

Possibilities

*T*his is my boss's family. Idella's case of nerves increased. "Are you certain you want MaMary to come work here, in the house?" Something inside made Idella question such a move. It sounded like a grand opportunity, and it wasn't that she didn't think well of Mr. Addison. From her viewpoint, he was a high-class man and whenever she interacted with him, which wasn't often, he treated her well. But Idella had to admit she had heard things, rumors about him: rumors about drinking, gambling and women. Idella had decided it was pure gossip. She ignored the rumors. The truth was it was a matter of survival. Addison Restaurant and Catering kept food on the table and allowed her to buy the medicines MaMary needed. Not that at seventy-two years old she needed that much. In general, MaMary was healthy . . . at least her body was, though her memory was not the best.

Idella looked away from Rachel's probing eyes. MaMary said a blow on the head she received during the fire that changed everything was the cause of her poor memory. Many times MaMary shared with Idella how she grabbed her up off the pallet right before a burning piece of wood came down in that very spot. It hit MaMary instead. MaMary said it was all she could do to get out of that house full of smoke. Her inner guidance led her to the door and out into the yard, where she collapsed with Idella pressed to her chest. Although MaMary said she was able to save Idella's life, her son, Idella's father, who had been drinking, didn't respond to her cries and burned to death in that fire.

Idella looked at Rachel. "It's not that I wouldn't like MaMary to work. If something was to happen . . . I mean if she wasn't able to do what was expected of her, I wouldn't want it to affect my job. You see, it's the only income we have."

"Why wouldn't she be able to do the work? She'll simply be a companion for my mother. It won't be difficult, Idella. And I do want to do something for you." She touched Idella's hand. "The more I think about it, the more perfect it sounds. Look at it this way. We both have needs. We need someone to be with my mother, Agnes. And you and MaMary could use the financial help."

Three strong knocks sounded from somewhere upstairs. "What in the world may I ask is going on around here?" a strong, elderly female voice demanded.

Rachel rose from the settee and made Idella stand with her. "Now you go home, and you talk to MaMary about this." She lowered her voice. "And come back tomorrow and let me know what she thinks about it. In fact, bring MaMary if you can. Will you do that, Idella?" Rachel led her toward the front door.

Idella looked into her kind eyes. "Yes, ma'am, I will. I will."

Rachel opened the door to let Idella out.

"What is going on around here, I said?" The voice was much closer.

"Goodbye, Idella." Rachel dismissed her.

"Goodbye, Miss Rachel," Idella replied as she glanced at the top of the staircase.

A thin, extremely fair-skinned woman was slowly heading down the stairs, with a grayish-white braid that tumbled over her shoulder and lay against her breast. Her dusty rose dress fit tightly down to her waist then opened into a wide belled skirt. She walked with a cane and Idella knew she had sounded the commanding knocks a few moments earlier. Idella felt she was looking at an old photograph, before Rachel closed the door.

"Who was that young woman?" Agnes demanded. "And why hasn't anyone told me what's going on around here?"

Rachel walked over to the staircase as her mother reached the bottom. "Her name is Idella, Mother, and we're thinking about hiring her grandmother to be a companion for you over the next month or so." Rachel's voice turned childlike. "You know you haven't been feeling that well."

"I am fine," Agnes replied. "I don't need a companion, a watch-dog or anything else. I told you that before."

"I know"—Rachel folded her hands—"but it's our job to look out for you, Mother. And at this point Roger and I think—"

"That husband of yours thinks?" Agnes walked away.

Rachel fell in behind her. "We believe a companion would be in your best interest and in the interest of the household. She could always do other things as well, Mother. You needn't worry. She wouldn't be underfoot all the time."

"And where did the girl come from?" Agnes asked. "She looks somewhat familiar. Is she a friend of Patricia's? Although, I believe I know all of them."

"No, ma'am, she's not. Actually she works for Addison Catering."

"Addison Catering?" Agnes clicked her tongue. "With looks like that, if she had the right family, she could go far. But I would assume being a waitress for us implies that her bloodline is not of the right type. If Patricia looked like her"—Agnes's eyes narrowed as she stared out the window—"there'd be no stopping us. But life dealt her the hand it has, and she's going to make the best of it."

Rachel crossed her arms as if to protect herself from the uncomfortable subject.

"How were we to know that Roger's family had such black sheep in it? And I do mean black. There's no other way Patricia's skin would be so brown if it hadn't been for his ancestors. It surely didn't come from my side of the family." She looked at Rachel. "But all that is spilt milk. And there's nothing we can do but wipe it up."

Rachel changed the subject. "I've asked Idella to ask her grand-mother if she would work here for a couple of months or so. And see how things work out, of course. And then we can make a decision from there."

"Her grandmother." Agnes showed dissatisfaction. "So all this hoopla is around a possible companion for me?"

"No, Mother." Rachel took a deep breath. "We had quite an incident."

"An 'incident'? Whenever you use that word, Rachel, it means so many things. Can you be a little clearer, please?"

"Well." Rachel paused. "Patricia had another one of her seizures. This time it happened in the front yard."

Agnes turned and looked at her daughter for the first time. "Patricia had a seizure on the front lawn?"

"Yes, Mother, she did. But we got her inside very quickly. It was Idella who found her, and helped her. She let us know poor Pat was on the—"

"Out in the yard!" Agnes nearly bellowed. "My granddaughter laying on the lawn for all the world to see having what you call a seizure. And of course they are not seizures. I have told you that once before. I don't care what that young doctor says. He is too young to be practicing medicine anyway. Epilepsy. There is no epilepsy in this family. None of my descendants have epilepsy. Something else is wrong with Patricia. I don't know what it is, but we will find out when we have a doctor who is qualified to diagnose it correctly. So at this point I don't want you or anyone else in this house to use that word, 'seizure,' again. Patricia does not have seizures." She shook her head. "What man would want to marry a girl who's an epileptic?" Agnes struck the bottom of her cane against the carpet. Then she stopped and pressed two fingers against her closed eyelids. "And how is she doing now?"

"She's resting in her room. A little upset to say the least. But I think she'll be fine. I've called Dr. Simpson to come and see her."

"After this I don't want that doctor in this house again." Agnes glared at Rachel. "You find somebody else, somebody who can give me a real diagnosis for my granddaughter, and you get him in and out of here before Gerald comes. He's coming here to see Patricia this evening—he and his grandmother. It would be a total disaster if he even got a whiff that Patricia was an epileptic." Her hand sliced the air. "Even that stupid doctor says that whatever she has can go away at any time. So I pray it goes away today. It has taken me quite a while to set this meeting up between Patricia and Gerald, and I won't have anything messing it up." Agnes squinted with determination. "Gerald is the right man for my Patricia. He's the right man for our girl." She looked at Rachel with pride. "A marriage between Patricia and a Campbell will be a match made in heaven."

The Decision

After her experience on East Parkway, Idella was more aware than usual of the shotgun houses on her street. She noticed how close they sat together and the front yards without grass that sported hard-packed dirt. But still, some of the older residents, like MaMary, did what they could to bring beauty to the street. They used ceramic or plastic planters shaped like animals, trees with the bottom of the trunk painted white, and rubber tires painted and cut like strange hybrid tulips.

"Boy, get back up here in this yard. He-ey, Idella. How you doing, girl?"

"I'm fine, Savannah." She looked at her neighbor, who sat on the stoop. "How you doing?"

"I'm good. Just having to deal with these children. I tell you they know they can wear me out, but I love 'em." Savannah's smile filled her pie-shaped face before her eyes took on a special gleam. "Late last night, you didn't happen to see Ricky's car parked out here, did ya?"

"No, I didn't."

"He claimed he came by and knocked, but I didn't open the

door. I knew he was lyin'." Savannah pursed her lips. "You lookin' mighty good today. Did you go to work? Where's your uniform?"

"I got off early." Idella stopped outside her gate. "I had an appointment at the Urban League. I plan to go to a job fair they're going to have. I can't see myself working for Addison Catering all my life."

"Well, you go, girl. I'm proud of you." Savannah crossed her legs. "But I just can't do it. I got too many babies. Here we are the same age and I got three babies and you don't have one. So there's no way I can work. By the time I pay someone to take care of them"—she took a dirty candy wrapper out of her baby's mouth—"I won't have no money left." Savannah popped her gum several times. "So I don't have a choice. I'm better off with the money I get from welfare and the food stamps they send me than I would be working for someone's minimum wage job."

"You got to do what you think is best, Savannah," Idella replied. "But you know MaMary don't believe in handouts, and that's what she says welfare is. Hey, and what can I say? She cleaned houses until I got out of high school and her motto is everyone should work."

"I know. And you can believe she wears me out every chance she gets. Constantly, MaMary reminds me how she promised my mama she'd do everything she could to make sure I did something with my life." Savannah looked frustrated. "She keeps harping on me about getting my G.E.D. and doing better for myself because she says I'm smart." A light entered Savannah's eyes. "She told Mama that before she died."

"And she's told me that many times. She said you could do a lot if you put your mind to it." Idella watched Savannah wipe her baby's palm with her own. "MaMary's from the old school and she's got a long memory. We moved here next to your mother a year before you were born and I was just a teenie baby. MaMary says Miss Barnes, who used to own both of these houses, still lived up the street then."

"I gue-ess." Savannah tightened a rubber band on her daughter's hair before she lit a cigarette.

Idella's front door opened. MaMary stepped outside.

"Hi, MaMary," Idella said.

"Hey, baby. I was getting worried 'bout cha."

"Hello, MaMary," Savannah called.

"How ya doin', Savannah?" MaMary replied.

"You shouldn't have been worried." Idella reached the front door. She kissed her grandmother's cheek before she went inside.

"Maybe." MaMary closed the door behind them. "But I expected you about a half hour ago. How did you do at the Urban League?"

"Good, I guess. I learned how to make the best of the job fair when they have it." Idella put her uniform on the couch.

"That sounds promisin'," MaMary said. "A door won't open unless you knock. That's for certain." She nodded. "Are you hungry? I kept the food warm for you."

"I'm starving," Idella replied. "But let me take off my dress before I get something else on it."

"You go right ahead. I'ma be in the kitchen."

Idella walked down the hall and quickly changed into a top and a pair of jeans. "Did you eat already, MaMary?"

"Naw, baby. I was waiting on you. You know I hate to eat alone."

Idella entered the kitchen. A plate of broiled chicken, steaming hot mashed potatoes and peas waited on the table. "Something exciting did happen on the way home."

"I knew you were later than what you should'a been." MaMary sat down across from Idella.

"Well, you were right." Idella smiled. "You know those big, fancy houses on East Parkway?"

"I sure do," MaMary said.

"I was walking pass one of them this afternoon, and this well-dressed black woman about my age just dropped to the ground right in front of me. She was having a seizure."

"Lord have mercy," MaMary said. Then she added, "Poor thing. I know how that can be. It's like a thousand bolts of electricity is going through your veins and you can't stop it, no matter how you try. It's one of the most helpless feelings in the world."

"You've told me that before." Idella looked into MaMary's bluing eyes. "That's why I went right over to her and did what I've done for you. I put something in her mouth to keep her from swallowing her tongue."

"Did ya?"

Idella nodded. "Then I ran to the door to get some help. But, MaMary, the truth is, at first I was afraid because it was a black woman that was having the seizure. I didn't know what the folks inside that house would do. If they would help her or not. Now this is what you won't believe." Idella leaned toward MaMary over her plate. "A maid answered the door and went and got one of the owners. She was black."

"Shut your mouth," MaMary said. "You mean black folks live in those houses?"

"Yes, ma'am." Idella paused for emphasis. "I couldn't believe it. I just couldn't believe my eyes. The woman who was having the seizure lived there."

MaMary shook her head. "I never would have thought it."

Idella nodded. "And as a result of me helping her, her mother invited me inside." Idella covered her mouth. "MaMary, it is one of the most beautiful places you've ever seen. It was just like looking at something you'd see on TV."

"Ain't that something," MaMary said. "Black folks sure have come a long way in this world, haven't they? Such a long way." She looked into Idella's eyes. "And one day you'll live like that. You've got the brains to do it and you've got the will."

"MaMary." Idella wasn't convinced.

"I can see it now," MaMary insisted. "One day you'll get us a fine house, I just know it. And we won't be renting this rundown shotgun no more. There's nothing like owning your own house, Idella. Even if you don't have the money to fix it up, it stills feels good." MaMary's eyes gleamed with the memory of the house she had owned outside of Clarksville, Tennessee.

"I'm going to make that happen one day, MaMary, because it's your dream."

"Ahhhh, child, you just go on ahead. I run my mouth too much. I've stuck myself right in the middle of your young life."

"Where else would you be?" Idella asked.

"You love your MaMary, but you don't know what life's going to bring you. One day I hope you'll have a husband and your own family. You won't have no place for MaMary then."

"That'll never happen. Wherever I go, you'll go. You've taken care of me all these years and I'm going to take care of you in your old days. It's my duty, MaMary. I feel it really is my duty," Idella insisted. "But I don't know if we'll ever own a house like this, MaMary." Idella's fork went up in the air when she raised her arms. "It was unbelievable. Unbelievable. There was a gardener and everything. And everybody was black. The gardener ran up the stairs carrying Patricia—that's the woman's name—like she was nothing but a feather. Afterwards, Miss Rachel, the lady of the house, had me wait for her in the sitting room while the maid served me ice tea."

MaMary chuckled. "My goodness."

"After that, Miss Rachel, Patricia's mother, who told the maid to give me the ice tea"—MaMary nodded she understood—"came floating down the stairs like Diahann Carroll. She asked me to sit next to her, and she talked to me, and I told her about you."

MaMary smiled.

"Yes, Miss Rachel seemed to be really interested in me, MaMary. She said she wanted to thank me for saving Patricia, and that's what she said, 'saving her girl.' "

"Saving her?" MaMary said.

"Yes. I think it was her way of expressing how much it meant to her. I could see it in her eyes." Idella took a breath. "She asked me quite a few questions about myself. And then, I tell you it was so strange."

"What?"

Idella leaned in. "Miss Rachel is Roger Addison's wife. That was my boss's wife I was sitting with and his daughter that I helped."

"My word." MaMary smacked the table with her palm. "That couldn't be nothing but fate."

"That's exactly what I thought," Idella agreed. "I thought all of it was just one big gift from God." She rushed on. "So when Miss Rachel said her mother had been sick recently and they were looking for a companion for her, she felt you would be perfect for the position."

"Me?" MaMary was taken aback. "Why would she think that? She's never met me."

Idella thought for a moment. "I believe it was how I talked to her. It seems Miss Rachel feels you did a good job in raising me. I think she put two and two together and decided you'd be a good companion for her mother."

"Maybe so." MaMary's gray, kinky hairline lowered as her dark brow creased. It was obvious she didn't know what to think about this.

"I hesitated when she first suggested it just like you're doing now," Idella said. "But then Miss Rachel told me to ask you how you felt. She said, go home and talk to your grandmother. And she promised it would be easy work, nothing heavy." She looked deeply into MaMary's eyes. "Because neither one of us want you to be cleaning house again. Then it hit me just like it hit you a few minutes ago." Idella smiled. "That it had to be fate. I helped Patricia, who ends up being Mr. Addison's daughter. And now his wife wants you to come and be a companion for his mother-in-law."

"It sure seems that way." MaMary began to eat again, then added as if she were talking to herself, "And we could catch up with our bills much quicker."

"I told Miss Rachel," Idella continued slowly, "that I'd let her know tomorrow if you were interested. She invited both of us to the house. She feels it is important that Patricia and I officially meet, and perhaps you should meet Miss Rachel's mother. That is, if you want to."

"Well, you know I've never been one to shirk from work." MaMary's brow softened. "And it could be a good thing. It would get me out of the house and we'd meet some new people."

"You can say that again." Idella's eyebrows rose. "The kind of folks I've never dealt with before."

"Yes, you could get to know those kind of people better." MaMary nibbled her thumbnail.

"Miss Rachel said she'd do what she could to help me in the community," Idella recalled.

MaMary looked at Idella. "It can't do you but good to get to know a girl like Patricia Addison. Can't do you nothing but good."

She sat up straighter. "So I guess there will be two of us working for the Addisons."

Idella put a forkful of mashed potatoes in her mouth. "It's kind of exciting, isn't it? And Savannah's going to get a kick out of this. Now, she'll be hiding from you when we come home. She says you make her feel guilty for not working."

"That child." MaMary shook her head. "I do tell her she needs to go to work. I know that's what her mama would say. She sits over there smoking them cigarettes, drinking that beer and waiting on Ricky to come over or call." She shook her head again. "She's always worried about where he's been and who he's seeing. That's her job."

"She asked me about him today."

MaMary licked her lips. "But I can't say she doesn't take care of those children because she does."

"She does. And she's got a point about getting money from welfare."

"Of course, she's got a point," MaMary replied. "She's got three babies and it truly would cost an arm and a leg to try and put them all in childcare. But Savannah's still young and she has an opportunity to look forward to the future, and that means some planning. Sometimes you gotta make some sacrifices. She'll never get out of the government's pocket if she doesn't make a change. That's all I'm saying. Long time ago, black folks didn't depend on no government. We got out there and we made our way. We had our skills and our farms. We made our own business and took care of ourselves. All this integration has done is made us dependent, that's what I say. I feel in my heart sometimes that we were better off when there was segregation. There was work for everybody because we knew who we were gon' do business with back then. Stuck with our own kind and we took care of each other. And once that fell apart"—MaMary's palms faced the ceiling—"now look at us. Every two or three of us got our hand out for the government to take care of us."

"Not the Addisons," Idella replied.

"No, not the Addisons. Folks like the Addisons living in a world like you've described here, you and me, Idella, didn't even know existed." She looked thoughtful. "I wish I had taken a greater in-terest in learning Swahili from my mother when she tried to teach it to me. I wish I had. Maybe I could have taught it to other black folks who were interested. Had me a business." She sighed. "But I'm glad for the little bit of knowledge that I did pick up from her. There's pride in that for me, Idella. Pride."

"I know, MaMary. I know." Idella hoped MaMary wouldn't start talking about Africa again. Sometimes it was a bit much. "Because you did learn how to bead from her." Idella diverted the conversa-tion a little.

"That I did. And I taught you," MaMary tossed back.

Idella smiled. "You did."

"That's the kind of knowledge we have to hold on to. My mother insisted that I learn beading." MaMary tapped the kitchen table with her forefinger. "Some of the colors and patterns she said come right out of Africa, but others were our family's personal message. Blue is a request. Some pinks are love. As a matter of fact, I finished a pretty little piece today, just as pretty as it could be." MaMary got up and walked over to the old end table in the kitchen where she kept all her beads and crafts. "You just gotta see this one, Idella. It's so pretty." She looked down at the table. "Now, where is it? I could have sworn I left it right here. Then I heard you outside talking to Savannah and I went to the front room." She walked out of the kitchen, then returned with a puzzled look on her face. "I just don't know what I did with it."

"Don't worry about it right now, MaMary. Just eat your food. Don't let it get cold. You probably put it in the bedroom or some-thing."

"That's what I probably did. I baked up a new batch of clay beads a couple of days ago." She looked at Idella. "My colors came out so good. I mixed some other things in the food coloring. So I bet I just thought I put that purse on the table before I heard you outside." She continued to talk as she walked to the bedroom, but came back with her brow creased even further. "I just don't know what happened to it."

"Please, MaMary. Don't worry about it. Sit down and eat. If you don't eat right now, I'm not going to eat either."

"All right." MaMary sat down and looked around the kitchen.

"Boy, I tell you," Idella said, "it could be kind of rough if some of those ladies at work find out that you're working in the Addisons' home. They're going to pester me for every bit of information they can."

"Don't they gossip enough already?" MaMary said.

"You know they do. And I tell 'em over and over again, I don't even want to hear that stuff. I don't wanna hear it. And Sadie loves to talk about Mr. Addison. Un-huh. The other day I told all of them, I personally have never seen Mr. Addison take a drink and I don't know nothing about his gambling away hundreds of dollars in gambling houses. So, what I haven't seen with my own eyeballs I'm not going to talk about. And it's not doing them no good either because he's still their boss, regardless." Idella got up. "I think I'll have a little more Kool-Aid." She opened the refrigerator door. Idella stared at the beaded purse and material scraps that sat on the shelf with the butter, Kool-Aid and cheese. She took them out.

"You mean I put it in there?" MaMary shook her head. "Sometimes my mind, Idella." She clasped her hands. "I can remember things my mother said just like it was yesterday, but then I do something like this."

"We all make mistakes," Idella assured her. "Don't worry, MaMary. We all do sometimes." But Idella was worried too.

Their eyes met.

"Don't worry," Idella mouthed, then said out loud, "everything will work out just fine."

High Status

Patricia Addison looked in the mirror. Basically, she was pleased with what she saw. Julia's Charm School had taught her well. She knew the perfect amount of eye shadow, facial powder and lipstick to put on for day or night; never too much to draw attention to her makeup, only to her face. She was glad Ultra Sheen manufactured a foundation for darker skin; it made her look more natural. But still Patricia couldn't bring herself to wear the powder that matched it. She used a lighter shade. Patricia examined her profile. Her hair pleased her most. Yes, her hair was her fine point as she had been told so many times by Grandmother Agnes. It was thick and long, and with a perm hung in a split-end free pageboy just below her shoulder blades.

Thank God there was no trace of the seizure she had earlier. With just the thought of lying on the front yard in convulsions, Patricia closed her eyes and clenched her fist. *I must have looked like a chicken that had just had its head cut off. Why me, God? Why me?*

She stared at herself. *I want to make something of my life. I want to make my mark as a part of this Addison family. A mark on the black community. The elite community. I—*

A sharp tap sounded at her door before it opened with no invitation. Grandmother Agnes walked into her room.

"Thought I'd come by and see how you're doing." She crossed the floor. Even with a cane her bearing was regal. The dark navy dress she wore accented her fair complexion.

"Just finishing up my makeup, Grandmother."

Agnes leaned in behind her and looked in the mirror at Patricia's face. "And you've done a wonderful job. You look absolutely wonderful," she repeated.

Patricia smiled into her grandmother's mirrored eyes.

"And that Nadinola skin cream is doing its job." Her old but barely wrinkled hands turned Patricia's face to show both profiles. "Make sure you put it behind your ears and all down your neck. You don't want your face lighter than your neck, do you?"

"I know." Patricia closed her eyes for a second, then looked at her grandmother. "You've told me before."

"Well . . . you look just beautiful," Agnes said. "And a soft, lemon-yellow dress like this is perfect for a skin color like yours. Because—"

Patricia said it with her. "Soft light colors lighten the complexion of a darker-skin woman." Their eyes met in the mirror again. There was a moment of silence.

Agnes patted her hair. "A complexion like mine can wear anything and, of course, darker colors like this navy blue make me appear even fairer."

Patricia got up from the vanity stool. She walked over and picked up the cleaner's bag that previously covered the dress she wore. She had to get away from Grandmother Agnes's assessing eyes. She felt she was always being judged. But what bothered Patricia most was she wanted to meet her grandmother's expectations. She wanted to fill them. But Patricia was afraid that being born who she was, it could never be done.

"I'm excited that you're going to meet Gerald tonight," Agnes said. "He's a fine young man from a fine family. I haven't seen him for years, but they're some good-looking people, and he was a very good-looking boy. If I remember correctly, his eyes are just about green, and his hair is black with the right amount of a wave."

Patricia's heart quickened. She looked at her grandmother again. "He sounds really handsome."

"Oh you can bet your money he is. I believe he takes after his mother's side of the family. It will be good to see his grandmother, Dorothy, tonight." Agnes sighed. "I haven't seen her in quite a while. We talk on the telephone, though. When you've been friends as long as we have, seeing each other isn't that important." She looked in the mirror. "So much time has passed, and Lord knows I'm not that easy on the eyes anymore."

Patricia walked over and took her grandmother's hands. "You're beautiful, and you always will be."

With genuine affection, Agnes touched Patricia's face. "And so are you, baby. So are you." She gave her a light kiss on the cheek. "Tonight you just be yourself. You've been raised the right way, given all the right opportunities and the woman that you are is perfectly charming. And I just know you're going to charm that Gerald Campbell right out of his pre-dental shoes."

Patricia laughed nervously. "That's right, he's going to be a dentist." She knew the answer. She simply wanted to hear it again.

"Yes, he is going to be a dentist," Grandmother Agnes said with certainty. "Just as his father, and his father's father before him. It would be wonderful to have a dentist in the family."

"Oh, Grandmother." Patricia's eyes filled with apprehension. "Aren't you planning the wedding a little early? I haven't met him yet."

"I know," Agnes said. "But his grandmother and I have been talking, and we think you and Gerald would be the perfect match. Dorothy and I have been a part of this society for a long time, and the Addisons and the Campbells coming together is a grand match. This kind of thing has been done by our kind of people for generations. If we didn't do it, things wouldn't remain as clear as they are. We marry our own kind, Patricia. I can't help it if it just happens to be the folks who look like us are the ones who are the professionals and the successful businessmen. So it's important to keep it that way. That's why we have Jack and Jill, Tots and Teens and the fraternities and sororities."

"I know, Grandmother."

"Yes, you do know," Agnes said with conviction. Obviously, she was perturbed by Patricia's "I know" attitude. She squeezed Patricia's hand. "If our way of life is to survive, Patricia, these are things we must do. And by God, life could be worse than looking forward to snaring a good-looking man like Gerald who's going to be a dentist."

About an hour later, the doorbell sounded throughout the house.

"That must be them," Agnes said.

Patricia watched Ruth walk across the foyer as Agnes arranged her wide skirt on the settee.

Rachel looked at her mother and then at her husband, Roger. "It's been quite a long time since I've seen Miss Dorothy. I remember Gerald too, but he was quite young." She smiled at Patricia.

"I don't recall the boy at all," Roger said. "I know his father, but I don't remember him." He put his hands in his pockets. "Now here he is coming to look my little girl over." He looked at Patricia with love in his eyes. "You can be sure, Miss P., that we're going to be looking him over too."

"There's nothing to look over," Agnes said. "He comes from a good family, a good bloodline and from my viewpoint he's just perfect for Patricia."

"Excuse me." Patricia's nerves got the best of her. "I just need to go to the ladies' room. I'll be right back."

"Are you feeling all right, honey?" Rachel looked concerned.

"Yes, Mama." Patricia waved her hand as if it was of no consequence. "I just want to check my powder." She found an adequate excuse. "You've both taught me a lady makes a mark when she makes an entrance."

"Patricia's right." Agnes straightened her back. "We don't want to appear like sitting ducks waiting for them to come in, now do we?"

Patricia smiled politely, walked out of the sitting room and entered the nearest bathroom. She could hear the hellos and exclamations of seeing each other again as she closed the door. She glanced in the mirror. All was still well. Patricia gave her hair one last pat, took a deep breath and opened the door. By the time she reached the sitting room, she entered with a practiced confidence. "Hello"—she smiled—"Miss Dorothy, it's so good to see you. I haven't seen you in such a long time." She took Miss Dorothy's hands in both her hands.

"Hello, Patricia. It's good to see you as well."

Patricia turned to Gerald with just enough of a smile. "And you are Gerald."

He reached out to shake her hand. "I am. It's good to see you. Actually, my grandmother told me I should say it's good to see you again."

"It's good to see you too, although I don't remember meeting you either." She smiled before she looked around the room. Gerald was far more handsome than Patricia had imagined. "Would you care for some lemonade or ice tea before we go in? Grandmother Agnes doesn't allow anything else to be served during dinner."

"I most certainly don't," Agnes spoke up. "I don't believe in drinking spirits." She glanced at Roger, who continued to smile as if he hadn't heard her.

"I can wait for dinner." Dorothy's pearlized gray linen suit hung on her elderly frame quite attractively.

"But we don't want to keep you waiting. Let me check and see if the food is ready," Patricia offered. "And if it is, we can go right into dinner."

"Please do, Patricia," Agnes said proudly.

Patricia discovered the food was ready and the table set. All of a sudden, on her way back to let everyone know, she realized how important the night could be. That something big was at stake: her future . . . the future of her family. Patricia was determined she would not fail.

Dinner went smoothly. An hour later, dessert was served.

"Would you care for some more peach cobbler, Gerald?" Roger Addison pushed the still-warm ceramic dish toward his guest.

Gerald put up his hand. "I think two servings are enough, Mr. Addison. I hope that shows that I truly liked it."

"I'm glad you did," Roger replied. "It's the best in Memphis, second only to your grandmother's, of course." He motioned toward

Dorothy. "And Addison Restaurant and Catering's peach cobbler." He laughed deep and easy.

"Of course." Gerald joined him. "This is one of the best meals I've had in a long, long time. I thank you all for having me." He looked around the table.

"It's a pleasure having Miss Dorothy and you in our home," Rachel said. She looked most elegant in a french roll.

"I hate to say this, but Rachel and I need to discuss a meeting that's coming up in a couple of weeks with Dorothy. I know it might bore you young people." Agnes looked at Patricia and then Gerald. "It involves your fraternity, Roger." She smiled at her son-in-law. "We could use your help if you can stand our chatter for a little while longer."

"I'll help in any way I can, Mother Agnes," he replied.

"Good," Agnes said with charm. "Patricia, why don't you take Gerald out on the screened veranda so you two can sit and talk awhile. I'll get Ruth to bring something out there for you to drink."

"That sounds like a good idea." Gerald pushed his chair back from the table, then stood behind Patricia's chair. "You'll have to lead the way, Patricia."

"I'd love to." She got up. "Right this way."

She walked a bit ahead of him. Patricia could feel Gerald's eyes cruising the back of her as they proceeded. She walked slowly and allowed her hips to sway just enough through her A-line dress. *A lady never hurries*, she thought as she walked. Their eyes had met several times during dinner, and Patricia felt there was a natural attraction between them. She knew for certain she was attracted to Gerald. What woman wouldn't be?

Gerald opened the door. Patricia was the first to step out onto the wide screened porch that traveled the length of the back of the house. They had a choice of furniture, so Patricia led them to a grouping of rattan chairs, a cocktail table and a small sofa. She sat in one of the chairs and crossed her legs. Gerald sat beside her in the other. They looked out onto the expansive backyard with its strategically placed lighting. There was a moment of silence, but then Patricia easily filled it.

"So you said you'll be in Memphis for about a month and then you'll fly back to Atlanta?"

"Yes, I've got to get back. I start my internship once I return."

"That's right, you mentioned that during dinner. But the summer starts soon, and that's when all kinds of events take place in my fair city."

"I hope to get to enjoy some of them," Gerald said. "I'll be back. I'll be spending plenty of time here now that my grandfather has passed away and my grandmother is alone. I've got to come down here and see about her." He smiled. "She spoiled me so much as a child. No matter what I did, I knew I could depend on Grandmother Dot to back me up. It seems to be the genetic makeup of our grandmothers, doesn't it? Looking out for us and our best interests." Gerald looked at her with focused concentration.

Patricia looked down. She thought about her paternal grandmother, Sandra Addison. Patricia was sure she would have had more input in her life if it hadn't been for Grandmother Agnes. Grandmother Agnes always stood guard at the gate as if God had appointed her the personal director of Patricia's life. She knew they both loved her. Grandmother Addison's love was more traditional. Grandmother Agnes loved her too, but she needed control. She needed to control everyone around her. "Yes, it does seem to be," she replied.

"But you know," he said, "I spent quite a bit of time here in Memphis when I was growing up. As a matter of fact, Grandmother Dot told me we were together at a few Tots and Teens events that we both were obviously too young to remember."

"Grandmother Agnes told me the same thing," Patricia replied as Ruth stepped out onto the porch with two glasses of lemonade. She quietly set them down on the table.

Gerald looked out at the sky. "Look at that. This is one beautiful night. Just look at those stars."

Patricia longed to gaze at Gerald. Reluctantly, she looked up.

"You can imagine if we can see this many stars with all these lights here in the city, how many must still be hidden from us. We just can't see them."

Patricia nodded.

"They're like you, Patricia," Gerald said.

"Like me?" She was intrigued.

"Yes. How is it that a good-looking woman like you hasn't been snatched up by some of these men here in Memphis? You must be hiding from them."

"Nope, not hiding at all." Patricia picked up her lemonade and took a sip. "I've had my share of lookers, but the right one just hasn't come along, that's all. Not the right one for me."

Gerald crossed his legs and leaned in a bit. "Are you so hard to please?" he asked.

"I wouldn't say that. But I've got my standards like any other woman who's been raised like me."

"And may I ask—before I even start thinking of asking you out to a movie, to dinner or all those things that a man will do when he's trying to show interest in a woman—may I ask, do I meet your standards?"

Patricia held her control. "You meet them very well." She tilted her head slightly.

Gerald leaned back in his chair and relaxed. "I thought so. It appears your grandmother has been pushing quite hard to make sure that we meet."

Patricia was shocked. "Well, I didn't hear from Grandmother Agnes that Miss Dorothy had any big objections. From my viewpoint, it was a mutual effort."

Gerald leaned forward again. He reached out and touched her hand. "Please, of course it was mutual," he placated her. "I didn't mean to imply anything different. My grandmother knows how many women have been after me through the years." He laughed in a self-assured way. "And now that I'm becoming a dentist, you could imagine how the women are acting." Gerald ran his hand over his sea of wavy hair. "So, obviously, when she told me she felt you were someone that I had to meet, you piqued my attention more than most."

Patricia wanted to be insulted by Gerald's arrogance, but the truth was she could imagine the women that had fallen at Gerald's feet. Just the thought of competing against some of the women she had grown up with, their fine features and hair that hung down their backs, caused Patricia to feel uncertain about her qualifications. But she wasn't about to let Gerald know that. Grandmother Agnes had taught her well when to speak, when to remain silent and when to bluff. "Well, I can't say you piqued my interest more than others. Certainly, I'm glad to meet you," Patricia said, "but I try not to get excited about anyone until I really get to see who they are. I need to spend a little time with them to see what kind of person he or she may be."

Gerald looked at Patricia with renewed interest. "That's smart. That's real smart. And that's only one of the reasons I am looking forward to doing just that with you."

Endings & Beginnings

"Idella."

Idella stopped in front of her screen door. She turned back toward the street.

"What's going on?" Bobby smiled through the rolled-down passenger window of his car.

Idella didn't smile back. "Hi, Bobby." She turned back toward the house and reached for the screen door handle.

"Wait a minute. Is that all I get after not seeing you for over a week?" He pulled the car over to the curb and parked.

Idella clenched her teeth before she faced him again. "I really don't have time to talk."

But Bobby got out of the car. He leaned on the top over the driver's side. "I didn't hear you."

"I really don't have time, Bobby. MaMary and I have somewhere to go."

"Look, you could at least give me a minute," he insisted. "I'm not gonna leave until you do."

Idella remembered the last time they broke up. Bobby had knocked on her door around midnight and woke MaMary up. She let go of the door handle, crossed her arms and walked toward his car. "A minute. That's all I'm gon' give you."

"Well, you sure have changed."

"You didn't give me a choice, did you?"

"I'm not just talking 'bout your attitude," Bobby said. "I'm talking about your hair too. What you got going on there? An Afro?"

"That's exactly what it is." Idella leaned into her hip.

"Why you trying to have an Afro? Your hair don't even wanna curl. I guess you're tryin' to fit in and be like everybody else around here."

"Not everybody. I decided I was gon' look like that girl you cheated on me with. She has an Afro, doesn't she? You talked about Black Power and all that stuff. 'The blacker the berry, the sweeter the juice' when I confronted you with her. So why you putting up a protest about what I do with my hair?"

"You gon' go there, huh?"

"Yes, I'm bringing her up. I'm never going to forget that. And you know what I wondered, Bobby? I wondered why in the hell were you with me in the first place. I didn't seem to fit your model of beauty." She continued to let him have it. "Or are you just another one of those brothers who talks black and really wants something else?"

Bobby licked his lips and looked up the street. "I don't even know why I stopped by here to talk to you."

"I don't know why you did either," Idella retorted.

"I'm outta here." He got back in his car.

Idella heard the screen door open behind her as Bobby turned on the car and pulled off. MaMary came and stood beside her.

"Whatever you said to him sure made him leave in a hurry."

"There wasn't nothing to say," Idella replied. "We said all we had to say over a week ago."

"I noticed he hadn't come by. But I was just waiting for you to tell me about it."

"I'm telling you now." Idella looked down into MaMary's face. "Bobby and I aren't seeing each other anymore."

"That's fine by me," MaMary replied. "It's time to move on, that's all."

There was a pause.

"I heard you out here"—she changed the subject—"and since we're going to walk over to the Addisons', I decided to join you."

"No problem. But I don't wanna wear my uniform over there," Idella replied. "I'll run in the house and change."

Idella emerged a few minutes later and they began their walk toward East Parkway.

"My goodness. I see what Bobby was talking about." MaMary studied Idella's hair. "I never thought your hair would get that curly."

Idella couldn't help but laugh. "I didn't either, so I gave it a little help. I bought some curlers that look like little pink bones and I washed my hair after you went to bed last night. Then I rolled it up."

"So that's how you did it." MaMary was impressed.

"Do you like it?"

"It may have to grow on me . . . but it's pretty. So many little, bitty curls."

"It's my version of an Afro, MaMary."

"Ohhhhhhh, is that what it is?"

Idella laughed again. "Bobby cheated on me with what he called a 'real sistah.' "

"A what?"

"A 'real sistah,' " Idella repeated. "And I saw who she was. She's pretty, MaMary. Dark, dark beautiful skin. Darker than yours. And an Afro that was perfect. Talk about two women who look different. When I first saw her, I wished I looked like her. Seeing that I'm trying to wear an Afro I guess I still do."

"There's no use in wishing you look like somebody else," MaMary said. "Even though a lot of folks would think it should be the other way around."

"Yeah, but these are the days of Black Power." Idella raised her fist in mock militancy. "And you know Bobby is one of the biggest promoters of Black Power in this part of Memphis."

"Sometimes I think that stuff is just talk. A man likes the kind of woman he likes, regardless of how he might see other things."

"Who knows?" Idella said.

"I know," MaMary replied. "After Henry, your granddaddy, died and I was still on the farm—now this was before you were born—there was one white man who was always after me and everybody knew he couldn't stand black people. That man was your mother's father. Mr. Joseph Wynd'm."

"What?" Idella's jaw dropped.

"Yes." MaMary nodded strongly. "And I believe because I, a black woman, never gave in to him, but his daughter, your mother, fell in love with and gave in to my son, was one of the reasons they burned us out of our house."

"Wow." Idella didn't know what to say.

"Yes. Men can be some strange creatures when it comes to women."

They continued in silence until they reached the Addisons' door.

"This is it, huh?" MaMary looked at the house. "It's one of the biggest on the street, and they are all fine houses," she said as Idella rang the doorbell.

"Wait until you see inside," Idella replied before the door opened.

"Hello," Ruth said.

"Hello," Idella replied. "Miss Rachel told me to come back today with my grandmother, MaMary." She paused. "So here we are."

"I know. She's expectin' you." Ruth opened the door.

Idella and MaMary stepped inside. MaMary took one look around and turned to Idella, who had an "I told you so" expression on her face.

"I think it will be okay to put you in the sitting room while I let Miss Rachel know that you're here," Ruth said.

"Who is it?" a soft voice asked from the stairs.

Idella looked up as Patricia descended the stairs in a houndstooth-check blazer, beige pants and a button-up blouse.

"It's the young lady who helped you out yesterday, Miss Patricia," Ruth replied. "Miss Rachel told her to come back today."

"Oh." Patricia's eyes softened with gratitude. "I'm so glad to meet you." She offered her hand. "I'm Patricia. Patricia Addison. I hope you recognize me standing up." She made light of the situation.

Idella smiled. "Of course, I do. I'm Idella Baxter, and this is my grandmother, Mary, but I call her MaMary."

"Hello, MaMary. It's good to meet you as well."

"Nice to meet you," MaMary replied.

"I'll take over from here, Ruth," Patricia said. "You can tell my mother that Idella and her grandmother are here."

"Right away, Miss Patricia," Ruth said as she walked away.

"Come. Let's go into the sitting room. I'm really very glad to meet you, Idella. I guess I scared you yesterday." She motioned for Idella and MaMary to sit before she sat.

"I was a little frightened," Idella admitted. "But I've seen a person have a seizure before." She made sure she didn't look at MaMary. "So I had an idea what to do."

"I'm glad you were there," Patricia said. "I hoped that I would have an opportunity to meet you again."

"I felt the same." Idella looked down. "That's one of the reasons we're here. And the other is your mother offered MaMary a job as a companion for your grandmother."

"Wonderful." Patricia looked at MaMary with renewed interest.

"She told me to bring her by so we could chat and see if things will work out."

"I think that was a good idea," Patricia replied. "But Grandmother Agnes isn't feeling well today. She's been in her—"

"Hello." Rachel entered the room. "I'm so glad that you took me up on my request and returned," she said to Idella. "And this must be MaMary." She went over to MaMary and shook her hand. "I am very, very glad to meet you. Your granddaughter was a lifesaver yesterday. I can't tell you how much we appreciate everything she did for Patricia." She glanced at her daughter.

"Idella's just that way," MaMary replied. "She sees somebody in trouble and she tries to do what she can to help. She's a really good girl."

"I'm sure she is," Rachel replied.

"So when she told me about the position here and how she

thought it would be a good idea if I considered it, I couldn't say no."

"I'm glad to hear that." Rachel smiled. "And now the girls got to meet each other." She looked from Patricia to Idella. "But I'm afraid my mother is not her best today. She stayed in her bedroom all day. We haven't seen very much of her at all. So I'm not sure if you'll get to meet today, MaMary."

"Miss Rachel," Ruth interrupted.

"Yes."

"Miss Agnes asked me who was at the door. So I told her." She swallowed. "Then she told me to tell all of you that she would like you to come to her room."

"Oh." Rachel smiled again. "I guess that settles it. You *will* get to meet my mother after all."

They left the sitting room and started up the stairs. Idella's eyes met MaMary's. She smiled ever so slightly as they reached the top. MaMary walked down the hall beside Idella before they entered Agnes's bedroom.

"I thought I heard the doorbell," Agnes said as they stepped inside. "And once Ruth told me who was here, I made it clear that I wanted to meet you." She looked at Idella and MaMary.

"We were discussing that downstairs, Mother," Rachel said. "I was trying to determine if you were well enough to receive them."

"Well, you couldn't decide that without me. And obviously"— she sat up a little straighter against the white eyelet pillowcases—"I am well enough not only to receive them, but to talk to them."

"Yes, we can see that you are," Rachel replied. "This is Idella." She made the introduction. "My mother, Agnes Sawyer."

"Nice to meet you, Miss Agnes."

Agnes nodded.

"And this is her grandmother, Mary."

"Good evening, ma'am," MaMary said.

"Good evening to you," Agnes replied. "I guess you are here to discuss the possibility of your becoming a companion of mine."

"Yes, that's exactly why I'm here," MaMary replied.

"Well, I don't know if Rachel has had the opportunity to tell you

this, but I don't think I need a companion. I do fine on my own."
Her chin rose. "But she insists that it will be better for everyone if I
have one." Agnes paused. "Have you done this kind of work before?"

"No, I haven't." MaMary glanced at Idella. "But as far as taking
care of someone, I've taken care of Idella all her life. And in my
mind when you care for someone it's very simple. You see what
their needs are, you pay attention to it and you try to follow
through."

"I don't know if being a companion of mine will actually be that
simple," Agnes replied.

Idella saw discomfort cross Patricia's face.

"The Addison household is a rather complicated place," Agnes
continued. "And I have overseen the running of this house for
many, many years. Therefore, any companion of mine would have
to be able to keep up with me and what I'm doing." She began to
cough. "I have many thing—" Her cough interrupted her.

MaMary walked over to a pitcher of water with lemon and cu-
cumber slices floating on top, picked up the empty glass beside it
and poured Agnes a glass of water. "Perhaps a little water will help,"
MaMary said.

Agnes took the water gratefully. "Thank you." She looked at
MaMary before she returned the glass. MaMary replaced it on the
table.

There was a moment of silence.

"The truth is," Agnes said, "I'm not up to par at the moment."
She wrapped her arms around her abdomen. "And based on Idella
helping our family, I don't mind seeing if you will work out, Mary.
But I'm warning you, if you don't, I won't hesitate to let you go."

"That's fair," MaMary replied. "I appreciate the opportunity."

Agnes did not reply. She openly studied MaMary, then Idella.

"And we appreciate you," Rachel compensated for her mother's
lack of tact. "But I think we should leave now and let Mother get a
little more rest." She moved toward the door. Idella, MaMary and
Patricia followed.

"When will you be able to start, Mary?" Agnes asked before they
exited the room.

"Today is Friday, so I can be here Monday morning at whatever time you suggest."

"Monday morning sounds good. Be here by eight o'clock."

"Eight o'clock," MaMary said before Rachel closed the door behind them.

Heartache

Rachel walked out of the master bathroom. She stopped, bent over and threw her long hair forward. Now it was easy to wrap it in a ball on top of her head. It was part of her nightly ritual.

"I left a couple of pieces of mail over here on the nightstand," Roger said.

"My goodness." Rachel's hair unwound in a mass of curls. "You scared me half to death. I didn't know you were in here."

"Well, it is still my bedroom, you know," Roger replied. "Even though the only thing we do in here is sleep."

Rachel ignored the remark. "You could have said you were here. I had no idea. I might have had a heart attack."

"I did call out to you. I can't help it if you didn't hear me. Have you seen the mail that I'm talking about? It was sitting on my night-stand." He sat on the edge of the bed to remove his shoes.

"No, I haven't. You need to ask Ruth because I haven't seen a thing." Rachel began to wrap her hair again.

"I've told you and Ruth more than once. Why don't you leave my things alone? I can't find them if you keep moving them around."

"She's not just moving them around, Roger. She's straightening up. Making the house presentable. That's her job."

He snatched a sock off. "I can't find anything around here. That mail is important to me."

"Tomorrow I'll ask Ruth if she saw it. If she did, I'm sure she'll be eager to point the way." Rachel slid out of a housecoat that matched her gown and placed it over a chair. Next, she propped up two pillows on her side of the bed, pulled down the covers and climbed inside. Once she was comfortable, she picked up her novel and started reading.

"And another thing," Roger said, "what's this I hear that the grandmother of one of the girls that works for me is now working here in the house?"

"You heard right," Rachel replied. "I just haven't had a chance to tell you about it. News sure does travel fast. We just hired her yesterday."

"That's the kind of thing I would like to hear from my family and not from my employees, if you don't mind."

"Roger, please." Rachel looked at the ceiling. "I was going to tell you today. I can't help it if you're gone most of the time. Not that we were trying to keep it a big secret or anything."

"Well, something like that, you need to tell me right away. I don't like being caught off guard like that."

"Caught off guard like what?" Rachel lost her patience. "It's not that we hired the girl. We hired her grandmother. Not unless there's something else you need to tell me about her." Rachel closed her book and looked at her husband. "Are you sure the only reason you are perturbed is because we didn't let you know, or is there something else you need to tell me about Idella? She is a mighty pretty girl. And we know how it is when it comes to you and pretty women."

Roger's jaw tightened. "Look, that is not why I brought this up. Don't start bringing the past up tonight, Rachel. It's been a long day. I'm too tired. It's been a good business day"—he squeezed the bridge of his nose—"but I'm not up to listening to you and your complaints about me, women, drinking, gambling or anything else. I just thought that out of all the people here in Memphis you could have hired someone who wasn't related to one of my workers."

She stretched. "But Idella happens to be the person who helped Patricia the other day when she had the seizure. I wanted to do something special for her, and I thought hiring her grandmother was the right thing to do."

"Patricia had another seizure?" Roger gave his wife a pointed look. "Why is it that this is the first time I'm hearing about that? Were you going to tell me about that tomorrow too? Or was I going to hear it from somebody else?"

Rachel opened her book again. "I was going to get around to telling you."

"When, Rachel? When were you going to tell me?"

"When the time was right," she said softly.

"Oh. And I know what that means when it comes to you." Roger leaned across the bed. He placed his face about a foot from Rachel's. "You're a good one for keeping secrets."

The smell of liquor hit her in the face.

"We both know that, don't we?"

"Now, Roger, you were the one who said we weren't going to bring up the past."

"I haven't brought your past up yet, Rachel. Not yet."

"Well, don't." She glared at him before she looked down at her book. "It's not going to do either one of us any good. And it surely won't do Patricia any. But this is why I didn't tell you. I knew it would start you down the wrong road."

"Start me down the wrong road." He laughed. "And what does that lead to in this household?" Roger answered his own question: "One bad turn deserves another."

"Please, Roger." Rachel closed her eyes. "I can tell you've been drinking. I can smell it on your breath."

"Yes, I've been drinking. I deserve to drink. Any man who takes a daughter to heart who is not his deserves to drink." Anger flashed and died in his eyes. "Especially when no one knows it but him and his above-reproach wife."

"You said we weren't going to bring up the past," Rachel pleaded.

"But we can't get away from the past. How can we when she lives in my house? Patricia. My baby." He laughed a troubled laugh. "You laid down with that black bastard. Epilepsy probably runs all through his family."

"I wouldn't have turned to him if you had been there for me," Rachel cried.

"Yesssssss." Roger moved back to his side of the bed and took off his other sock. "Blame it on me. I can shoulder all the blame. Let the world think Roger Addison is the thorn in the Addison family's side. I'll continue to take the blame, but I'll always know my little wife is the real thorn. Is the real whore." He cut his eyes toward her. "And my child is not my child. And her babies will not be my grandbabies." He threw his dirty sock. "And as long as that's true I will continue to drink, gamble and do whatever I please."

"You weren't," Rachel accused. "You weren't there for me so I turned to somebody else. I'm human, Roger. What did you expect?"

"You're right." Scorn burned his eyes. "I was not there for you. But guess why? Do you remember why, Rachel? I wasn't there because I was trying to prove myself to your mother, who always felt I wasn't good enough. Who always thought her daughter needed somebody better, who had more money, more prestige in the community. So I was out working my ass off trying to prove myself to Agnes. That's the truth of the matter."

"Roger." Rachel covered her ears. "I don't want to talk about this anymore. Do we have to go over this again tonight?"

"Yes, we do." His words slurred a bit. "I feel like going over it tonight. I wanna talk about it. Just like you use to talk about and accuse me of all those women. That I was going with Sylvia and I had Marlene." He shook his head. "I didn't have any of those women and I told you so, but you didn't trust me. You were listening to everyone but me, Rachel. You listened to everybody but me. So we stopped making love then and when you closed the candy store"— he leaned closer—"what was I to do? I did what any man would do. I looked for comfort somewhere else. I want you to remember you forced me into that, Rachel. You forced me."

"We can't change the past now, Roger. There's nothing we can do about it. So why do you torture me with this? Why?"

"Because," he spoke through his teeth, "every time I look at Patricia, who I love so much, who should have been my child . . . I know that she's not. And if I had the guts, the self-pride, I would have let the world know a long time ago." He shook his head again. "But I kept quiet because I loved you, and I wanted this family to work. I wanted my family name to mean something, so I never told a soul. Not even after"—he seemed to be talking to himself—"not even after I confronted you with it. She was in your arms and I was looking down at her knowing she wasn't mine. And I told you I was going to tell the world what kind of woman you were. That you were an adulterating whore." Roger looked at Rachel as if he couldn't bear to see her. "But I couldn't bring myself to do it because I thought it would make me look like less of a man. I told myself over and over again that I was going to get out of this mess. I would let the world know the truth. Then fate stepped in. I stumbled across your pitiful, secret meeting. He was standing in the alley. You were at the back of the flower garden. I saw you." He swallowed hard. "I saw him put his rough, ashy hands on your arm in such a way. You closed your eyes, not in disgust, but because you wished he could do more." Tears formed in Roger's eyes. "But then you told him you would never see him again. That it was over," he sniffed. "I thought about Patricia, who was six months old. I thought about the life we had made together and the life we could possibly have if I could just hold on. Try to forgive you and myself for being so weak."

"Roger." Rachel reached out and touched his arm. "I'm so sorry."

He flinched away. "I know you are, Rachel. I know you are and wish that sorry could do it. But every time Agnes looks at me with that look . . ." He paused. "And the sly comments she makes about Patricia's skin color and how it had to be my people who made her that way, I want to turn around and say, 'Blame your daughter, don't blame me.' " Roger closed his eyes. "But then I think about the Sawyer money. How it has benefited me and Addison Catering and I continue to keep quiet."

A deep hurt crossed Rachel's face. "But even the Sawyer money won't last forever, Roger. What are you going to do when it runs out?" she asked softly. "Are you going to turn on me and Patricia then?"

Slowly, Roger opened his eyes. He looked at her as he got up from the bed. Then he showed Rachel his back as he went into the bathroom and closed the door.

Contentment

Two weeks later, Idella walked up the Addisons' driveway to the back of the house. By now, stopping by the Addisons' and walking MaMary home in the afternoon was a familiar routine.

"I'll tell Mary that you're here," Ruth said. "She was in the kitchen a minute ago. I don't know where she went."

"That's fine. I'll wait," Idella said. "I'm in no hurry."

Idella felt comfortable in the Addisons' kitchen. She leaned against the counter and looked at an array of drinking glasses through a glass cabinet door. There was no doubt in her mind the Addisons had style and taste beyond any that she knew was possible. She admired the ample counter space and a lemon meringue pie that cooled in a decorative spot. How clean things were, and orderly. *A house this big wouldn't work without Ruth or Sam*, Idella thought. *When you have a house this big, you need a maid.* The Addisons weren't being highfalutin. They were being practical.

"I'm ready, Idella." MaMary adjusted her sweater as she came through the swinging door. "I had to go upstairs and tell Miss Agnes where her favorite handkerchiefs are. I put them in a special place for her." MaMary smiled.

"Her favorite handkerchiefs." Idella made a face. "Hey. Can I borrow you for a day or two?" she whispered. "You sound like you'd be really handy to have around."

MaMary chuckled.

Idella reached for the door, but it opened from the other side. Roger Addison walked in.

"Well, hello, Idella."

"Hello, Mr. Addison." It was the first time she had ever seen him in his home.

"Is everything going okay for you?" he said in a familiar yet businesslike manner.

"Absolutely, sir," she replied. "And, of course, you know my grandmother, Mary."

"Yes, I know Mary. How you doing this afternoon?"

"I'm just fine, Mr. Addison," Mary replied.

"Good." He walked away. "You all have a good evening."

"You do the same, sir," Idella said.

"Good evening, Mr. Addison," MaMary added. They went outside and walked up the driveway toward the street.

"Did you really go back upstairs to tell Miss Agnes about her favorite handkerchiefs?" That was still on Idella's mind.

"I did," MaMary replied. "She needs to know where they are."

Idella shook her head. "It's just . . . sometimes when I come to walk you home, I don't know what to expect."

"What do you mean?"

"It's the way you talk and act when you're around Miss Agnes. It's so different, MaMary."

"That's because she's my boss. They hired me to be her companion, Idella."

"But there's something about it that gets on my nerves. I didn't think being her companion would mean you'd have to act and talk the way you do." Idella looked down. "It's not slavery, you know."

MaMary's features turned thoughtful. "Of course, it's not slavery. I know that. But it's just like when you spoke to Mr. Addison a few minutes ago. You didn't speak to him like you would speak to me. There was a change in your voice; you acted different too."

"I did, didn't I?" Idella's brow creased.

"You did. And there's nothing wrong with that. After all, he is your boss and pays the bills."

"But I guess when it comes to you and Miss Agnes, you two being about the same age and all, it just feels different to me."

"Well." MaMary patted her back. "It is different. It's a lot different. There are worlds that separate me and Miss Agnes. And that's just the way it is. She comes from a life of privilege and money and she knows it. I don't. And she knows that too." She leaned her head toward Idella. "So the roles we're playing are very clear."

"Does she really make you feel below her, MaMary?" Idella was remorseful.

"I can't say she does, and you know, actually Miss Agnes isn't that bad." MaMary looked down.

"No?" Idella replied.

MaMary shook her head. "I had one of my moments the other day," she said softly.

Idella's eyes widened. "What happened?"

"I was bringing Miss Agnes some water. You know how she likes it with cucumbers and lemon slices in that little crystal pitcher."

Idella nodded.

"The next thing I knew I entered the room and there was a pitcher of water already there. I looked at the water I held in my hand and I tried to remember how the other had gotten there. But I couldn't." She looked at Idella. "Then I looked at Miss Agnes. She cocked her head and said, 'Don't you remember bringing me water a few minutes ago?' I just kinda stood there for a second. Finally, I said, 'Truth is, Miss Agnes, I don't.' For a moment we just looked at one another. Then she looked back down at the magazine she was reading and said, 'Well, I don't need but one,' and we just went on from there."

"She didn't question you any further about it?" Idella asked.

"No, she never said another word," MaMary replied. "But don't get me wrong, Miss Agnes never lets me forget that I am the companion." She acted as if she were tapping a cane on the floor. "Never lets me forget my place." They laughed. "We belong to two different classes of people. She and I know as long as we keep it

clear, there shouldn't be any problems. But when I was younger"—
MaMary's face brightened—"I never would have stood for some of
this stuff. I was feisty back then."

"You've told me." Idella giggled.

"I definitely was. I tell you I didn't want to work for anybody, and
as twisted as it may sound, definitely didn't want to do housework
in the house of a black person." She smirked. "Now, the truth is I
didn't personally know any well-to-do black folks. But I knew this,
we were all scrambling for our identities, and I wasn't going to
make myself available to help my own folks feel better at my ex-
pense. We were all scrambling to make a place in the world."

MaMary wiped the perspiration from her face. "And it had to do
with the color, and the shade of your skin. There was no denying it.
Not like today where it's somewhat subtle and all." She chuckled.
"So I was ready to stand up and be counted. I knew I was dark, but
I also knew I wasn't too bad to look at either and you weren't going
to just walk all over me. I wasn't going to help folks feel above me
so I started my vegetable stand."

"I believe you, MaMary," Idella replied. "You're not bad to look
at now."

"Oh please." She waved her hand. "That's your love talkin'. I'm
serious." She gave Idella the eye. "Your white granddaddy definitely thought so. But he thought he was slick too."

"How so?" Idella asked.

"He put me in an awkward position. You see, no matter how I
was feelin' about myself, meanin' that nobody was above me . . .
some of the white folks around there were already saying that I
didn't know my place. He knew that. And he used it because he
wanted to get his hands on me. Yes, he did. One day, he and some
white woman, who stayed in the car, drove by my stand real fast.
Then he stopped abruptly and got out. He didn't want no vegetables though. What he did was offer me a part-time job. Now, he
knew most black maids would have considered it an honor to work
at his house, seeing that he was an up-and-coming white man in
the community. And we both knew if I turned the job down, it
would make me look more uppity than I should. We needed the
money because Henry had just lost his little piece of a job."

MaMary squinted. "So I took it because I thought I could play the game and come out on the winning side. But lo' and behold, when he tried to force himself on me, I up and quit fast. That day I didn't care what them white folks were gonna say about me." Her features turned serious. "Afterwards, I told a few folks what happened so the word could get around. I had to. That way it wouldn't seem like I was uppity. I was simply a moral woman with a husband."

Idella shook her head. "We don't talk about that side of my family much. But the more I hear, the surer I am that I don't like my grandfather. When I think about the fire, which I hardly do, I feel I could hate him." She looked at the ground. "If I thought you hated him, I'm sure I would."

"Oh, Dee. It was just the sign of the times." MaMary looked at her. "I believe the evil that entered his heart when he got older and caused him to burn us out, came out of his feeling he was this big, respectable white man around town. And he couldn't stand the thought of folks knowing his untouchable white daughter laid down with a black man and her baby, you, was the proof." She paused. "But I feel when we were younger, he was really smitten with me. Boy, he must have hated himself for that, seeing how he felt about black people." MaMary paused again. "But I could see it in his eyes when he watched me in his house. There was lust, all right, but there was something else too. I think Mr. Wynd'm felt he could make me want him if I was near him. Then he found out he couldn't and he went too far."

Idella's face hardened. "To think he'd try something like that."

"He was known to be a womanizer, now. And he was a really, really handsome white man. But he'd lie in a minute to lay down with whatever woman he wanted." MaMary smiled. "But he could have been pure gold and I wouldn't have had him. I had my Henry." A soft smile lit her face. "I was a nice little prize when Henry married me. We made a good life together right outside Clarksville until he died."

"It's hard for me to imagine staying with a man until he dies, MaMary. I haven't even found one to begin with yet."

"Oh, it's coming. It'll come in its own time."

"I'm gon' hold you to that," Idella replied.

But MaMary continued to speak of the past. "Yeah, I was a pretty good-looking old girl until the fire. It changed everything. Everything. You can imagine with your daddy, John, dying in it that alone almost killed me. Then you and I leaving town because I didn't feel it was safe for us no more. We lost everything. The strain and the worry nearly turned my hair white overnight."

"It must have been really hard." Idella felt the story every time MaMary told it.

"It was hard, Dee. It was mighty hard. But who said life was going to be other than that? And when life is hard, but you keep your faith, you can believe the Man upstairs gives you what you need to make it. If He didn't, none of our ancestors would have made it over here to this land. So what happened? God gave you and me old lady Price, a stranger who let us live with her right here in Memphis until I got on my feet." MaMary looked proud. "We made it despite everything. And life is looking pretty good for us right now."

"It sure is," Idella replied.

They turned the corner onto their street. "We got some money in our pockets. I've got two weeks' work under my belt, and if things keep going like this, in two or three months we'll be caught up."

"Can you believe it?" Idella looked at the sky. "We've been behind so long, catching up sounds like magic."

"Yes, we'll catch up," MaMary said. "And while we're catching up, I'll keep working and acting like I'm suppose to act in the Addisons' household. And you and Patricia, I hope, will continue to get to know each other."

"Patricia has been one of the biggest surprises out of this whole thing," Idella said. "She's so kind and considerate, MaMary."

"I know. I've seen you two together. You genuinely like each other and that's good, Idella. It's a door that's been opened for you in this world. So you just walk right through it, you hear me? Don't stop and say nothing. Just take this gift that's been given to you, 'cuz you can believe connections are everything in this world." She squeezed Idella's hand.

Then MaMary's tone changed. "Idella?"

"Yes?"

"Do you remember the dream I told you I had the night you were nothin' but hours old, and you were left on my porch by your mama?"

Idella looked at MaMary. "Yes, I remember. You said you had asked me what was my purpose for being born?"

"I sure did." She nodded. "Your daddy was out of town and I had put you in my bed with me. You looked so much like a little, white baby, and I thought about everything that had happened, but I loved you all the same because you were of my flesh and blood." She looked at Idella. "At that moment, I wondered what you should be called, so I asked you that question."

MaMary looked into the air. "That night I had the dream. An old African spirit came to me. I believe it was you in a previous life. She told me you would become the ideal person to prove skin color doesn't mean a thing. She said the soul has no color, so how could color be important? That we put on these bones, muscle and skin in whatever color that best suits us to fulfill our life's purpose." MaMary smiled. "I told your daddy the dream and that's when we decided to name you Idella."

"I know," Idella said.

"We got to remember that."

They looked into each other's eyes.

"No matter who it is and how important they may think it is, know that in the end skin color don't mean nothin'."

Suspicion

"Well, aren't you looking happy with yourself this morning?" Agnes said. She was still in her nightdress.

"Actually, I'm feeling pretty happy this morning, Grandmother. Gerald and I had a really nice time at the get-together. He's such a social charmer." Patricia chuckled. "Everybody likes him." She tightened her robe. "Plus, he treats me like such a lady. I feel good when I'm with him." Her smile brightened her entire face.

"Didn't I tell you?" Agnes said. "Didn't I tell you that you two were meant for each other?"

They both laughed.

"Everybody's in such a good mood. What's going on in here?" Rachel entered her mother's bedroom. "I could use some of that this morning."

"I bet you can," Agnes replied. "I wasn't feeling well last night and I couldn't sleep. So I was awake when Roger came in last night. He nearly knocked the table over in the hallway. My God, Rachel. Is the man ever going to stop drinking?"

"Your guess is as good as mine when it comes to that," Rachel replied. She looked at Patricia, who crossed her arms.

Agnes glanced at her as well. "She's old enough for us to talk about him in front of her. We hid it for all these years. I'm tired of hiding it," Agnes said.

"I've known for a while that Dad drinks," Patricia replied.

Rachel covered her hand with hers.

"I wish he wouldn't, but he's my father regardless," she defended him.

"He is that," Agnes said.

Rachel looked down.

"When they were younger, your mother loved her some Roger." Agnes looked at Rachel and turned a sour smile. "No matter what I said, no matter what I did, she was going to have Roger Addison. So here we are, and here you are." She leaned toward Patricia a bit. "I'm not upset about it in the least now that you and Gerald seem to be hitting it off so well." Agnes continued, "All I can see is roses coming up for us in the future." Her eyes brightened. "How many times have you two been out now?"

"Four times." Patricia didn't hesitate.

"That's good." Agnes smiled. "Now go on and tell us what you did last night. Where'd you go? Who'd you see?"

"It wasn't who we saw or where we went that was so exciting. Because we just went over to Deborah Bentson's house. I don't know if you know her."

"I know her folks," Rachel replied.

"I know that, Mama. I didn't know if Grandmother did." Patricia liked the positive attention. "Deborah's house is okay, but it's not as big as ours. And what made the evening great was being with Gerald. I could talk to him until I'm blue in the face."

Agnes chuckled again. "That was one thing I enjoyed about your grandfather. We could talk from one subject to another. We started a conversation at the very beginning of our courtship that lasted for years."

"How old were you, Grandmother?" Patricia asked.

"Oh, I was probably about your age. High time to have gotten married," she said. "But I was a little headstrong, quite different from you." Agnes looked smug. "My mother and father had an idea of what they wanted for me but I had a few ideas of my own.

So, in the beginning, I had to do it my way and although they backed me up . . ." She shook her head. "It nearly killed me."

Surprised, Rachel looked at her mother. "What did?"

Agnes's eyelids became veils. "Some of the decisions that I made." She looked directly at Rachel. "It won't do any good to go into details now. It was so long ago. But in the end, my mother did what Rachel and I have done for you, Patricia. She took the bull by the horns and arranged my meeting with your grandfather, Ronald. Ronald Sawyer. We hit it off from the very beginning. We hit it off because I was ready. No more of the crazy dreams that I had. You know back then quite a few of us who could, passed." She looked at Rachel. "Still do to this day. Your grandparents did everything to provide a wonderful life for me. They wanted me to be happy even when I flirted with that idea."

Patricia groaned. "Grandmother Agnes, the idea of you trying that is too much for me. I'm going to get dressed." She stood up. "Idella has a half day off today and I told her to come by so we can go shopping." She left the room.

Rachel sat back. "You had a relationship with a white man."

Agnes nodded slowly.

"And you were passing at the time." Rachel's eyes widened. "What happened? Did you love him?"

A stillness came over Agnes's face. "I loved him more than I ever loved any man." She paused. "Including your father."

"Mother!" Rachel was shocked.

"It's the truth." Her face softened as she remembered. "I met him at a party. A fancy, fancy party. I had been passing for a short time, and although my mother warned me before I left that I needed to be low key to make it work, it just wasn't in me to do it that way." Agnes leaned back. "I dressed that night like I've never dressed before. I had hired me a maid, Peggy; a young, brown-skin girl who was new in town. She helped me that night." She sighed. "I wanted to fit into white high society so bad. I did an excellent job too, because that night I caught the eye of one of the most charming, one of the richest men there. That man . . . he was so handsome. The most handsome man I'd ever seen in my life, and when I looked at him, something struck me right in the middle of my heart." She looked down. "Eventually, he asked me to dance. He led me on the floor and took me in his arms." Agnes appeared as if she felt it all again. "And the truth is he had me. I didn't have a chance from that moment on."

"I can't believe you're telling me this."

Agnes shrugged and the room went silent.

"So you got together?"

She nodded.

"Why did you break up?"

"I was betrayed." Agnes's face turned into a mask. "In more ways than one."

"What was his name?" Rachel asked.

"I'm not telling you that." Agnes shook her head. "I've said more than I needed to already. Good morning, Mary," Agnes said as Mary appeared at the door.

"Good morning, Miss Agnes. How ya doin' this morning? Miss Rachel?"

"Morning, Mary," Rachel replied, then she focused on her mother. "But, Mother, did it happen here in Memphis?"

Agnes took in the dark circles around her daughter's eyes. "No, in Clarksville, Tennessee."

"That's where I was born," MaMary said.

"You were?" Rachel turned toward her.

"Yes, ma'am. Out in the country. I sure was."

"How old are you, MaMary?" Rachel asked.

"I'm seventy-two."

"So you and Mother may have seen each other."

"I'm sure we might have. But our social circles were different, wouldn't you say, Miss Agnes?" MaMary smiled comfortably.

Agnes's face became somewhat drawn. "Yes, I'm sure they were."

"My goodness, it's later than I thought." Rachel looked at her mother's clock. "We've been sitting here talking and the day is starting to get away from us."

"There's no harm in sitting and talking with family," MaMary said. "I think it's a good thing to do."

"Speaking of good things, Patricia and Idella are going shopping today. Did she tell you?" Rachel asked from the door.

"She sure did," MaMary replied. "It sounds wonderful. Idella could use getting out a little more. She stays home entirely too much." She picked up Agnes's sweater and hung it in the closet.

Agnes remained quiet as she watched MaMary close the closet door. "Mary, what is your last name again?"

"Baxter," MaMary said. "My name is Mary Baxter."

Slowly, Agnes settled into her propped-up pillows.

Discovery

"I have never shopped in Goldsmith's before," Idella said to Patricia as they climbed the Addisons' staircase.

"Never?" Patricia looked down at her.

"Never," Idella replied.

"Well, as they say, there's always a first time for everything." Patricia led the way up the hall. "Come on, let's go look at the things that we bought."

"I'm so excited," Idella replied. "So excited."

Patricia opened her bedroom door and they went inside. Unceremoniously, she dumped her shopping bags on the bed. "You almost have as many bags as I do."

"I know. I hit the clearance rack." A big smile lit Idella's face. "But clearance rack or not, I got some great things." She pulled the first dress out of the white paper bag with a corded handle. Idella held the deep pink garment up against her, then turned to Patricia's mirror. "I love it."

They both laughed.

* * *

Agnes felt winded when she reached the top of the stairs. She held on to the round ball at the top of the banister, and examined herself in the full-length mirror that had been in her family for years. She was still a good-looking woman. Frailer than she would like to be, more wrinkles than she ever thought she would have, but in general a good-looking woman.

Even now, Agnes knew there were many people who never questioned her race. They presumed she was white, and a part of her still reveled in that, although she had long put away the dream of passing. She had learned to embrace her blackness within her social circle, the wealthiest group of blacks in America, the elite of black society. Within that group, Agnes was among the top members. You could go no higher than what her family name brought to the plate. Her father had been a savvy, some would say crafty, politician when many blacks were afraid or didn't know they could vote. Yes, Agnes was the crème de la crème of the black elite. She knew it was where she belonged. She had accepted long ago that had she been successful at passing for white, she would simply have been another white woman playing mistress to a well-off white man.

She looked deep into her grayish-blue eyes. There she could still see her youthful self. There she still held the pain, the hopes and the acceptance of what had happened so many years ago.

Agnes heard Patricia and Idella laugh in Patricia's bedroom not far down the hall. The question that had plagued her ever since Mary said she was from Clarksville surfaced in her mind. Could it possibly be the same Mary? Could it? Agnes walked softly down the hall. Could life have come full circle and brought her and Mary together again? The chances of that were astronomical, Agnes thought, nearly impossible.

She passed Patricia's cracked door. She could see the two young women looking at the clothes they pulled out of their shopping bags. The irony of it all, Agnes thought when she looked at her own granddaughter beside Mary's, is most people would assume Idella was her blood relative and Patricia was Mary's.

Quietly, Agnes continued on her way. She reached her bedroom and sat down in a cushioned chair. There, Agnes listened to the laughter and wondered if what she felt was true.

"You should love it." Patricia dug into one of her bags and laid out a matching sweater and skirt set. "That's a great color for you."

"Oh, but look at your sweater set," Idella chimed.

"It's me." Patricia stood beside Idella and checked herself in the mirror.

"It is you," Idella said. "We have two different styles, don't we?"

"I'd say so," Patricia replied.

"But that doesn't stop us from getting along." Idella smiled.

"It sure doesn't."

"I don't think I ever had a friend like you, Patricia. As a matter of fact, I know I haven't."

Patricia simply laughed. "Now . . . when are you going to get an opportunity to show off your new clothes?"

"Well." Idella thought about it. "Just off the top of my head I don't have the slightest idea."

"I do," Patricia said.

"Where?" Idella's hazel eyes beamed.

"I am going to have a barbecue. It's going to be the weekend after next, and you've got to come."

"Really?"

Patricia shrugged. "Why not? You'll get to meet some of the people I know. Young people like us."

"Young people like *you*," Idella said.

Patricia knew what Idella meant. "Well . . . still young people all the same."

"I don't know." Idella looked down. "Like you said, our taste is different."

Patricia waved her hand. "You'll fit in fine." Her tone changed. "Better than most."

Idella looked at her. "What do you mean?"

"It's the way you look. You'll fit in perfectly." Patricia looked at Idella's hair. "Can I ask you something?"

"Sure."

"Why do you wear an Afro?"

"I like it," Idella said. "I think it's cool. And it's the fashion nowadays." She looked at Patricia's permed pageboy.

"I know it's the trend," Patricia said, "but it's a little too militant and harsh for me. I think you'd look much prettier if you just allowed your hair to be natural. You know, straight."

"But my hair isn't naturally straight."

"It's not very curly." Patricia came close and examined her hair. "I can tell by your roots."

"It's got some wave to it."

"Well, just think about this," Patricia said. "At least for the barbecue, you should wear your hair straight. Your hair is a lot like Grandmother Agnes's, so if you just blow-dry it"—she snapped her fingers—"you'd be gorgeous."

"You really think so?"

"Absolutely."

Idella's eyebrows rose. "No one's ever told me I was gorgeous."

"They haven't?" Patricia looked totally surprised.

"No."

Patricia ran her hand through her own hair. "You just haven't been around the right kind of people. Believe me, you are gorgeous. You just need a little tweaking here and there."

"Okay." Idella laughed. "Will it be worth my while? You plan on inviting some good-looking guys?"

"Definitely. Most of the guys I've grown up with have been."

Idella put her hand on her hip. "And you haven't claimed one of them as yours?"

"Nope. I'm waiting on the best one with the best offer."

Idella dropped her jaw. "I heard that. Well, you can count me in."

They laughed.

"So I guess that means you don't have a boyfriend either," Patricia said.

"No, I don't," Idella replied. "I did for a while but when it came down to it, I don't know if he really liked me or not. Seemed like the women he claimed were so beautiful didn't look anything like me, so . . ."

"Obviously, he wasn't the right man for you."

"I guess not." Idella clicked her nails.

"Was he your first boyfriend?" Patricia asked.

Idella looked at her "What is this? Let's find out all of Idella's business?"

"No. It's just that"—Patricia hesitated—"we've never talked about men before. You know, boyfriends and all that. So I felt this would be as good a time as any. That's all."

Idella shrugged. "I guess it is." She looked at Patricia. "And no, he was not my first boyfriend. Not real boyfriend, if you know what I mean."

They looked at each other.

"I know exactly what you mean."

There was a moment of silence.

"My first one was called, get this"—Idella leaned in—"Black Stallion."

"Nooo," Patricia said.

"Swear to God." Idella put up her hand.

"Black Stallion."

They laughed together.

"His skin was dark and smooth and he moved like a proud horse," Idella said.

"Woooooooo-whew," Patricia remarked. "Normally, he wouldn't be the kind of man I'd be interested in, but he sounds like he could have been quite the prize."

"He was," Idella said. "But he was too much for me to deal with. There we were, both of us poor, and he was always talking about how I was suppose to buy him stuff."

"No, he wasn't," Patricia said.

"Yes, he was." Idella crossed her arms. "There is one day I will never forget. It was Christmas, and I didn't have any money. I had saved up to buy him some jeans, but they weren't any brand-name jeans. I didn't have money for those. They were no-name jeans and he was sooo insulted. First, he acted like he was going to hit me with them, and then he threw them down on the ground and said don't ever buy him anything like that again."

"No way," Patricia said.

"Yes, he did. And that was enough for me."

"That was some introduction to love," Patricia said.

"It sure was. And it didn't do much for my self-esteem, I can tell you that."

Patricia touched Idella's shoulder. "The guys you meet at my barbecue won't be anything like that."

"Thank you, Lord," Idella replied. She smiled. "I'm looking forward to dressing up and meeting your friends."

"You're going to have a great time."

Idella looked at her watch. "I better head downstairs." She returned her clothes to her shopping bags. "MaMary is probably waiting for me in the kitchen."

"All right," Patricia replied. "But don't forget—it's next weekend."

"No way," Idella said as they went out into the hall.

"Is that you, Patricia?" Agnes called from her bedroom.

"Yes, ma'am. It's Idella and me."

"Send Idella in here. I'd like to speak with her."

Patricia and Idella looked at each other.

"What does she want?" Idella whispered.

Patricia shrugged, but motioned her forward.

Idella walked up the hall and quietly entered Agnes's bedroom. "Hello, Miss Agnes."

"Idella." Agnes nodded. "How are you?"

"I'm fine." She held up her shopping bags. "Patricia and I went shopping."

"Seems like you did pretty well for yourself." Agnes shifted in her chair.

"I did." Idella smiled. "It was the first time I've ever shopped at Goldsmith's."

Agnes ignored her. "I won't hold you long. I have a few questions."

"Yes, ma'am." Idella turned serious.

"Exactly where were you born?"

"Outside of Clarksville, Tennessee."

Agnes looked at her lap. "Did you go to school there?"

"No, ma'am. MaMary and I left Clarksville when I was a tiny baby."

"And your parents, did they move up here with you and Mary?"

"No, ma'am. My father's dead. As a matter of fact, I don't remember him at all. He died in a fire, but MaMary was able to save me. Our house burned to the ground."

Agnes nodded her head slowly. "That's a shame." But there was no emotion in her voice.

"I never met my mama." Idella was encouraged by her response. "So I don't know much about her or her side of the family."

"I see," Agnes said.

"Miss Agnes"—Idella hesitated—"why do you ask?"

Agnes smiled a stunted smile. "This morning Mary said she was from Clarksville, and I lived there for a while. I didn't get a chance to ask Mary today, so I thought I'd ask you."

"Oh." Idella replied.

"Well, that's all, Idella. You have a good evening. And thank you for answering my questions."

"Good evening, Miss Agnes." Idella left the room.

Agnes got up and walked around her bedroom. Idella had confirmed her suspicion. It was the same Mary Baxter. *Although, it's difficult to believe. I wouldn't have recognized her. She looks so different.* She walked over to the bedroom window, moved the curtains aside and watched Idella and MaMary walk up the sidewalk. *Although, I only saw her a few times, and the only time I really paid her attention was when Joey stopped at her vegetable stand that day and I stayed in the car. He offered her a job as a maid in his house and I asked him about it. Joey said it was because she had been pressuring him. Had asked him over and over again about coming to work there.* Agnes's eyes narrowed. *She wanted to get next to Joey. Wanted him for herself.*

She looked at MaMary and Idella again. *Yes, it's the same Mary Baxter. The one who Joey threw up in my face when he found out I was black.*

Attraction

Ruth opened the door. "Well, look at you!" she exclaimed as Idella stepped inside. "You look mighty pretty tonight. If I didn't know it, I would take you for one of Miss Patricia's longtime friends."

Idella smiled somewhat shyly. "You would?"

"No doubt about it." The maid closed the door.

"Well, the truth is"—Idella exhaled—"I'm a bit nervous."

"And why's that?"

"Because I haven't been to that many parties in my whole life, and now to come to Patricia's barbecue . . ." She looked uncertain.

Ruth nodded. "I can only imagine. Well . . . they're all in the back-yard underneath Japanese lanterns." She nudged Idella. "There's party favors too."

"Japanese lanterns?" Idella replied. "And there's lots of people back there?"

Ruth nodded again. "I think you are guest number fifty. So you win the door prize."

"Oh, I don't know about this." Idella covered her mouth. "I didn't want to be the first person here, but I sure don't want to be singled out as I go in."

"I'm just kidding you." Ruth patted her on the back. "Go on

back there, girl. People are people, no matter what they may think." She laughed before leaving Idella to her own devices.

Idella took her time as she walked toward the backdoor that she'd entered so many times. She could see many young people gathered in the backyard through the large windows. Various people clung together, then parted and joined another group. It was obvious these people knew each other quite well. Their laughter was easy, and their conversations appeared to be effortless.

Idella felt more out of sorts than ever. "Sometimes you got to fake it to make it," she said beneath her breath as she opened the door and stepped out onto the long porch. Her eyes searched for Patricia. She finally found her. But Patricia was too far away to get her attention. Idella didn't know what to do.

She watched Patricia enjoy a deep laugh before she spoke again in a very engaging but easy fashion. It was like someone had turned the light on inside of her. Idella could tell Patricia was deep in her element; as deep inside her element as Idella felt outside of it.

The smell of barbecue was everywhere, and Idella was definitely hungry. She walked toward a long table filled with backyard barbecue favorites—from hot dogs, to steaks, to hamburgers, grilled corn, potato salad and desserts. You name it, it was all there, and done in an elegant fashion. Idella picked up a small plate and a few potato chips. She wanted to go straight for the ribs, but decided that wasn't a good idea. Her stomach complained loudly as she tossed a couple of chips in her mouth. Idella caught herself and began to nibble at one of the larger ones.

"There's more where that came from," a rich voice said from behind her.

Idella looked up into a very handsome face.

"Would you like me to get you a plate?" he offered.

"No. No, I'm fine." She looked around. "I just got here and I'm trying to figure out the lay of the land."

"There's no lay of the land. It's always the same at these gatherings. Everybody here basically knows each other. We talk about where we've been, who we know, what our plans are, where the next party's going to be and who's getting married."

"You folks sure do cover a lot of ground." Idella looked around again. "It's quite obvious that everybody knows each other."

"Just about everybody, but I've never seen you before."

"My name is Idella." She smiled. "Idella Baxter." Idella balanced her plate of chips in one hand and stuck out the other.

"And I'm Gerald Campbell." He took her hand. His hand was soft, his grip gentle.

"Nice to meet you, Gerald."

"Likewise," he said with an inquisitive look. "Now, why is it I've never seen you before?"

"I guess I'm rather new to all of this." Idella munched on another chip. "I met Patricia not too long ago, and we've become friends. So she told me about her barbecue and now I'm here. What about you?"

Gerald licked his lips. "Patricia and I go back rather far, as do most of the people here. Our grandmothers know each other, so you can say it's somewhat of a family affair."

"Your families are friends?"

"Aren't most of the families in this circle?" He smiled.

Idella shrugged. "I wouldn't know, to be honest with you. You make it sound as if you all belong to a private club."

One eyebrow went up. "In a way we do."

Idella clicked her tongue. "Shame-shame. Patricia didn't tell me the secret code that I needed in order to get in."

He laughed. "No. No secret codes. No secret codes at all. Are you hungry?"

Idella looked at the food.

"I am," Gerald said. "I'm very hungry, and I would love for somebody to eat with me. I think everybody else, especially the women, are too busy trying to make sure they don't get barbecue sauce all over their hands or on their dresses. You will share a rib or two with a brother, won't you?"

"I wouldn't mind at all," Idella said. "To tell the truth, I'm rather hungry myself." They walked over to the meat platters.

Gerald leaned close to her ear. "I could tell that you were by the way you stuffed those potato chips in your mouth."

Embarrassed, Idella replied, "Was I stuffing them?"

He laughed. "But I must admit you still looked good. Very beautiful, indeed."

She concentrated on the ribs she put on her plate. "You sound like you've had a lot of practice at this. And I think you like to move rather fast."

"I don't call that fast." He looked innocent. "I call it telling the truth." His voice lowered. "You wouldn't want me to lie, would you?"

Idella shook her head.

"And if you're pretty, you're pretty. But if you're a downright knockout, like you are"—their eyes met—"so be it."

"I see I'm going to have trouble out of you," Idella replied, a little breathlessly.

Gerald smiled. "No, no trouble at all. Do I look like a man who would cause trouble?"

She looked at him, from his perfect haircut and trimmed mustache down to his polished shoes. "Trouble with a capital *T*," Idella replied.

"You just don't know what *T* stands for. It might stand for 'tempting,' but not for 'trouble,' " Gerald replied.

Idella threw back her head and laughed.

"Idella, you made it," Patricia said as she approached.

"I sure did. I was going to come over and speak to you but you were in the middle of a group of people, and you know me, I'm not one for crowds."

"That's okay," Patricia replied. "I'm just glad you're here." She looked at Gerald. "And obviously you two have met."

Gerald took a bite of the rib he held between his fingers as he nodded.

"Yes," Idella replied.

"Good." Patricia smiled at the two of them, but her gaze lingered on Gerald's face. "There are so many people I want you to meet. So finish your food, but be careful with that sauce. They used too much and it gets all over your hands."

Gerald smiled when Idella looked at him. By then a group of people had joined them at the meat trays and different conversations erupted all around.

Idella finished eating and Patricia introduced her to so many people she could not remember their names. Throughout the introductions, she would find Gerald in the crowd and he was always looking at her. Then Idella was on her own, chitchatting here and there, but mostly she listened. On several occasions she saw Gerald and Patricia interacting with the same groups and once he put his arm around her waist. When Idella was done and Patricia was engaged in conversation elsewhere, Idella made her way to the sweet tea. Gerald met her there.

"And here you are." He bumped his shoulder against hers.

Idella looked at him. "If I wasn't sure, I'd think you were following me."

"You can be sure that's exactly what I'm doing. Following you and staring."

"And why is that?" Idella flirted. "With all these lovely ladies, I can't believe you would choose just one."

"See, you got me all wrong. I'm a one-woman man. I don't have time for anything else. No, not Gerald Campbell. Life is too short, and everything's got to count. Every move I make. Every step I take."

Idella took a drink of tea. She couldn't pretend she wasn't attracted by Gerald's looks and his style.

"Which brings me to the question," Gerald continued, "what do you do when you're not going to barbecues?"

Idella looked at him. "I work."

"That sounds like a useful thing to do." Gerald nodded.

"Yes, I believe it is. If I want to eat, it's a very useful thing to do," Idella said.

He looked at her as if he didn't know if she was kidding or not. "So are you working in the field in which you acquired your degree?"

Idella shook her head. "No." She looked him straight in the eye. "No degree. No degree at all."

"No degree." Gerald's silky brow went up.

"No, didn't even go to college. I had a chance though." She looked down. "They were going to give me a scholarship to Fisk, but things just didn't work out that way. I had to stay with my grandmother. She needed me. And she had taken care of me all my life, so I figured I could sacrifice for her."

"I see." His features softened.

"And what about you?" she asked.

"I'll start an internship in a dentist office in about three weeks. As a matter of fact, it's in the office of a family member."

"So you're a dentist?" Idella misunderstood.

"Going to be a dentist," Gerald replied patiently. "For several generations now, we Campbell men have been dentists, and so I'm following the family tradition."

"Good for you," Idella said sincerely. "You must be pretty smart, huh?"

Gerald laughed. "I can say the same about you. You had a scholarship to Fisk University."

"Well . . ." She shrugged.

"I got some advice I'd like to give you," Gerald said.

Idella looked at him, not knowing what to expect.

"I think it would be a good idea if you took up with a fellow who was on the road to being a dentist, who could take you to other barbecues, the movies, a restaurant."

Idella was surprised. "Are you saying you want to see me again?"

Gerald looked purposefully undecided. "Well . . ."

Idella smacked his arm. "I see now you are a tease."

Gerald laughed, then whispered in her ear, "So can I call you?"

Idella looked at the well-to-do crowd. Patricia was looking at her. She was willing to bet no one here, including Gerald, could understand having your telephone cut off because you didn't have the money. And if Gerald didn't understand that, how could he understand or accept living in a shotgun house on Raynor Street? *If he's interested in me, he'll have to understand,* Idella decided. *But I don't have to open up my life, MaMary's life to him so quickly. It would probably do Mr. Campbell some good to jump through a few hoops.* Idella lifted her chin. "You can meet me at the library."

"The library?" Gerald's brow creased.

"I'll be at the library on Norwood Street day after tomorrow at six," Idella replied.

Gerald studied her for a moment, then laughed. "The library it is."

Hostility

Rachel let the screen door close softly. "Well, Mother, I'm surprised to find you out here."

"I don't know why," Agnes replied. "I like fresh air as much as anyone else, particularly the night air." She looked at the backyard through the screen.

"I know you do, but it's been such a long time since you came out here to sit like this." Rachel sat next to her mother in a chair.

"I use to do it all the time, years ago. You could always find me out here gazing into the night during the summer months. Suddenly, I missed doing it," Agnes said. "I missed it a lot. So I said regardless of how this body of mine may be feeling I'm going downstairs and I'm going out on the porch. So here I am." She took a deep breath. "I get sick and tired of sitting in my room. It's not the most exciting place, you know. But when your body starts turning against you like mine has started turning against me"— she closed her eyes—"sometimes it takes control. But today I wanted it to know I'm in control. I'm in control of these old limbs of mine." Agnes rocked slowly. A satisfied smile lifted the corners of her mouth.

"I definitely like coming out here," Rachel said. "I probably got that from you. I don't expect Roger for a while, and Patricia's out with Gerald, I guess."

"Let's hope." Agnes closed her eyes.

"Young love is a wonderful thing, isn't it, Mother?"

"I guess so," Agnes replied. "But I'm certainly no expert on love and I don't think you are either."

"You don't have to be an expert," Rachel replied. "But I can remember what it feels like, and you told me a couple of weeks ago, you do too."

Agnes just shook her head. "I don't want to remember. Love didn't do me much good. I can tell you that."

"Mother, you didn't love Papa at all?"

"I loved your father." Agnes continued to rock. "I loved him. I definitely did. But it wasn't the kind that took my breath away, where I couldn't think, eat or sleep. No, no. By the time I met your father, I knew that kind of love wouldn't do me any good. So I chose a much more sensible kind. And my life blossomed because of it."

"I know all about sensible," Rachel said. "But there seems like there's something wrong with putting love and sensible together."

"My theory is," Agnes said, "you can love the right man—a smart, rich man easier than a poor, smooth-talking one."

Footsteps sounded in the kitchen, then a cabinet door closed.

"Roger?" Rachel called. "Patricia? Is that you in there?"

The footsteps came closer. Finally, the screen door opened. "Yes, it's me, Mama." Patricia stepped out onto the porch.

"We didn't expect you back so early," Rachel said.

"Well, here I am." Patricia flopped onto a cushioned rattan chair.

"Short dates are never good." Agnes looked at her granddaughter. "Did Gerald have some type of emergency?"

"I don't know what Gerald had," Patricia replied. "I haven't seen Gerald today."

"You haven't?" Agnes stopped rocking.

"We just assumed when you said you were going out, it was with Gerald," Rachel replied.

"No, I didn't see him today, yesterday or the day before. As a matter of fact, I've barely talked to him much since the barbecue."

Rachel and Agnes glanced at each other. Patricia acted as if she was interested in her nails.

"And why is that, may I ask?" Agnes pressed.

"You can ask, but the truth is I don't know any more than you do. All I know is he doesn't call me as much as he used to."

"Well, that's not a good sign," Agnes replied. "That's not good at all."

Patricia looked at her out of the corner of her eye. "Grandmother, I know it's not good. I feel it. That's why I don't care to talk about it."

"What is he saying?" Agnes ignored Patricia's hint for her not to pry. "Is he busy with Dorothy? Is he sick? What is he saying?"

"He hasn't said, Grandmother Agnes." Her voice dropped. "But I can guess."

"Guess what, baby?" Rachel asked.

"I think he may be seeing somebody else."

"Oh no," Rachel sighed.

"How do you jump to a conclusion like that?" Agnes sat forward. "Have your girlfriends said something? Have you heard something about him around town?"

"No." Patricia shook her head. "None of our friends have seen him either."

"Well, why do you think it's another woman?" Agnes asked pointedly.

"Because I noticed at the barbecue he paid an awful lot of attention to Idella. An awful lot. And since then I haven't seen or heard from him that much. Her either."

Agnes sat back.

"Idella? You must be mistaken," Rachel said. "Idella wouldn't talk to Gerald knowing that you and he are friends."

"But how would she know that, Mama?"

"You mean you didn't tell her?" Rachel said.

"There was nothing to tell her. We hadn't established anything for me to tell her. We went out on a few dates. We had fun, but there was no huge romantic spark." She looked down. "Obviously, not on Gerald's part there wasn't. So I couldn't tell Idella we were going together."

"Idella," Agnes said. "You mean to tell me that little hussy has come up in here and in one evening snatched Gerald from underneath your nose."

"Now see." Patricia pointed. "This is why I hadn't mentioned it to you before, Grandmother. I know how you can act up, and I know how you can talk. And I'm going to be honest with you: I don't want to hear that this evening."

"Well, I'm going to be honest with you." Agnes's voice trembled as she tried to keep it level. "I don't care about what you don't want to hear, Missy. This is important. You and Gerald are the future of this family."

"I know that was your plan, Grandmother. But how can you plan something like that?" Patricia threw up her hands. "I can't make that man want me if he wants Idella. There is nothing I can do about it."

"I don't understand that," Agnes replied. "He must only want one thing. Other than that, how could he want her? She has no family background and she comes from no money."

"Come on, Grandmother Agnes." Patricia looked at her. "You know how he could want her as easily as I know. Her looks pass all the rules easier than mine ever could." She sounded angry as she counted off on her fingers: "Light skin. Light eyes. Straight hair."

"I just don't believe it," Rachel said. "I think the simple thing for you to do, Patricia, is to sit down and talk to Idella about this."

"You would think that," Agnes said. "You have always been the worst when it came to making decisions. What is Patricia going to say? 'Oh, Idella, I hear you're talking to Gerald, but you need to leave him alone because I like him.' " She rolled her eyes. "Gerald is probably the best man in Idella's pitiful life that has ever paid attention to her. So do you think she is just going to lie down for our Patricia?" Her face hardened. "Absolutely not. But I blame you for this, Rachel. I blame this on you."

"Me?" Rachel exclaimed.

"Yes. You brought her and her grandmother into this house. You brought them into this house."

"Mother, wait a minute. Wait a minute. I think you are forgetting that Idella's the one that helped Patricia that day."

"Patricia didn't need her help. She did not need her help. That girl was plotting all the time to try to get into this house. She's never been in a place like this before. She's been plotting all the time." Grandmother Agnes got up. "I bet her little brain was clicking more than ours ever could. She has pulled one over on us. And shame on us for that."

"Grandmother Agnes, I don't think Idella was thinking any such thing," Patricia said.

"I do," Agnes replied. "Because I know the kind of people she came from. I know." She shook her finger. "It came to me. I remember Mary Baxter from Clarksville."

"You do?" Rachel said.

"Absolutely. Mary Baxter was a manipulator and so is her granddaughter."

"What do you know about MaMary?" Rachel asked. "You never said anything."

"Don't you worry why I didn't. But I've got my reasons." Agnes crossed her arms. "I know who these people are. And they are not going to use me and my family to move up the social ladder." She shook her head. "No, they are not. They will only do it over my dead body."

Withering

"Good morning, Miss Agnes. How you doing today?" MaMary said as she entered Agnes's bedroom. She didn't wait for an answer. "It's such a beautiful day today. And I really enjoyed my walk over here this morning." She lifted the window a bit to let in the fresh air. "Walking past some of these yards is just like walking through a huge garden. The flowers are in full bloom and the colors, oh my Lord." MaMary stopped and looked at Agnes. "But you didn't say how you're doing today."

"You didn't give me a chance," Agnes replied. "Not that I think you really care."

"Well, of course, I care." MaMary walked over to her. "I definitely do. Why would you say a thing like that, Miss Agnes?"

Agnes's eyes hardened. "Because my family invited you and your granddaughter into our lives, and you wasted no time in stabbing us in the back."

MaMary stood as straight as her body would allow. "Why, Miss Agnes, you are angry with me this morning."

"I am that and more," Agnes said.

"But why?" MaMary's arms hung at her sides. "I don't know what you're talking about. What have we done?"

"Your granddaughter, Idella, is just like every other apple that doesn't fall far from the tree."

"I beg your pardon?" MaMary's brow creased.

"Idella is just like you when you were younger, giving the appearance of respectability, but you didn't hesitate to latch on to a man if you thought it would benefit you."

"Miss Agnes, I just don't know what you're talking about. You didn't even know me when I was younger. And as far as Idella is concerned, she's not that kind of girl."

Agnes's eyes spit fire. "You're mistaken on both accounts. I did know you in Clarksville. You use to live on that farm on Slow Creek Road. You sold vegetables from a stand."

MaMary's mouth opened. "Yes, I did."

"I know you did," Agnes said.

"But I was a happily married woman back then. There was nobody in my life but my husband." Hurt entered her voice.

"I bet this is the same innocent act and look you used back then. Men are suckers for this kind of thing. But I'm not. You had a reputation for bringing attention to yourself, Mary, so you could get what you wanted." She looked down her nose. "And I don't think it mattered to you how you got it."

"I was known to be outspoken," MaMary said. "Yes, ma'am, I was. But I didn't have anything to do with any men."

"Didn't you do cleaning at the Wyndhams' house?"

"Yes." MaMary looked surprised. "I worked for Mr. Joseph Wynd'm for a little while." Her pronunciation was totally different from Agnes's.

"The word was out that you purposefully sought a position there and you weren't interested in cleaning."

"No, ma'am, Miss Agnes. That is absolutely not true. I took a part-time job there when my Henry lost his job. And I can assure you all I did for Mr. Wynd'm was clean his house." MaMary's brow creased again. "That's crazy talk, Miss Agnes. I don't even wanna think about those people. That man was after me and . . ." MaMary started to say more but changed her mind. "They're responsible for my boy dying and for us being burned out of our home."

"You can call it crazy talk if you want," Agnes replied, "but there had to be some truth in it."

"But it wasn't true," MaMary argued.

Agnes stared at her in an uncanny way.

"It wasn't." MaMary's voice trembled. "I swear."

"Well, where did Idella get her sluttish ways?"

MaMary clasped her hands. "What did Idella do to make you talk like this?"

"What did she do?" Agnes repeated. "Came to Patricia's barbecue, that Patricia was kind enough to invite her to, and secretly made advances toward Patricia's boyfriend."

"I can't believe it," MaMary said. "That doesn't sound like Idella."

"Are you saying I'm making it up?"

"No. Of course not, Miss Agnes. I'm not saying you're making it up." MaMary's hands went out in explanation. "But maybe there's some misunderstanding here."

"No, this situation is clear. Your granddaughter has repaid my family's kindness by offering herself to Patricia's boyfriend," Agnes said. "And although Rachel and Patricia may not have the stomach to tell you, I have no problem doing it."

Silence filled the room.

"I think I better go downstairs and get your breakfast." MaMary sought an excuse to leave the room.

"Go," Agnes said with her face averted. She couldn't stand to look at Mary any longer. Agnes could see Mary felt she was telling the truth about Joey Wyndham and that incensed her. *Who did she think she was to say a white man like Joey was after her?*

As quickly as Agnes's anger rose her memories smothered it.

But Joey had wanted her. The pain of it washed over Agnes. *Even my maid said so that evening. God, that was a horrible time. Peggy came in that day and told me she'd heard some disturbing things about Joey. One of them she knew was true. The other she wasn't sure of.*

"What did you hear?" I asked her.

"Miss Agnes, I know this is going to hurt you, but I swear it's true. You see, you and I are new around here."

"What is it?" I demanded.

"Mr. Joey is married, Miss Agnes. He's been married for a couple of years now."

"Married!"

"Yes, ma'am."

I started to cry and I couldn't stop. "What else did you hear?"

"I heard he tried to force himself on one of his maids. But she wouldn't have him. They say she even quit working for him."

Peggy continued to talk, but I was so hurt because Joey was married that I sat down and wrote him a letter right then and there.

May 17, 1921

Joey,

At this moment I am so shocked I cannot confront you face to face. To discover that you are married and have taken advantage of my innocence hurts me beyond compare. I trusted your intentions toward me were honorable and that I would be the future Mrs. Wyndham. I demand an apology for your misleading me.

Devastated,
Agnes

I couldn't wait for Joey to read the letter. I knew where he was that night so I had Peggy deliver it. His response . . . Agnes clenched her eyes in an attempt to protect herself from the memory. *He scrawled his response on top of my writing:*

One nigger wench is the same as any other and could never be my wife.

After all those years Agnes was surprised by a tear that ran down her cheek.

My world crashed . . . but I couldn't let go. I confronted him face to face and I found out Joey was not the man I thought he was. To say he preferred Mary Baxter to me—a dark, nappy-headed maid to me.

Agnes's anger flared. *I won't let Mary Baxter get the best of me. And*

I won't let her conniving granddaughter get the best of my Patricia. Mary will pay for being a liar and a manipulator just as Joey has paid for disgracing me. He said I was a nigger. She looked in the mirror. Her image reassured her that he was wrong.

Agnes's gaze dropped to the large jewelry box that sat on her dressing table. She had used it many times through the years and now Agnes decided she would use its hidden contents again.

MaMary tried to avoid Agnes as much as she could the rest of the day. She was relieved when the workday was over and she was able to meet Idella.

"Hi," Idella said as she approached MaMary, who was standing on the sidewalk in front of the Addisons' home. "Did you get off early?"

"No. I just thought I'd meet you out here today."

They began to walk in silence. Idella glanced at MaMary a couple of times. "Is everything okay?"

"As well as it could be, I guess."

"What do you mean by that?" Idella replied.

"Miss Agnes was in rare form today. Boy, I tell you something put a fire underneath that woman and she refused to let it go out."

"So she took it out on you?"

"In a way," MaMary said softly.

"But that's not fair."

"In this case she feels it is."

"Do you?" Idella asked. "Is it something that you did?"

"Not recently."

"Huh?" Idella sounded confused.

"No, Dee. It's something that she claims you did."

Idella's hand flew to her chest. "Me? I can't imagine what that could be."

MaMary looked at Idella's perplexed face. "I know, child." She threaded her arm through Idella's. "I'm sure there's some kind of mistake. But Miss Agnes has got it in her mind that you purposely came on to Patricia's boyfriend at her barbecue a couple of weeks ago."

"Gerald is Patricia's boyfriend?"

MaMary stopped walking. "Gerald? Who's Gerald?"

"Remember I told you I recently met a young man that I liked?"

"Yes. You did mention somebody, but you didn't say much about him."

"Well, I met him at the barbecue. And he's so different, MaMary, from everybody I've been out with. I'm just beginning to know him." Idella paused as she wondered about her own motives for keeping MaMary and Gerald apart. "He's a really nice guy. I've never had anybody treat me the way Gerald does. He treats me like I'm somebody special and he makes me feel good about myself," Idella tried to explain. "And God, is he good looking."

MaMary looked at her. "From the way you talk about him, you really like this boy."

"I do." Idella returned her gaze.

"But you haven't introduced him to me."

Idella drew a deep breath. "I know, MaMary. It's kind of complicated." She looked down. "It's just that from the way he's been brought up I know coming down here and seeing where we live would take a little adjusting to for a man like him." Idella rushed on: "But it's not that I'm ashamed of us or anything. You know I'm not."

MaMary looked away.

Idella gently tugged her arm. "I wanted to give him a little time to see me just as another human being before he drew any conclusions about who we are based on where we can afford to live. And MaMary, you've got to consider, I've introduced you to a couple of guys who just weren't right, and I didn't want to make the same mistake again."

"Well," MaMary sighed, "either way, this Gerald has caused quite a stir. Agnes says you've stabbed them in the back, the entire family."

"But I had no idea that Gerald and Patricia were seeing each other. She never told me that, and he didn't either."

"Well, in Miss Agnes's eyes, he's spoken for. And from the way she talked to me today, I don't think she's gon' back down from this or forgive you, if you did it or not."

"This is ridiculous." Idella shook her head. "I want to see what

Gerald has to say about it. We've been talking for a couple of weeks now and never once did he mention Patricia."

"Well, the truth is," MaMary said, "do you think it would be in his best interest to?"

Idella went silent.

MaMary patted her hand. "This is something that's got to be straightened out, Dee, or it's going to give us trouble. I've never seen Miss Agnes like that. She attacked me in so many ways I just can't tell you."

"Well, I'm going to talk to Gerald," Idella said. "I wish our phone was back on. But we won't be able to pay what we owe and the reinstatement fee for two more weeks."

"Catching up takes time," MaMary replied.

"I could call Gerald from a phone booth, but this just isn't the kind of conversation I want to have over the phone." She exhaled long and hard. "I'll wait until tomorrow. We're going to get together tomorrow evening to have a bite to eat." Her brow softened. "I'm sure there's some kind of explanation for this." They turned the corner. "Are you going back to work tomorrow?"

"I certainly am," MaMary replied. "I sorta enjoy it. I'm sure we'll get this thing straightened out."

"I'm sure we will," Idella replied, but she hoped that didn't mean giving up Gerald because the Addisons had claimed him.

Blame

*I*t's a perfect day, weather-wise, MaMary thought as the Addisons' house came into view. She noticed the strange car parked in the driveway, but her thoughts focused on the inside of the house. MaMary hoped the weather was good inside as well, and that Miss Agnes had calmed down from yesterday.

As she approached the building, two men with concerned faces came out. They got in the car and MaMary watched them drive away before she entered the house.

"What in the world is going on here?" MaMary asked as she stepped into the kitchen.

"You'll find out soon enough," Ruth said uncomfortably. "And this is nothing. Last night the ambulance was here."

"The ambulance," MaMary repeated.

"Yes."

"And the men that I saw leaving, who were they?"

"They were doctors."

"Did Patricia have another one of those seizures?" Concern descended on MaMary's face.

"No. They were here to see Miss Agnes."

"Oh no." MaMary's hand went up to her dark cheek. "What happened?"

"I don't think it's my place to tell you," Ruth replied. Her eyes avoided MaMary's. "Miss Rachel is upstairs. I think you need to talk to her about it."

"All right," MaMary replied. "I will." She walked through the kitchen toward the staircase. MaMary mounted the stairs as quickly as her body would allow and headed down the hall. Rachel came out of Agnes's bedroom before she reached the door.

"Morning, Miss Rachel. Ruth told me the ambulance was here last night for Miss Agnes."

Rachel's normally smooth brow wrinkled. "Yes, Mary, it was." She paused. "I need to talk to you."

"You bring her in here." Agnes's weak voice still held a commanding tone. "You bring her in here. I want to see her."

MaMary searched Rachel's face for an answer as to what was going on, but Rachel looked at the floor as she stood aside for MaMary to enter the bedroom.

Slowly, MaMary walked over to Agnes, who was propped up on her pillows. Her skin was chalky.

"Miss Agnes," MaMary said. "How you doing?"

"I'm here," Agnes managed to say. "But that's no thanks to you."

"Beg your pardon?"

"I said no thanks to you, Mary." Her voice grew stronger.

"How do I figure into any of this?" She looked at Rachel, then back at Agnes.

Agnes's eyes narrowed. "Bringing you here was a far bigger mistake than I could have imagined."

"Don't say that, Miss Agnes. We had a rough enough time yesterday." MaMary shook her head. "And you're going to need your strength to get well."

Agnes closed her eyes. "I should have known there would be trouble when I saw you forgetting things around here. But I decided to let it go, and now you've nearly killed me."

"Wha-at?" MaMary's hand went to her heart. "Why you saying this to me?"

"Because you nearly did, Mary. You left a double dose of the liquid medicine for me, and I took it." Agnes swallowed. "It nearly killed me. It's the truth."

Mary was visibly stunned. "I did? Are you certain?"

"The ambulance wouldn't have been here last night, and these doctors wouldn't be traipsing in and out of here this morning. I'm telling you I nearly died, Mary. Whatever happens in that no-good brain of yours nearly killed me!"

"I'm so sorry, Miss Agnes." MaMary sat down in Agnes's chair, something she never did. "I'm so sorry."

"I'm sure you are, but sorry isn't going to change any of this."

Silence filled the room.

"You know you can't work here anymore. There's no telling what you might do." Agnes looked at her from beneath heavy lids. "And this has upset poor Roger so badly, he doesn't want Idella working at the catering service either."

"Oh no," MaMary said. "What will we do if Idella loses her job too?"

"You should have thought about that when you took this position. Didn't you know something was wrong with you?" Agnes's voice was suddenly weak.

"There's no need for that, Mother," Rachel warned. "You can see Mary is distraught over what has happened."

Agnes turned her face away from both of them. "I can see she is, but there's nothing I can do about that now. The woman nearly cost me my life."

"I want to talk to Miss Rachel, right now," Idella said from the hall.

"Just wait a minute and let me see what Miss Rachel wants to do," Ruth replied.

"I've got to talk to somebody," Idella insisted.

Rachel and MaMary turned toward the bedroom door as Idella walked in.

"Miss Rachel, I tried to tell Idella to wait downstairs, but she wouldn't listen to me."

"I'm sorry, Miss Rachel," Idella apologized. "But I couldn't wait. What is going on here?" She looked at Agnes lying in her bed. "I got to work and Mr. Addison told me I was fired. But when I asked him why, he told me he had too much work to do, and that I could ask you, MaMary, once I got home." Idella looked at her grand-mother. "So I went home. But you weren't there. So I came here. What is going on?" She looked around the room.

"It appears that Mary accidentally gave my mother a double dose of medication and she had a very, very bad reaction to it. She nearly died last night."

"What!" Idella said.

"Yes." Rachel looked saddened.

"But how did MaMary give her a double dose of medication last night when she leaves in the afternoon?"

"Before I leave, I measure the liquid out for her," MaMary replied.

"Well, Miss Agnes, didn't you see that it was more than usual?"

Agnes turned steel-gray eyes toward Idella. "That was one of a few duties that Mary had around here. She made a mistake. An awful one. And instead of you being apologetic, you turn it on me?"

Idella shook her head and looked down. "I am sorry, Miss Agnes. I'm so sorry, but I'm just shocked by this whole thing."

"You should be shocked," Agnes replied. "And ashamed of your-self for coming in here with such an attitude."

"I am sorry, Miss Agnes," Idella apologized again. "But I was just fired. And if I've been fired, I assume MaMary won't be working here any longer." She looked at her grandmother.

MaMary shook her head.

"This is horrible. We've both lost our jobs and I don't know what we're gonna do. So excuse me if I'm not reacting the way you think I should."

"Well, it could be worse." Agnes looked at her again without compassion. "Last night, I thought about filing charges against her and having her committed."

"No-o," Idella said.

MaMary's eyes widened.

"Yes, I did," Agnes said. "I was so sick." She closed her eyes. "I was so sick. And when they told me it was because I had overdosed on my medication, I knew what had happened. She should never have taken this type of position knowing she had mental problems. And you shouldn't have allowed her to take it if you knew it."

They were both stunned into silence.

"And I still might do it. I still may have her committed," Agnes threatened.

MaMary started to cry quietly. Idella knelt down and put her arms around her grandmother. "MaMary, don't cry. Don't cry. Please, Miss Agnes, don't call the authorities. I don't think we could live through that."

"Mother, please," Rachel said, "Aren't things bad enough?"

Agnes sighed. "I guess they are. But I can't handle having her work here anymore."

MaMary's shoulder trembled as she held her hands over her face.

Rachel passed her a tissue.

"And if Roger has fired you, there's nothing I can do about that. He runs Addison Catering," Agnes said.

Idella placed her hand on her grandmother's hand. "I just don't know what we're gonna do." Tears came to her eyes.

"Maybe once things cool down," Rachel said, "we can get Roger to take you back."

"But how long will that be?" Idella asked. "We're already behind on our bills. We thought we could catch up with both of us work-ing."

There was silence again.

"I know by now you think I'm heartless," Agnes said in a tired voice. "But I'm not." She paused. "The daughter of a friend of mine owns a house on Martha's Vineyard. When I spoke with her, she told me Janice is in a bind, and needs some summer help. It would just be general maid work, of course, but perhaps it will help you for a few months until you can find something else," Agnes said.

"Martha's Vineyard? Isn't that in Massachusetts?" Idella asked.

"Yes, it is," Agnes replied.

"But what about MaMary? What will she do while I'm gone?"

"We'll stay in touch," Rachel said, "and make sure she's doing okay."

Idella's and MaMary's eyes met.

"If I go there to work, I'd live at the house and wouldn't have any expenses."

"Yes, you would live at the house," Agnes confirmed. "You'd be a live-in maid."

"A maid," MaMary said. "Idella, I don—"

"Then I could send my money back to you, MaMary," Idella reasoned. Fresh tears fell down MaMary's face. "This job would keep us afloat."

Idella looked at Agnes. Everything had happened so fast. She didn't know how she felt—if she wanted to scream or cry. Idella knew neither would do any good. Finally, she asked, "When would I start?"

"Once I feel up to it," Agnes said in a tired voice, "I'm going to give Alicia a call and see if Janice still needs a maid. And if so"— she looked at Idella—"the sooner you leave the better."

Sadness

"Knock-knock. It's me, Savannah."

"Come in," Idella called out. "We're back here in the bedroom."

Idella heard Savannah giving instructions to her children as they entered the house. "Come on, y'all," Savannah said. "And don't be touching things either. Stay right with me."

Savannah appeared in the door. "I had to finish giving them dinner. And then I decided to go ahead and give them their bath." She bumped the baby farther up on her hip. "I hope I didn't take too long."

"No," Idella said. "I wanted you to come over because I need to talk to you about something. I'm leaving in the morning."

Savannah scanned the bedroom as Idella opened a drawer and removed some clothes. MaMary's face looked drawn and older than usual. She stared at the open suitcase in the middle of the floor. "Where you going?" Savannah asked.

"I'm going to take a job this summer at a place called Martha's Vineyard."

"Martha's Vineyard. Where is that?"

"It's up in Massachusetts."

"Massachusetts?" Savannah repeated.

"It's up north," Idella explained. "On the east coast."

Savannah's face wrinkled as she tried to picture it.

"Not far from New York." Idella sought an image Savannah could understand.

"Oh-h. That's far away," Savannah said.

"Yeah." Idella looked at MaMary, who simply closed her eyes. "Yeah, it's sorta far away, but it's only for this summer."

"But I thought you was working for Addison Catering."

"Not anymore," Idella replied. "Neither MaMary nor I have a job at the moment."

Savannah's jaw dropped. She looked at MaMary. "Something happened."

"Yes, something did happen, but we're not going to talk about that right now, Savannah," Idella replied. "That's not real important. Right now I want to talk to you because you've been our next-door neighbor practically all my life. Your mama and MaMary were good friends. And now MaMary's going to be here by herself for the next couple of months." She looked in Savannah's eyes. "I know neither one of us has a telephone, but I hope within a couple of weeks I'll have enough money to pay the phone company what they need so I can call home. You hear that, MaMary?" Idella touched her knee.

MaMary nodded, but said nothing.

"Are you okay, MaMary?" Savannah sat down beside her and put the baby on her thigh.

A couple of tears ran down MaMary's cheek.

"You're crying," Savannah said. Alarm was in her eyes when she looked at Idella again. "Don't cry, MaMary." Savannah put her arm around her. "I'll be right next door if you need anything."

The baby pulled up to its feet on Savannah's thigh. She pressed her cheek against her mother's as she looked at MaMary's face. Instinctively, the baby reached out for MaMary. She took the baby in her arms and held her close as tears continued to fall.

"MaMary, please don't cry." Idella's voice trembled. "I can't stand to see you cry."

MaMary nodded. She wiped her face with one of her hands. "It's my fault. It's all my fault," she said softly.

"It's not anybody's fault. It's what happened," Idella replied, although she wished she could change it. "We'll be out of this in a few months. Things will straighten out." Idella glanced at the clock. "I gotta meet a friend of mine in a half an hour. He's going to meet me at the library."

"That library up on Norwood?" Savannah asked.

"Yes." Idella looked at the clock again.

"You got some business up there that's got to do with your leaving?" Savannah pried.

"No. It's definitely not business," Idella half-explained. "It's a guy I like. I've just been cautious about telling him where I live."

"Well, if you haven't told him that, then he must not be someone you need to deal with."

"It's not that." Idella patted her clothes inside the suitcase. "I wanted to find out some things first. Get to know him a little better before I make my life an open book. I'm not always as clear as you are when it comes to men." Idella lifted an eyebrow.

"Yeah, right." Savannah dismissed Idella with a wave. "Lord knows I could have done without giving some of those Negroes I messed with my address." She shook her crossed leg.

Idella touched MaMary again. "I'm going to have Gerald bring me home this evening, MaMary. In light of everything that's happened, I guess it doesn't really matter now. But I want to introduce him to you. I hope you like him." She tried to smile. "He's really nice."

Love beamed from MaMary's eyes as she looked at Idella. "I'm sure I will. Yes, you do that. Bring him on home to meet me. Your life can't stop because of this."

"And yours can't either." Idella put more clothes into the suitcase.

"How you getting to Massachusetts?" Savannah asked.

"I'm taking Greyhound."

"That's gotta be a long, long ride."

"It's going to be a mighty long ride." Idella felt a little fear. She had never been away from home. "I leave early in the morning, and I'll travel for at least one day before I get there."

"This could be kinda exciting," Savannah said. "Going to a new place. Meeting new people. I don't think I'll ever get out of this hole. Put that down." Savannah pointed at her eldest son. "You two sit over there. Sit right there and do not move." The two kids, with hurt puppy eyes, followed their mother's instructions.

"That's about it." Idella looked around. "And I don't want to be late." She got up off her knees.

"I think we'll be going too," Savannah replied. "I know they're sleepy so I might as well go on home and put them to bed. Ricky's coming by tonight." She smiled. "He's bringing me a little something." Savannah batted her eyes, then pointed at the kids. "So y'all better be sleeping when he gets here."

Idella, Savannah and the children walked outside together. MaMary stood on the other side of the screen door.

"I almost forgot." Idella looked at MaMary. "Day after tomorrow, you need to pick up my last check. With that I want you to pay something on our last bills. That's the only money we'll have for the next two weeks, since most of your money paid for my trip."

"I won't forget, Dee," MaMary promised.

"Good. I'll be back," Idella said, "with Gerald."

MaMary put on a small smile, but the yellow light over the stoop seemed to exaggerate the deep lines in her face.

Idella hurried up the street. Her heart pounded as she thought about everything that had taken place. She wasn't sure what to tell Gerald, but Idella knew if he was going to be a part of her life, she would have to tell him the truth regardless of the relationship he had with the Addison family. She also felt bitter that she and MaMary had both been fired. Still, Idella reluctantly acknowledged, Miss Agnes had shown some compassion by arranging a job for her on Martha's Vineyard—a job that meant the difference between having a roof over their heads and being out on the street.

Idella took the bus and got off at the appropriate corner. She walked over to Norwood and entered the library. Immediately, her eyes went to the large clock. She was five minutes late. Idella walked to the wooden table and chairs where Gerald had met her on three other occasions. The last time they met they had gone to a movie. He teased her about not allowing him to come to her home. Idella remembered how, in a playful manner, Gerald claimed he must not be good enough. She sat at their table and recalled how she promised to take him home the next time to meet MaMary.

Despite everything, Idella smiled. She liked being with Gerald. It didn't seem to matter that they were from different backgrounds. The attraction they felt made it easy for them to find a way to bridge their worlds. The limited time she had spent with him seemed immense. Gerald was able to make her see her own possibilities. To him, the world was a bowl of opportunities and Gerald felt he was born with a large spoon to taste it all. Idella believed that with a man like Gerald by her side she could do the same.

She looked at the front door again as a young woman and her son entered the library.

Since the barbecue two weeks ago, Idella had seen Gerald three times. It was after the movie that she had allowed him to kiss her. Talk about sweetness. Idella never knew a kiss could be sweet, but Gerald's was. What impressed her was it was a kiss and nothing more. He didn't push for anything. Idella decided Gerald was a gentleman, and she liked that.

She continued to wait as the time slipped away. Idella walked around the library. She looked at the countless books on the shelves. Finally, after thirty minutes, she went to the pay phone and called the number Gerald had carefully written on a slip of paper. No one answered.

Idella waited for an hour before she got back on the bus and returned home. She didn't know what to think. She feared something may have happened to Gerald, but a little voice deep inside asked, "has he deliberately stayed away?" Idella didn't know and she wouldn't find out before she left for Martha's Vineyard.

She entered the house and closed the screen door quietly behind her. MaMary was sitting on the worn-out couch, beading. Immediately, Idella recognized the black pattern. It was MaMary's way of relaxing her mind and expressing her sadness.

"You're back already?" MaMary said.

Idella nodded. She went and stood over MaMary. "He didn't come."

They looked into each other's eyes.

"I'm sure he had a good reason, Dee."

Idella nodded again.

"When you get to Martha's Vineyard, you should call him," MaMary said. "Make sure he's okay." There was pause before she repeated, "I'm sure he had a good reason." MaMary grabbed Idella's hand and held it.

It took Idella more than a day on the bus to reach Martha's Vineyard. When she wasn't sleeping, MaMary's haunting eyes entered her thoughts more than she ever thought anything could. She remembered MaMary's hug and how she gave her the bag of beads that sat beside her on the bus seat.

"Maybe you'll find time to do some beading while you're there," she said. "It's been awhile since you made a purse. And you know how it is—when you don't bead, you tend to forget how."

Idella knew it was MaMary's simple way of trying to find something to keep her mind off things during the months she'd be away, but it was also a personal bridge between them. She reminded Idella, "Beading is something I gave you. Just like my mother gave it to me, and her mother before that, and her mother before that, all the way back to the Ancient Mother."

Idella looked down at the bag of beads. It symbolized the special bond between her and MaMary. It was something the two of them alone shared.

As the miles rolled by, Idella wondered if she had done the right thing in agreeing to the job so quickly, but she knew they had to continue to take care of themselves somehow. The thin, distant lifeline of Martha's Vineyard seemed to be the most logical choice. Three months was not a long time out of a lifetime, she told herself.

When Idella arrived, she retrieved her suitcase from underneath the bus and took a cab to the address that Rachel had given her. In the early morning hours, she knocked on the back door.

Elsie, who introduced herself as the cook, let Idella in and showed her a small room where she would sleep. She told her to hurry and dress in the proper uniform because the Thorns were expecting early guests. After so much drama, Idella thought her introduction into the Thorn household would have been more eventful, but it was nothing of the kind.

Ill Will

Patricia had looked in on Grandmother Agnes earlier, but she never knew it. Her sleep was so deep her skin was nearly as pale as her pillow. It frightened Patricia to see Grandmother Agnes that way. Her mother did the best she could to tell her what all had taken place: MaMary's mistake, Grandmother Agnes's flirtation with death, and Idella being caught in the middle. Grandmother Agnes had remained in bed for two days and the whole house seemed to be filled with whispers. The constant doctor visits fueled the quiet talk. But they had to come. Agnes refused to go to the hospital.

Slowly, Patricia opened her grandmother's door and looked inside again. Her favorite crystal lamp was on and it gave soft light throughout the room. Patricia's vision adjusted to the change as she tried to see if Agnes's eyes were open or closed.

"Pat," she said softly, "come on in."

"I didn't know if you were awake or not, Grandmother."

"I'm awake. Come on in. Let me see your face."

With careful steps, Patricia went over to Grandmother Agnes's bed. She sat down beside her. "How are you feeling?"

"Fair to middlin'," Agnes replied. "Much better than I felt last night."

"Actually it wasn't last night," Patricia said.

"What is today?" Agnes inquired.

"Today is Thursday."

"Ohh." Agnes nodded. "Better than I felt night before last."

"The amount of time isn't important," Patricia assured her. "What is, is that you are feeling better."

Agnes smiled.

Patricia shook her head. "What happened is really horrible."

"Yes, life can be horrible, can't it?" Agnes replied. "But Mary never should have worked here, Pat. Her mind is bad."

Patricia nodded. Her eyes filled with concern. "But it wasn't that obvious to me."

"You had to be around her a lot to know," Agnes said.

"So you think Idella knew?"

"Yes, I think she knew. But Mary's her grandmother." Agnes's eyes almost closed. "You can tell she loves her. And when you love people, you tend to look over their faults."

Patricia looked at her grandmother's face. She knew exactly what she meant.

"And really, the girl is better off working at Martha's Vineyard for the summer. She could also be in danger with Mary being like that."

"You think so?"

"Yes." Agnes nodded. "Yes, I do. I noticed some other things too. But I kept quiet because I wanted to help them out." She looked straight into Patricia's eyes. "Mary is definitely a harm to herself and to others."

"I never would have guessed it," Patricia replied.

"And Idella being in such a delicate condition and all, she needs to be careful. A woman has to be careful at this time of life."

"Delicate condition?" Patricia's brow wrinkled.

"Yes." Agnes's gaze poured into hers. "That's why I said what I said. Mary could be a danger to Idella because Idella is pregnant."

Patricia sat back. "How do you know that?"

"Oh, Dr. Taylor told me." She rested her eyes. "But of course it was confidential."

"Pregnant," Patricia repeated the word.

"Yes. She is in trouble."

"By who?" Patricia was afraid to ask.

"By one of those boys that she's been dealing with. People we don't know, of course. With a girl like that, you never know what to expect. She seemed so innocent and all when she came here, but I never really bought it. She's just like so many girls in Memphis who grew up in that place."

"What place?" Patricia asked.

"P.V. It's a housing project with a nickname that is not used in polite society. The girls there are so poor and they have no morals. They will sleep with anyone." Agnes paused. "I know about it because through the years I've dealt with all kinds of people." She touched Patricia's hand. "But we've tried to protect you from those kinds of things."

Patricia's curiosity deepened. "What does 'P.V.' stand for?"

"Substitute a *P* word for a woman's private parts, then add 'Valley.' "

Shock widened Patricia's eyes.

Agnes continued. "I wouldn't be surprised if Mary didn't know she was pregnant."

"I just don't know what to say," Patricia replied.

"You see, Idella got her ways, if not her looks, from Mary. Mary was born and raised out in the country near Clarksville, Tennessee. Those people didn't know anything about morals. Most of the women who lived there were tramps." Agnes looked down. "So Idella going up to Martha's Vineyard is good thing. Maybe she'll stay there long enough where she can have the baby and come back and continue with her life."

"So you were thinking about her despite everything that had happened."

Agnes closed her eyes. "I was thinking of both of them." She nodded slowly. "Gerald's grandmother, Dorothy, called me today. She wanted to know how I was doing. We talked awhile. I had to tell her the truth about the situation. We've been friends for a long time. She thought I was mighty kind to continue to help them in light of everything. And I told her to tell Gerald the truth about Idella." Agnes looked at Patricia. "A young man with a future like

Gerald does not need a woman like that in his life." She paused. "I told Dorothy that eventually she may have blamed the baby on him. Yes, mental illness and a woman with an illegitimate child is not the kind of association Gerald needs. Dorothy is my longtime friend. I was obligated to tell her."

Agnes and Patricia's eyes locked.

"So perhaps Gerald will come to his senses now," Agnes continued. "Young men's eyes tend to wander, you know. Dorothy and I talked about that too. When we were done, I told her we'd love to have them back over to dinner when I'm feeling better."

Patricia looked down. She wondered about the convenient timing of it all. "What did she say?"

"She said they'd love to come, and for you to let Gerald know when the time is right."

Patricia nodded.

"Is your father home?" Agnes shifted in the bed.

"Yes. He's downstairs."

"Would you tell him I'd like to see him, please? Alone."

"Sure, Grandmother." Patricia gave her grandmother a soft kiss on her cheek. "I'll get him. But after you talk to Dad, you must rest."

"I will. I will be able to rest after I talk to your father."

Agnes watched Patricia close the door. Her body felt weak. She could feel something inside was dreadfully wrong, but despite her physical discomfort, Agnes believed with all her heart she was doing the right thing. *As a politician, my father taught me lying or using what you know for a good cause is never wrong. Yes, I've lied, and I'll continue to lie to ensure Patricia's future. There's not much I wouldn't do to make sure my family will be well taken care of after I'm gone. Even though that overdose I took may bring that on earlier than I ever envisioned.* She inhaled. *Idella is out of the way. Mary Baxter's grandchild is out of the way. She's no longer able to bring the past into the present and remind me how Joey said if he wanted a black woman, he'd prefer that nigger, Mary, over me.*

Agnes focused on the tap at her door.

"Mother Agnes," Roger called.

"Yes. Come in, Roger," she commanded in a weak voice.

He did as he was told and came and stood by her bed. Roger looked uncomfortable. He always looked uncomfortable when they were alone. He had good reason. "I hear you're feeling better than ever," Roger said.

"I am feeling better. Yes," Agnes replied. "But I'll feel even better when some things are taken care of."

A nervous twitch moved the corner of Roger's mouth. "Well, right now, Mother Agnes, I think you just need to take care of yourself. Get a little stronger. You don't need to think about anything but your health."

"Are you really that concerned about my health, Roger?" she asked. Her weak eyes were still able to pierce him. "At this point in our lives I can say to you straight out, I doubt it. Once I am gone, then the Sawyer money will be yours for the pickings. Rachel's not like me, she doesn't have my strength. She won't be able to keep you from draining every penny we have."

"I can't believe that this is what we're talking about tonight."

"There's no better night to talk about it. Time is important," she replied. "But I must say, I have come to like you more than I thought I ever would." Her face softened just a little.

Roger looked down before he looked into her eyes again.

"It's been a mutual give and take of sorts," Agnes continued.

"I guess that's one way of looking at it." Roger remained standing.

"If I hadn't quietly attended to your gambling debts throughout the years, Addison Restaurant and Catering would have closed a long time ago. But on the other hand"—she took a deep breath with effort—"I wouldn't be able to have the things done that I needed."

Roger shook his head. "And I tell you, Mother Agnes, that's not something I'm proud of taking part in."

"Pride?" She would have laughed if she could. "You and I are all about pride. Our personal pride, pride in our family name and the image that we have. Your snooping around for me and making sure things were to our advantage, and I do mean our advantage, Roger, I think it's a small price to pay for your pride."

Roger simply looked at her.

"But this time I got something a little more complicated that we need to do."

Roger ran his hand over his hair. "I still think you need to rest, Mother Agnes. You may think I don't care about your health, but I do. You need to rest before you embark on any of your missions."

"Missions . . . is that what you called them? Well, let me tell you, this might be my most important one yet." She closed her eyes. "I know it will be one of the most satisfying."

"How so?" Roger asked.

She looked at him. "The future of our family depends on this. Patricia's future depends on this."

Roger's eyes narrowed. "Patricia's future?"

"Yes. Your daughter's future depends on you getting Mary Baxter out of this city."

"What?" He stepped back.

"Mary Baxter's a threat to the wheels that I've put in motion. I've managed to get Idella out of here long enough for Gerald to get her out of his system. Once the folks we know find out about her condition"—she paused for emphasis—"and her family background of mental illness, they won't want anything to do with her." She closed her eyes again. "And the only person that can challenge any of what is being said is her grandmother."

"Now, wait a minute." Roger put his hands up. "Wait one minute. What are you telling me you want me to do?"

"Let's put it this way, I've got an old friend in Clarksville, Tennessee, who owes me and he knows it. His name is Joseph Wyndham. He's a white man with importance and clout. I'm going to send him a special letter," she said softly, "reminding him of things he never wants anybody to know." A bitter smile touched her lips. "I have no doubt that he will pull whatever strings are necessary to have Mary Baxter quietly committed under whatever conditions I say."

"You've got to be joking," Roger said.

"Do I look as if I'm joking, Roger?" Her face turned ugly with revenge. "Do I look as if I'm in a position to joke?"

"No, you don't but . . . I'ma tell you, I don't want any part of this," Roger said. "No part at all."

"You think you have a choice?" Agnes asked. "Let me make it clear to you, you don't. I simply kept the wolves at bay when it came to your debts, but I never paid all the money you owed. No. Just enough to keep them at bay."

"What do you mean?" Roger stared at her.

"It means that you're not totally out of the woods, Roger. And you won't be until I hand over some more money."

"I don't believe this." Roger walked away from the bed. "I don't believe it." He turned to Agnes. "How can one woman hold so much evil and hatred inside of herself? How?"

"Life and my father taught me how. They taught me it's either you or me. Them or us. That you have to look out for your own and a lot of times that means someone else has to fall." One thin brow lifted. "In the big picture, self-preservation is the strongest urge we have and I have only looked out for my own, meaning my daughter, Rachel, my family's money when it came to you, and now my family's future when it comes to Patricia." Agnes paused. "My dead husband's money, and my inheritance from Father, who taught me everything I know, has enabled me to do that."

Roger dropped into a chair. He looked down and shook his head.

"It shouldn't be that hard, Roger. Shouldn't be that hard at all. We've got a few days to work things out. Initially, your job is to make sure that Joey Wyndham gets my letter and that he has set things up." Agnes exhaled. "Just give me a few days. I need to work out the details," Agnes said.

Roger sat back. "And you are a master at doing that, aren't you?"

"I think so," Agnes replied. "It's the details of people's lives that are important and what they are willing to pay for."

Roger looked at her with disgust.

"What are you calling me in your mind right now? An extortionist? A blackmailer?" She turned her head. "Call me what you like, it does not matter."

"So that's how you see it," Roger said.

"I'm too old and tired to see it any other way." Agnes closed her eyes again. "I just need to let the dust settle around everything that's happened and I'll need Idella's last check from Addison Catering." She inhaled with difficulty again. "I'm tired now. You can go."

Agnes listened to Roger leave the room. With what strength she had, she got out of bed. Agnes crossed the floor and opened her old jewelry box. It frustrated her when it took several tries to remove the velvet bottom, but once it was done, she saw the yellowed letter inside.

Agnes took the letter out as a sapphire pendant on a thin chain fell to the top of the dressing table. Immediately, she recognized it. Not because it was expensive like the majority of her jewelry. She recognized it because Joey had given it to her the third time she'd ever seen him. He had come to her place for the first time.

"Here," he said as he stood in the door. "I don't dare come in. How rude of me to come unannounced and uninvited. But I couldn't help myself. I saw this sapphire and I knew it would be the perfect stone to bring the blue out in your eyes. But there's a catch. I want you to have dinner with me tonight and I want you to wear this. If you don't, my heart will be broken."

Agnes stared at the sapphire. "His heart broken." She slung the necklace into the bottom of the jewelry box.

Deceit

MaMary opened her front door. She was surprised to see Sam standing on the other side of the screen. "Hello, Mary. I know you wasn't expecting to see me."

"No, I wasn't," MaMary replied.

"But since you don't have a telephone and don't live that far away, Miss Agnes sent me over here to get you. She said there's something at the house that only you know where they are. If you would come over for a few minutes this morning, it would help straighten things out. Miss Agnes said she'd greatly appreciate it, Mary. Just this one time."

"I don't have a problem coming, Sam," MaMary replied. "Let me get my shoes on. I'll be right on out."

MaMary got in the car with Sam. He drove them to the Addisons' house where she went directly to Agnes's room.

"Mary, I appreciate your coming." Agnes attempted to sit up in the bed with little success. "Seeing how things happened so quickly a couple of days ago, only you can answer a few things for me."

"I understand, Miss Agnes. I didn't have any problem with coming today," MaMary said slowly. "But if you don't mind me saying so, from the way you sound, you're not doing much better." She clasped her hands. "I really feel bad about that. But with Idella gone, I haven't done too well myself."

Agnes ignored what she had said about Idella. "I'm very sick, Mary. I haven't been able to get out of this bed for days."

"And I'm truly sorry, Miss Agnes. You're the one who's laid up. At least I'm walking around. But I'm very, very tired. So tired." She closed her eyes. "It's a lot to deal with. Idella being gone and all. Even though I know she'll be coming back."

"She will," Agnes said. "And I hope you see I was trying to show my kindness by finding Idella that job on Martha's Vineyard. You do understand we couldn't keep you on here."

"I know," MaMary said.

"And like I said, it truly was Roger's decision to let Idella go. I had nothing to do with that."

MaMary nodded. "There's no need for you to go on about it. I was the one who made the mistake and I tell you it haunts me almost every minute of the day."

"Yes." Agnes nodded with false empathy. "It's a pretty bad situation we've got ourselves in, but we'll all get through it."

"Do you think so, Miss Agnes?"

"Yes," Agnes said.

"I'm glad to know you feel that way." MaMary shook her head. "This morning, when I was about to come over here, I felt so turned around I didn't know my head from my feet."

"Life can do that to us sometimes," Agnes replied. "But we must go on regardless."

"Yes, ma'am." MaMary closed her eyes and nodded. "Yes, we must. It's just that I've never been away from Idella since she was a little bitty baby. We've always been together. And it's mighty hard on me at this age. It seems like life is just determined to play its worst tricks on me at a time when I don't have the strength of youth on my side."

"How I understand," Miss Agnes replied. "And with your being so tired and all, Ruth can handle a couple of things I had in mind. Your health is more important. So I need to know one thing. Where are my vitamins that I take every day? I believe if I started taking them again, regardless of what Dr. Taylor said, I'd get my energy back much quicker."

"I know exactly where they are. They're in the breakfast room," MaMary replied. "I'll go get them for you."

"Thank you, Mary," Agnes said, grateful that Mary had taken the bait. She was certain Patricia and Gerald were still there.

MaMary walked slowly as she left the room. Her feet felt heavy, and she had no words to describe how she'd been feeling since Idella left. It was as if the light had gone out of her life and she had nobody to blame but herself. If only she had been in her right mind and had given Agnes the proper medication, none of this would have happened. Idella would not have left her, even for a short while. The heavy guilt pressed down on MaMary as she reached the bottom of the stairs. She crossed the dining room and approached a small breakfast area. Without hesitation, she opened the breakfast room door. MaMary was surprised to see Patricia sitting with a young man. "Oh, excuse me. I'm so sorry."

"That's okay, MaMary." Patricia looked surprised as well.

"Your grandmother got me over here to tie up a few loose ends."

"There's no need to explain to me, MaMary." Patricia looked uncomfortable. She glanced at Gerald. "MaMary, I don't know if you've met Gerald. Gerald, this is MaMary. Idella's grandmother."

"Hello." Finally, he stood up and shook her hand. "I've heard about you."

"So you're Gerald." MaMary looked from Gerald to Patricia. She started to say more, but kept quiet.

Silence blanketed the room.

"Can I help you?" Patricia asked.

"I'll be out of here in a moment." MaMary glanced at Gerald again. "But I need to get past you, Patricia. I need to get something from one of the drawers."

"Sure." Patricia got up from her chair. MaMary stepped behind her and went to the built-in cabinet. She removed a bottle of vitamins. "Your grandmother takes these after she has her breakfast down here. But I guess she'll be having breakfast in her room now."

"I believe so. At least for a few days," Patricia replied.

"Hopefully." MaMary's eyes filled with apology. "All right, I'll leave you two young people alone now." She pulled the door closed behind her. MaMary stood there thinking about Idella and the things she'd said about Gerald. She was certain Gerald was not the man Idella thought he was.

"I didn't know what to say," Gerald said inside the room.

"At first, I didn't either," Patricia replied, "but I guess it was much more awkward for you, considering you and Idella had become quite close."

There was a pause. MaMary moved closer to the door.

"I liked Idella," Gerald replied. "But I never thought she'd be a part of my future. How could I? Listen, Patricia, the last time our grandmothers talked it was a serious conversation about us. Your grandmother . . ." Gerald hesitated. "Actually, both of them are willing to put everything our families have acquired into our future. That is, if we decide that's what we want."

"I'm not talking about our grandmothers. I'm talking about Idella."

"Idella knew how I felt." There was another pause. "I think you're mistaken about how close we got. I saw her a few times. She's a pretty girl. It doesn't mean I lost perspective. I'm basically cautious when it comes to women. Plus, I knew I was holding back for some reason. I just knew it."

"Oh, you were the one that was holding back," Patricia said skeptically.

"Yes, I was. When she never allowed me to come to her home, and she never wanted me to pick her up from there, I knew something was wrong."

"Well, they don't live in the best neighborhood in the world, you know," Patricia said. "And I could see how she'd be a little embarrassed by that."

"Also by her grandmother," Gerald replied. "Wouldn't you be embarrassed if Miss Agnes didn't have all of her marbles? Would you introduce her to people? I don't think so."

There was silence again.

"We are lucky," Patricia said. "We have families with good names, an education and bright futures ahead of us. But poor Idella, as long as she is who she is, most likely life is always going to be a disappointment."

"I'm just glad that I found out everything before it was too late," Gerald replied.

"Are you certain that it's not too late?" Patricia said.

"Absolutely," Gerald replied. "She and I were friends. We never went any farther than that."

MaMary couldn't listen anymore. She felt a pain in her heart. It was such an ache, and she knew it had nothing to do with the physical. It was a horrible thing to hear her loved one being discussed in such a way; a horrible thing to be seen as a detriment to Idella. She had never felt so useless in her life. MaMary felt like a trace of herself as she walked back to Agnes's room.

"Goodness, Mary," Agnes said when she entered the room, "is something wrong?"

MaMary shook her head.

"You didn't look like that when you left here. What is it?"

"When I got downstairs, Patricia was with her boyfriend. The one you said Idella had tried to come between them."

"I didn't realize Gerald was here." Agnes played ignorant.

"I heard them talking after I walked out."

"Really?" Agnes had not anticipated this.

"I don't think you have to worry about them. But I am concerned about Idella."

Agnes relaxed. "Worry is part of being a parent and a grandparent."

MaMary gazed out the window. "Tell me the truth, Miss Agnes. You're a woman of the world. You know how things work." She looked at Agnes. "I want Idella to have a good life. I'm the only relative she knows."

"Of course, you do. I want the same for Patricia."

MaMary's eyes bore into Agnes's. "Do you think Idella will be held back because she has a grandmother like me?"

Agnes never blinked. "If I was you, I wouldn't think about what

Patricia and Gerald said. Young people live in a different world. They have no idea what it means to get old. They'll say one thing about us today and regret what they said tomorrow."

MaMary sighed. She placed Agnes's vitamins on the nightstand next to her bed. "I'm tired. I'm gonna go, Miss Agnes."

"Thank you, Mary. We'll stay in touch and make sure everything is going okay with you."

"Thank you, ma'am. I appreciate it." MaMary could not smile. "Goodbye." She turned to leave the room.

"Wait a minute. You left your bag in the chair."

MaMary turned back. "Ma'am?"

"The bag that you had when you came in, you left it in the chair."

MaMary looked at the bag. "I didn't have a bag with me."

Agnes argued, "Yes, you did. I've been here in bed all this time and no one else has come in my room. I remember, you brought that paper bag with you when you came in."

"I did?" MaMary walked over to it. "I don't remember."

"Oh, Mary." Agnes sighed.

"I don't." She picked it up and opened it slowly. "What is this?" MaMary reached inside the bag and pulled out several bits of yellow paper. "I don't know what this is."

Agnes remained silent as MaMary emptied the pieces of paper onto the chair. "Oh my God."

"What is it?"

"This is Idella's check. It's been torn to pieces and I don't remember none of it. I don't remember going to get it or bringing it here. And I surely don't remember tearing it up and placing it in this bag."

"This is not good," Agnes said. "This is not good at all."

"No, it's not. It means I'm losing my mind." MaMary's eyes were frightened. "I'm totally losing my mind."

Agnes shook her head. "I don't know if that's true, but it's obvious you have a problem. And I know if you're like me, you're not so concerned about yourself. But you are concerned about Idella."

"Yes." MaMary covered her mouth with her hand. "Why did I tear it up? Why did I tear up her check?" MaMary asked, tormented.

"I musta been mighty angry to do something like that. So angry and I don't even remember. I could end up hurting somebody. I could end up hurting my Dee. I don't care about myself, but I love Dee so much." Her fists clenched. "I've torn up her check. The only money we have coming in the house for the next couple of weeks."

"Don't worry about it," Agnes said. "I'll tell Roger to make out another one for you. It'll be between us."

"But what if something like this happens again? Who's gon' cover up for me then?" MaMary shook her head. "I don't remember this." She looked at the pieces of paper. "I'm in trouble. I'm in deep trouble."

"Maybe Idella has to come back," Agnes said softly.

"No!" MaMary exclaimed. "What can Dee do for me? No. I don't want her to know about this."

"You need professional help, don't you, Mary?"

MaMary looked at her.

"You do. You need professional help," Agnes stated with certainty.

"I do," MaMary said. "With the way things are going, I might end up hurting myself or somebody else. Look at what happened to you." MaMary began to cry.

"Don't cry." Agnes's eyes were bright. "You know, sometimes when God closes a door, he opens a window." She paused. "I'm going to get my son-in-law to help us. I know a place northeast of here that I'm sure I can get you in. You can be seen by doctors who can help. They can straighten you out before Idella comes back."

"You think so?" MaMary said. "You really think so?"

"I hope so," Agnes replied. She feigned excitement. "They know me, and I can have everything set up before you get there. All you'll have to do is sign whatever papers they present. I'm sure I can get them to do it." Agnes smiled. "They'll take care of you."

"And when Idella comes back, there's a possibility I'll be much better." MaMary nodded.

"Of course, there is. And it will be our secret. I'll have Roger take you there." Agnes's certain eyes bore into MaMary's confused ones.

"I've got to go," MaMary decided. "I want to get better. I don't want Idella to have to worry about me. She's got her whole life ahead of her. She doesn't need to be worried about a grandmother whose mind isn't there. That's too much for a young person her age to have to bother with." MaMary's jaw set. "I am willing to go if these people can help me."

Agnes smiled again. "Mary, I'll make sure they take good care of you."

MaMary pressed her fist against her mouth.

"What is it?"

"I don't know if I can leave. We've got to continue to pay our bills." She looked at Agnes. "Idella is going to send me the money from Martha's Vineyard."

Agnes waved her hand. "Don't worry about that. We'll take care of your mail, your house and everything," she lied. "You can't think about those things. You've got to get better."

MaMary went over and touched Agnes's hand. "How will we ever be able to thank you for all you've done? I don't know how we'll ever do it."

Agnes removed her hand, slowly. "It's my pleasure," she replied softly.

Discovery

Idella entered the market. It was her second week on Martha's Vineyard and she hadn't acquired any love for the place. It amazed Idella that when it came to relationships how today was no different from the day she had arrived. She knew the name of her employers, the names of the other workers in the house, which included Elsie, another maid, a gardener and a butler of sorts, but they had had very little conversation. They knew nothing about her and she knew practically nothing about them. It didn't seem to matter.

This was Idella's third visit to the most popular grocery store on Martha's Vineyard. All kinds of people shopped there but she headed for the fresh vegetables feeling like a ghost among the living. Idella had come to realize what it felt like to be the invisible one. Her worth was in the work that she did and how well she performed it. Outside of that, no one seemed to care. Idella could not say the other workers or her employers were unkind, but they were definitely distant.

Carefully, she picked over the tomatoes, choosing the ones that were firm but not hard. Her time spent on The Vineyard had given her plenty of time to think about lots of things, most of all MaMary.

Idella was worried about her. She had never seen MaMary cry like that, so apparently helpless as if she were caught in a rapid she was not equipped to handle.

Idella knew MaMary had a problem with her memory. They both knew it. But despite her forgetfulness, MaMary had continued to be a source of inspiration and strength for Idella. To see her reduced to tears of insecurity hurt Idella's heart, and she was determined to have the telephone reconnected as soon as possible. She needed to hear MaMary's voice, to be able to reassure her that things would be okay. Although Savannah and even the Addisons claimed they would look after MaMary, the miles between her and MaMary were tough to bear.

Idella placed several tomatoes in her basket and moved on. She had attempted to phone the Addisons with no luck. She had called Gerald too but his grandmother answered the phone. Her tone turned cold when Idella requested she inform Gerald that she had called. Dorothy's change in attitude was so apparent Idella couldn't help but wonder why.

She riffled through several bunches of spinach before she reached for the healthiest one. Her hand collided with another shopper's.

"Oh excuse me," the woman said. "Go on. You can have it. There's plenty here."

Idella looked into the pleasant features of a young woman near her age. They shared a moment of silence as they continued to put spinach in their baskets.

"I saw you in here one other time," the lady began. "But I'd never seen you before that. My name is Angela." She stuck out her damp hand.

Idella was surprised. She hastily extended her hand. "My name's Idella."

"I thought I knew who you were. You're working for the Thorns, aren't you?"

"Yes, I am. I just started two weeks ago."

"I know you did. I know the woman you're replacing. She's a local like me who's also a worker. She got lucky." Angela winked. "She and another summer worker hooked up. And bam! Right before summer season was about to start, he sent for her. Now she's out of here."

"So that's what happened."

"Yep. That's exactly what happened."

"I didn't know," Idella said. "No one explained it to me."

"Oh it's not that easy to get people to talk to you when you're new around here."

"You seem to be friendly enough," Idella replied.

Angela shrugged. "I'm just like that. My mother said I was born talking and I guess I'll die talking, hopefully."

They laughed.

"So how you liking The Vineyard so far?"

"I don't know," Idella said. "I'm still getting my bearings."

"In general, there's plenty of workers like us on The Vineyard. We're definitely here in Oak Bluffs where most of the black people live. But most of the workers are like me, they're locals. We live here on the island, basically in our own community. We don't have to interact so much with the owners, unlike folks like you who are live-ins."

"I see," Idella said. "You even have your own terms for it, huh?"

"What do you mean?"

"Locals. Workers. Owners."

"Oh yeah. Definitely. All that makes a difference here on The Vineyard. If you live on the island full-time and you're an owner it's because you have money. . . . Status is yours." Her eyebrows went up. "If you have one of the summer homes here, that's pretty impressive as well. Then you've got the renters. Now, of course, those who are owners who have maids, like the Thorns, are some of the most impressive people." She paused dramatically. "Then you have the locals like me. We have lived here the majority of our lives, but at this point can barely afford to stay. We work for the owners. Then there are general workers who come here to work for the owners."

"My goodness," Idella said. "It's enough to make my head swim."

"I guess it would be confusing to an outsider. But for those of us who've lived here all our lives, it's just the way it is."

"I guess so," Idella replied.

"So how long do you plan to work here?"

"For a couple of months. Then I'm going to return to Memphis. Memphis, Tennessee. That's where I live."

Angela looked surprised. "Do the Thorns know that? I heard they didn't want anybody that was just going to be temporary. They wanted someone that was going to take over that position full-time."

"Well, I hope they know it." Idella made a face. "Because I do not plan to stay here. I've never felt like this in my life. It's like being invisible. And the people that I work for and the folks they associate with . . ." She shook her head. "Never in my wildest dreams did I think black people lived and acted like this."

"You've been here what, all of two weeks, you say? You haven't seen nothin' yet. You got here in time to experience the busy summer months. July and August. Talk about what all the rich folks do here. Pleeze." Angela squeezed a couple of onions, then placed the last one in her basket. "Those folks do some of everything, including take trips on their yachts."

"Yachts?" Idella repeated.

"Yes. Yachts," Angela said, with an added sophisticated flair. "Wait until the tennis tournament starts. And the cookouts are over the top. The Thorns definitely like putting those on. They even go clamming in high style."

"They do what?"

"Clamming. Going to get clams. You know, the shellfish."

"I've never seen any in my life," Idella exclaimed.

"You've never had clams?" Angela said.

"No. Never. And I surely didn't think that people just went out and picked them like vegetables."

"In a sense they do," Angela said. "But they don't go out dressed like regular folks do. They wear nautical attire," she said in a mimicry fashion. "It's really something to see. Yes, there's some fancy black people that live and come to Martha's Vineyard."

"It blows my mind," Idella replied.

Angela nudged her. "One day, if you get a chance, say about three o'clock or so, there's a beach around Nantucket Sound.

You've got to go down there. Talk about good-looking black folks."

"Is the beach just for us?"

"You can say it's for us, but that 'us' is basically the rich black people who own houses here. It's for them and their friends and other regulars who come during the summertime. Those are the kind of people that are down there. You might see a couple of workers or locals, but we're probably coming to bring them something." She chuckled.

"I don't think I like feeling like a second-class citizen," Idella replied.

"Well," Angela said, "I guess none of us do. But in this country if you're black you're second class anyway. Now with them, they got enough money that they can create their own world so they don't have to feel it as much as we do. But being black in America, you are second class in most white people's eyes."

"I know that. But I'm not working for a bunch of white people. I'm working for black people. The same kind of people I felt I was becoming friends with in Memphis."

"Really?" Angela leaned back. "You've accomplished something many of us who've lived here all of our lives have not been able to do. And that's break into that sacred circle."

"I wasn't trying to break into anything," Idella said as they continued to shop. "That wasn't my intention at least."

"Well, you can be certain on The Vineyard that as long as you're working in the Thorns' house as a maid, you won't have that problem. But you can come on over to my part of the neighborhood after hours if you like. I'll introduce you to some people."

"We'll see," Idella replied. "Because I didn't come here to socialize. I just want to do the work I came to do and go back home. My grandmother needs me, and a guy I started seeing recently is waiting for me."

"Is he one of those new friends that you mentioned?"

"Yes he is." Idella placed some cooking sherry in her basket.

"Well, I tell you this." Angela put on a deadpan look. "I grew up around here. My mama grew up around here. And from what I've seen and from what she's told me, relationships between the haves and have-nots never last."

Idella felt instant anger. "You don't know me and you don't know him, so don't judge us."

"I'm not trying to judge you." Angela threw up her hands. "Hey. Forget I said it. But my invitation stands." She started to walk away, then turned back. "Tell Elsie that Angela invited you to her part of The Bluffs. She can tell you where I live."

Jealousy

It was a good day for Agnes. Not that she had been able to get out of bed. She had been bedridden for three weeks now and a plethora of pills had been added to her diet. But there was a sense of peace that Agnes had felt all day long. Even Rachel and Patricia had commented on how good she looked today.

Agnes smiled. "Perhaps it's not the end for the old girl after all." She looked at the blue sky through her window as she waited for Roger.

Agnes wondered about her good mood. She wondered if knowing Mary was in the institution had anything to do with it. Agnes was sure it did. It felt like she had buried something that had haunted her from the inside out. She felt free. It was as if Mary were dead. *Perhaps that's why, when Alicia Wallace called and thanked me because Idella was working out fine, I told her that was a godsend because her grandmother had died suddenly. The lie slipped so easily from my tongue. I didn't have to think of it beforehand. It was like it was the truth.*

Agnes was amazed at how easy it had been to get Mary to go, like a lamb being lead to slaughter. *How could anyone be so trusting and gullible?* she thought. *Maybe I really did her a favor by getting her put away. Her mind is as simple as a little child's. No old person should be so simple. And to think Joey compared me to her . . . even said if he had to have a black woman, he'd prefer a real one like Mary.* She tossed her head.

My family, the Sawyers, had nothing to do with people like Mary Baxter. If we did, they worked for us and nothing more. Joey was wrong for saying that. He sparked something in me beyond vengeance when he put me on the same level as that woman. From the time I was a teenager I saw a white woman when I looked in the mirror. So when I decided to pass, although my parents were unhappy about it, they supported me when I moved to Clarksville from Memphis. They told everyone they knew I had decided to live in Europe. She watched the clouds float by.

Passing was easy, and if I had gone with a simple white man, I might still be passing today. But everything I felt about life I got from my daddy. He taught me power and influence was everything. So when I fell for Joey Wyndham, it wasn't just for his white good looks. It was because he was an up-and-coming powerful man in Clarksville. Everyone knew that.

She closed her eyes. Suddenly, her thin-skinned body could feel the heat of Joey kissing her neck, her breasts. Agnes started to pant before she opened her eyes abruptly. *God, I'm too old for this, but how I loved that man and he said he loved me.* She shook her head. *Things could have been so good. I thought I had snared the right partner and I would be his wife. But then I found out he was married. And that I had not been the first woman he'd made a fool of. Talk about hurt. But it hurt even more when he said he'd found out I was black through rumors and that I was the first nigger woman who had tricked her way into his bed. The hate in his eyes was brighter than the love had ever been.*

Agnes sighed. "You paid for that, Joey," she spoke out loud. "I made it my business." A cynical smile touched her mouth. *And before my maid, Peggy, died, for years after I left, she was my source in Clarksville. I kept up with Joey and his family.* She could see the past clearly. *That's why how he handled the birth of his half-black grandchild—Idella's birth—only played into my hands.*

There was a soft tap at the door. *Why does everyone tap so softly?* she thought. But Agnes believed she knew why. They were afraid of what they might find when they entered her room, afraid she would be dead. "Come in," she answered.

Roger stepped in and closed the door. He looked weary as he walked across the room and sat down.

"You look more tired than I do," Agnes commented.

"I'm tired enough," he replied.

"Did they give you any trouble?"

Roger shook his head.

"Did she give you any trouble?"

He seemed to think, then shook his head again. "And that's what's draining me." He rubbed his eyes. "She was the most pitiful thing I've ever seen. So quiet. Compliant." He looked at Agnes. "I don't know what you did to her, or what you told her, but you stripped every bit of her will away. I can tell you that."

"It was her decision in the end," Agnes replied. "The blame is off my shoulders."

Roger looked away.

"So you saw Joey Wyndham?"

He looked at her again. "I saw him for a moment. Tracked him down at one of his places of business in Clarksville. I didn't have a choice since you demanded that I put the letter in his hand."

Agnes focused on Roger's face. "How did he look?"

"How did he look? Like any old, rich white man. That's how he looked," Roger snapped. "His name is on so many businesses in Clarksville, but you can believe he didn't have Wyndham plastered on that place." Roger shook his head. "I bet he wouldn't be caught dead in that place. Not dead."

"It was that bad." Agnes looked down, but for only a second.

"Not on the surface," Roger replied. "When you first drive up, you just think it is one big old mansion, well painted, tucked back in a beautiful setting of trees. The reception area, where I left Mary, is nice enough. But there was a strange kind of deadly peace about the place so, before I left, I decided to walk around the building. It had these large windows. Very large. Perhaps to let the sunshine in. Lord knows it needs sunshine." He bit down on his lip. "I could see some of the people inside. There were so many women with dingy white gowns in one of the rooms, just too many of them, like rats in a cage. They were talking to themselves, picking at their hair, spitting—"

"Well, what do you expect at a mental institution?" Agnes replied.

"I don't know." Roger rubbed his eyes. "But seeing them sure didn't make me feel any better about my part in this. And I'm going to tell you now, Mother Agnes, this is the last time I let you pull my string." He squinted. "This is the last time. Putting a human being away in a place like that is just about as low as you or I can go. And I won't have any other part in this."

"Don't you tell me what you won't have a part of." Agnes's eyes shot fire. "If it wasn't for you and your family, I probably wouldn't have to go through all this to secure Patricia's future. You and the blood of the dark-skinned Negroes that runs in your veins. You're just like ignorant children. You don't know anything about holding on to money and don't know much about making it. You need someone like me to help make sense of your pitiful lives."

"Is that right?" Roger stood up. "Is that right? Well, let me tell you something, Mother Agnes. All these years you've rubbed in my face that Patricia's brown skin is my fault. You've even called my family niggers. So I know this will come as a surprise to you"—he paused dramatically—"but Patricia doesn't have a drop of my blood flowing in her veins, Mother Agnes. Not one." Roger stuck up his index finger.

"What are you talking about?" Agnes said with disdain.

"I mean Patricia, my daughter and your precious granddaughter, is not my child." He pounded on his chest.

"What kind of foolishness is this?" Agnes put her hand up over her eyes and rubbed her forehead.

"It's not foolishness at all. It surely isn't foolishness to me. When I realized that Rachel had had an affair, and as much as you hate dark-skin Negros, well . . . one of them is Patricia's father. He's almost blue-black he's so black. And your daughter wanted him. She w-wanted him. I saw it with my own eyes."

Agnes's eyes grew large. "Why are you lying like this, Roger?" Her breath sounded short.

"I don't have a need to lie, Mother Agnes. Not anymore. Because that's what keeping quiet was: a lie. So at this very moment, I decided you needed to know the truth." He crossed his arms. "I want to set the record straight with you for the first and last time. Patricia is not my child. And if you want any further details about it, you need to ask your daughter, Rachel."

Agnes's body shook suddenly and her eyes glared toward the ceiling.

"Mother Agnes!" Roger leaned over her. "Mother Agnes. Oh my goodness." He looked at the door. He tried to decide if he should leave and get some help. "I should have never told you this right now." Roger ran his hand over his hair. "I should have never said it."

Agnes's body stilled as she took a deep breath. "No, you should never have told me that lie," Agnes said. "I nearly killed myself with that medicine and now you've helped with your lie." Her words were barely discernible. "You lie. You lie," she repeated until the words became a harsh deep breathing.

"Rachel!" Roger rushed from the room. "Rachel! Something's happening to Mother Agnes."

Rachel and Patricia joined him in the hall. Rachel was the first to enter the room. "Mother. Mother, can you hear me?"

Agnes was breathing as if she could not get enough air.

"My God, call the ambulance, Roger. Hurry up," Rachel commanded.

"Grandmother Agnes, what's wrong?" Patricia said from the other side of the bed.

Agnes's eyes rolled upward as if there was something that only she could see. "Hold on, Grandmother. Daddy is calling for help."

But Agnes's breathing stopped and a gurgling noise erupted from her throat before her body stilled.

"Grandmother!" Patricia said.

Rachel looked into Patricia's eyes as tears began to stream down her face. "I think she's dead, Pat. I think Mother's gone."

"No," Patricia said. "This can't be happening. Grandmother! Help is on the way," she assured what looked like an inanimate body.

Roger reentered the room. "I've called the ambulance."

Stunned, Rachel sat back in her mother's chair and looked up at him. "I hope it's not too late."

Confusion

"I've never seen so many people in my life." Idella untied the apron from her waist. "If I don't see another tray of oysters Rockefeller, tiny crème brûlée or miniature quiche, it will not be too soon." She watched Angela sweep a tray of used napkins into the garbage.

"That's why Miss Thorn called in support. And when you're a part of The Socialites, a key part, you have to do things right. That group of women, when they band together, honey, they put on a show." Angela talked while Elsie and another called-in maid, Betty, worked not far away.

"Talk about a show, what are they going to do with all that art-work that's left over?"

"They will eventually sell it," Angela said. "I don't know anything about art, but I do know this: the ferries over there at Woods Hole have been mighty busy. That means there are a lot of folks on The Vineyard this summer. And I bet you most of them, like the folks here today, love to buy and collect black art. That art isn't going to stay around long. Somebody will buy it."

"Did you see the prices on those paintings?" Idella asked softly.

"I could barely figure some of them out, there were so many zeros," Angela replied.

"Yeah." Idella's brow wrinkled. "I wonder if the Addisons will come here."

"Say what?" Angela said.

"I was just talking to myself," Idella said.

"Woman, tell me, what did you say?"

Idella made a face, but she had become accustomed to Angela's forthrightness. "I've been trying to call some people back in Memphis to find out how my grandmother's doing. And I can't get anybody to call me back, send a letter or nothing. At this point, I don't even know if my grandmother knows exactly where I am. It's just bizarre." Out of the corner of her eye, Idella thought she saw Betty look at her, then roll her eyes.

"I'm sure things will straighten out with a little more time," Angela replied.

"How much time does it take for one of them to contact me? I've been here for a month, and it's really beginning to bother me."

"I'm going to leave you ladies to it," the butler said. "But I'll be back bright and early in the morning." He started toward the back door.

"Oh, Idella, these came for you." He handed her three letters tied together with postal string. "I don't know if they informed you or not, but when you have mail coming to this house, it must be sent in care of the Thorns."

She took the envelopes. "I haven't given anybody this address."

The butler left with no reply.

Idella looked down at the slim bundle. "These are the letters and checks I sent to MaMary."

"What is it?" Angela walked over and took a look.

"This is what I've been sending to my grandmother to live on while I'm here." Alarm filled Idella's eyes. "They've all come back to me."

"That's not good," Angela replied.

"I wonder if she even has a grandmother," Betty mumbled.

"I beg your pardon?" Idella was tired of the woman's negative energy.

"Look, we don't have time for this," Elsie said. "We need to organize and clean up this kitchen."

"No. I want to know what she said," Idella insisted. "I could have sworn I heard her say something about my grandmother."

Betty just looked at her.

"You know what?" Idella smacked the envelopes against the counter. "I'm tired of the attitudes of some people around here. Everyone except for Angela acts as if something is wrong with me. What I say is overlooked. My suggestions are laughed at most of the time." She looked from Elsie to Betty. "And it's not that I talk all the time. I could see folks ignoring me because they figure I run my mouth from morning to night. But I don't talk that much. And when I do, it's like I haven't opened my mouth." She got angrier. "Now I've come to accept it from the owners and the renters on this island, but I'll be damned if I'm going to take it from some of you around here who aren't any better than I am. Particularly you," Idella called Betty out.

The maid never turned around. "Maybe you need to tell the truth some time."

"I do tell the truth. What are you talking about?"

"Don't let her rile you, Idella," Angela said. "She's always messin' with people. You just have to cut her some slack."

"I don't feel like cutting her any slack today, Angela. The letters I have sent to my grandmother have just come back. I don't know what has happened to her. I can't get anyone in Memphis to call me and tell me anything. Now I get this from her." Idella walked over to the woman. "What made you say I don't tell the truth? You don't know anything about me. So I don't appreciate you saying that. I don't appreciate it at all." Idella stood very close.

"You better get back off of me." Betty looked at her. "You can tell Angela all them lies about what you gon' do when you get back to Memphis in two months and your plans for going back to school and all that stuff. But you're not fooling me. Or most of the other folks on this island."

"Betty, why?" Idella asked. "Why would I try to do that? What would I gain by trying to fool you?"

"I don't know." She gave Idella the eye. "But you better get back off of me and think about that baby that's in your belly."

"Baby!" Idella said. "You've lost your mind."

"You the one." Betty put her hand on her hip. "You the one. You better be trying to figure out how you gon' do this work while you big and pregnant. Can't stand people acting like they better than the rest of us just because they light skin-did. Don't talk to nobody. Don't socialize with nobody. All we get to hear is what you gon' do when you leave here just 'cuz the rest of us can't leave. Humph." She turned her head.

"Baby!" Idella looked at Angela, who looked down. "Angela, do you think I'm pregnant too?"

"Idella, it don't matter to me if you're pregnant or not."

"It matters to me because I'm not pregnant. And it matters to me if that's what everybody around here thinks." Idella looked at each of them. "Where did that come from?"

"Idella, you need to keep your voice down," Elsie warned. "You're going too far now."

"Well, what is this about my being pregnant?" Idella demanded.

Elsie's lips stiffened. "If you must know, it came from Miss Thorn."

"Miss Thorn!" Idella was shocked.

"Yes. I know because she told me you were expecting. Now, I don't know who else she's told, and I don't know how Betty knows because I didn't tell her."

"Well, I'm telling you all right now, I'm not pregnant," Idella announced.

"All right. Okay, you're not." Elsie lifted her shoulders. Betty rolled her eyes again.

"Is that why everyone treats me the way they do? Like I'm some pitiful person who's asking for a handout from everybody. Is that why I'm being treated that way around here? Well, you know what, I'm going to get this straight right now." Idella stormed over to the door that led from the kitchen to the house. "I'm going to make sure Miss Thorn and everybody else knows that I am not pregnant.

And, as a matter of fact, I don't need this job. I don't need how I've been treated here. I can go back to Memphis and do just as good for my grandmother there. Better, because at least I'd know what's happened to her."

Idella stormed out of the kitchen in search of Janice Thorn. She found her at the front door. Idella waited as she said goodbye to the last of The Socialites. Janice closed the door and was visibly surprised to see Idella.

"Yes, Idella. Is there something you need?"

"I think so, Miss Thorn. I don't mean to be rude or anything. And since we haven't had one conversation before this one, I hate that this will be the first. But I need to get something straight."

"Yes." Janice crossed her arms. "And what is that?"

"For some reason or another, you told Elsie that I'm pregnant. I don't know where in the world you got that idea from—" Idella's chin rose.

"It was more than an idea. My mother told me. She got that directly from Agnes Sawyer. The Sawyers and the Addisons have been long-time friends of our family. And I don't believe that she would simply make it up."

"Miss Agnes said that?" Idella was stunned.

"She most certainly did." Janice looked perturbed to be forced into such an exchange.

"I can't believe Miss Agnes told you that I was pregnant when I'm not."

"I beg your pardon." Janice was outright offended. "She did not tell me that. I have not spoken to her in I can't tell you how many years. It was my mother who set up everything for you to come here, and that is what she told me."

"Well, I am so sorry." Idella shook her head, confused. "I am not pregnant. I am not."

"Fine." Janice looked apprehensive.

Idella's hand covered her heart. "If Miss Agnes told your mother that and it's totally not true, I'm more concerned than ever. My God. This is crazy. Today I got these letters back! They have money orders in them. I had sent them to my grandmother. She was supposed to pay our bills with these." She showed the bundle to Janice.

"They've all come back to me." Deep concern marred Idella's face. "I've got to go back to Memphis now. I need to know what's happening with my grandmother."

Miss Thorn looked down. "I don't know what to say, Idella." She took a step toward her. "I'm sure this is probably the worst time for me to say this, in light of what you just told me. Obviously, there's been some confusion. But . . ." Janice hesitated.

"What is it?" Idella asked.

"It's just like you said." Janice took a deep breath. "I hate that this is the first conversation that we've really had and that this is how it has gone." She paused again. "I'm glad to know that you are not pregnant. And I'm sorry if there was some kind of misunderstanding on my part." Janice gave a thin smile. "Now, would you send Elsie in here, please? I just want to talk to her for a moment."

"Yes, ma'am," Idella replied. She went back in the kitchen. "Elsie, Miss Thorn wants to speak with you."

Elsie left the room and Idella began to pace. "I just don't know what's going on here. Why did Miss Agnes tell people that I was pregnant?" she said to Angela.

"Sometimes people misunderstand things," Angela replied.

Silence filled the kitchen.

Elsie reentered the room. She had an uncomfortable look on her face. "Idella, can I speak to you in private?"

"I guess so." She looked at Angela, then Elsie. "Don't tell me she's going to fire me now. I told Miss Thorn I was ready to quit anyway. With all that's going on I need to go back to Memphis and find out about my grandmother." Idella talked as she followed Elsie into her bedroom.

Elsie closed the door. "Idella, I know we have not had the best relationship. It's nothing against you personally. That's just the way I am. I work here and I try to keep the lines pretty clear between work relationships and personal relationships. And I try to get to know somebody before I lend my hand or my heart. You understand that?"

"I can understand that. Yes," Idella replied.

"The truth is I hate to be the one to tell you this."

"What? Did she fire me? Is that what it is? I already said I'm ready to go back to Memphis."

"No, she didn't fire you, Idella. She did not fire you." Elsie drew a deep breath.

"What is it?"

"Miss Thorn told me to tell you this because she just didn't have the guts to." She shook her head.

"Tell me what?" Idella pleaded.

"Miss Thorn says there has been a lot going on. A lot has happened. And in the midst of it all there was a death."

"A death," Idella repeated.

"Yes," Elsie pressed on. "And things have changed completely. There's no way for you to go back to your grandmother in Memphis because your grandmother is no longer there."

"What? There was a death." Idella searched Elsie's eyes before her eyes filled with horror. "MaMary died and nobody told me. Oh God, no!" She slumped to the floor.

Fear

The female attendant walked past the tiny room MaMary shared with three other women. A woman carrying an invisible baby walked behind her. MaMary hurried to the door. "Excuse me, ma'am. Excuse me." The woman with the child kept walking, but the attendant turned and looked. "Yes, Mary?"

MaMary felt and looked nervous. "I've got a problem."

"What is it?" the woman asked.

"I've been here now for a couple of months and no one has really talked to me about my situation. I haven't been given any test or anything. I came here because I thought I would get some help."

The attendant's eyes narrowed.

MaMary looked down. "But I haven't talked to one doctor." She thumbed behind her. "Unlike some of the other women in here, I haven't been given no medication or anything. So I'm beginning to worry that I'm not gon' be able to get any help here."

The attendant blinked several times. "Well, at this point, attendants like myself are simply following the directions we've been given by the doctors. And that is to keep an eye on you and to make sure that you're comfortable. The other patients are not your concern." She started to walk away.

MaMary couldn't let her. "But I'm not comfortable." She glanced at a woman sitting in a corner, who seemed to never stop crying. "It's hard to be comfortable. And giving people medicine and keeping an eye on everybody is all you seem to do here." Her voice rose a bit before she brought it down. "It's just that I don't think y'all are helping me at all at this point. I dreamed about my granddaughter last night." MaMary's voice broke. "She will be coming home in about a month and I hoped my memory problem would have been better by then."

"I see," the attendant said.

"So, will you please, ma'am, check with the doctors and see when someone is going to start working with me?" MaMary put a hand on the woman's arm. The attendant drew back, carefully. "I want to be back home by the time my granddaughter arrives."

"All right, Mary. I will do exactly as you asked. But you must go back into your room. Patients are not to be out and about in the corridors."

"Yes, ma'am," MaMary said. "I'll go back. But how long do you think it will be before you let me know something?"

"It will be as soon as I have the answer. Now go back in the room," she ordered.

MaMary nodded and went back inside. Two of her roommates looked at her with dazed, medicated eyes. MaMary couldn't understand how one woman slept, which she did the majority of the time, despite the incessant crying of the fourth roommate.

"You wanna go home?" one of the ladies said.

"Not until I'm better," MaMary replied. She was uncomfortable talking to the woman, who exhibited extreme moods.

"Maybe they'll let us all go home," she said. "We'll be so happy to go home. Wouldn't we? Going home would be so wonderful. Yes! Yes! Yes, it would. Hooooome. Hooooome." The woman howled the word until MaMary sat on her bed, covered her ears and turned her back.

She wondered about everything that happened in the place, which included being nude in front of strangers, fed and treated like children, and even being beaten. In the beginning, no matter what MaMary saw, because of the guilt she felt, she believed she belonged there. It was a far better place than jail, wasn't it? She had nearly killed Miss Agnes and murderers were sent to jail. So MaMary was determined to have patience because she believed she would be helped.

But her patience wore thinner as days and weeks passed and no one seemed interested in her at all, although neglect appeared to be standard procedure. Outside of giving medication, she never observed doctors and patients talking. Still, MaMary had to admit, it would be impossible to talk to some of the patients, although she felt beating them was no answer. As a result of what she'd witnessed at The Lilac Home, her nerves were constantly on edge.

The only time MaMary relaxed some was craft time when she was allowed to do beadwork. But these were not her beads. These were large, plastic objects, nothing like the beautiful beads she would bake in her oven at home. Baking beads here was out of the question. MaMary was certain they were afraid she might hurt herself. She might stick her head in the oven like one of the patients who escaped to the kitchen had managed to do. She had burned herself horribly.

Idella must be terribly worried about me by now. MaMary wished she had told Miss Agnes and Mr. Roger to let Idella know what she had decided to do: that she had decided to seek some help for her mental challenges, all because she didn't want to be a burden to Idella, or anyone else. MaMary covered her face as the dream she had the night before began to play itself again. *They both were in cages, although they could not see each other, and they had lost the ability to speak. MaMary had accepted her silence, but Idella's muteness was extremely painful for her. So painful that it had turned into a cancerous sore deep inside her.*

MaMary looked up at the door. They needed to start her treatment or let her out because she was certain Idella needed her. *Patience. I have another month. Patience,* MaMary urged herself as she sat with her back to the wall. She waited like that until lights-out time came and the day was gone.

Early the next morning, several doctors were out on the floor and MaMary was determined they would not leave without talking to her. She waited as a nurse administered pills to one of her room-mates, while a doctor outside her room looked at some papers on a clipboard. Soon the nurse joined him, but moments later they disappeared out of sight.

MaMary couldn't stand it any longer. "What about me?" she shouted. "What about me?" she heard herself say again.

The nurse rushed back into the room, the doctor behind her. He looked at the chart of bed assignments on the wall. "Mary, what is it?"

"What is it?" MaMary wanted to scream. "I've been here for two months and no doctor has said a word to me. Nobody's given me a test to find out what's wrong. Nothing has taken place to help me or to give me a reason for staying here." Her arm swept the room. "When I came here, I had no idea it would be like this. I thought I would come and somebody would help me. But I haven't had a soul even look my way until now."

"I'm sorry about that, Mary," the doctor said as he thumbed through some papers. He stopped and looked like he was reading. "Actually, this says that you're here for observation and rest."

"Observation and rest? I didn't need any rest!" MaMary ex-claimed. "I needed somebody to help because my memory was get-ting bad. I agreed to come here because I was told I would be helped. I don't need no rest. I can rest at home." She looked at them as if they were crazy. "How long am I supposed to be here without someone doing something?"

"Well, there's an indefinite period for your stay."

"Indefinite period?" MaMary's brow wrinkled. "What do you mean by that? 'Indefinite.' "

"It means that how long you'll be here has not been decided yet."

"I decided it when I signed the papers when I first came here. I told the lady as she took me to change my clothes that I had to be out of here in three months' time. That my granddaughter would be back. I made that clear to her."

He glanced at his clipboard. "What I have here is that you have been sent to this institution for an undeterminable amount of time, and what you are suffering from is something that needs to be observed before any treatment can begin."

"But this is what I'm saying, doctor. I've been here for two months." She tried to make them understand. "In that time, nobody's observed something because nobody's talked to me. This is the first conversation I've had with somebody like you. Don't you think there's something wrong with that?" MaMary pressed.

"In all honesty"—he nodded—"I think there is. And I'm glad you brought it to our attention. So from this day forward, we'll be mindful of that. I'll direct Amy"—he looked at the nurse—"to take notes."

"But, sir, my granddaughter, she's coming home in a month. I need to be there."

"I'm sorry, Mary. I can't guarantee that you will be out of here in a month's time now that we're just starting observation."

"But that's not my fault." MaMary poked her chest. "It's not my fault that you're just starting the observation. I've been here."

"Mary, there's no need to get excited," the doctor warned.

"I don't want to get excited, sir. I've been patient. You can ask this lady or any of the attendants."

He looked at Amy.

"Yes, she's been mighty cooperative, Dr. Nelson. I have to admit that."

MaMary pressed on. "And now I'm getting worried because the time is short, and I can't possibly be any better." Her eyes pleaded. "By now my granddaughter has to be worried sick about what's happening to me. I haven't been able to talk to her or anything."

"Well, you're allowed phone calls, ma'am. You could have called your granddaughter."

"Well," MaMary paused. "Where she is right now, I don't have her phone number."

Puzzled looks crossed their faces. They quickly changed to disbelief.

"I'm telling the truth," MaMary said.

Dr. Nelson placed the clipboard by his side. "Like I said, Mary, we're going to conduct more observations."

"No." MaMary's eyes filled with fear. "Please, sir. Don't leave. You say I can make a phone call?"

"You are allowed phone calls, yes."

MaMary thought quickly. "Well, I got some people that I would like to call, if you don't mind."

"All right. But you can't make the phone call right now. You have to wait until I finish my rounds. One of the attendants will come back and take you to a telephone."

"Thank you. Thank you very much." MaMary hoped the attendant would return soon.

About an hour later, an attendant wearing thick glasses entered her room. "Mary?"

MaMary stood up. "Yes."

"You can come now and place the phone call that Dr. Nelson approved."

"Thank you, ma'am. I really 'preciate it," MaMary said as she followed the nurse up the corridor. "I want to be outta here in about a month because my granddaughter is coming home." She wrung her hands. "But now it doesn't look like I'll be able to, and Dee's gonna be outta her mind with worry if she comes to the house and I'm not there. She has no idea where I am."

The nurse simply nodded, but continued to walk. They stopped in front of a small room. "You can go right in there." She pointed toward a telephone sitting on an old desk.

"It's not a local call, ma'am. It's a long-distance call."

"All right. Well, we'll have to charge your account something for that." She started to leave.

"But, ma'am," MaMary called nervously.

"Yes?"

"I don't know the phone number," she rushed on. "But I know the name. Would you please get the number and place the call?"

The woman groaned. "Yes, I will. But let's hurry."

MaMary swallowed, "The name is Addison. Roger Addison. And they live in Memphis, Tennessee." She sat down and began to wring her hands again.

"Operator. I'd like a Roger Addison, please, in Memphis, Tennessee. Yes, Addison. A-D-D-I-S-O-N," she said as she looked at

MaMary. "Yes." She wrote the number down on a pad. "Okay, would you put the call through for me, please? Thank you."

MaMary began to sweat. Her breath came faster and faster.

"Are you okay?" the attendant asked.

"Yes. Yes, ma'am." She sounded as if she were on the verge of hyperventilation.

"Okay." But the attendant didn't look convinced. "Tell me who you want to speak to."

"I want to speak to Agnes. Miss Agnes."

"Hello," the attendant said into the receiver. "Yes, this is a call for Agnes. Yes, Agnes. Oh, I see." She looked at Mary. "And when did this happen? Oh. Well. Could you hold on for a moment, please?" She covered the receiver. "I'm sorry, Mary. I'm afraid I got some bad news for you. It seems that the person you want to speak to is in the hospital. She's been there for a couple of weeks."

"Oh. My God," MaMary replied. A pang of guilt tore through her.

"Is there anyone else that you would like to speak to?"

MaMary tried to focus. "Miss Rachel or Patricia."

"Hello? I have someone here by the name of Mary, Mary Baxter. She is asking to speak to either Rachel or Patricia." The attendant's eyebrow rose. "You've been instructed not to take any calls from Mary Baxter." She looked at Mary. "All right then. Thank you for your help. Goodbye." She hung up the telephone.

"She was told not to take any calls from me." MaMary's pupils darted from side to side.

"Yes, Mary. That's what the woman said. So please, you've had your phone call. You've got to go back to your room now."

"But what am I gon' do?" MaMary remained seated. "How am I gon' tell Dee what's happening with me here?"

"I don't know, Mary. If there is someone else you can ca—"

"There is nobody else to call. There's nobody." She stood up. "And I don't know how to call my granddaughter. I don't. I feel like I've just been thrown away in this place. I've been sitting here for months rott-nin', and nobody has even asked my name. I'm surprised nobody has asked my name."

"Mary, you're not rotting away. These kinds of things take time."

"Well, how do you know how much time if nobody has even asked me what's wrong with me? It's like I've been locked away in here and nobody even cares. Nobody. Nobody." She started crying.

"Really now, Mary. You've been a good patient up until now, but we can't have this kind of disturbance."

"What kind of disturbance? Why doesn't anybody understand?" MaMary pleaded. "I've been here for months and ain't nobody helped me at all. All I've been is locked away from the one and only person in my family. Only one, and she don't even know where I am. Told not to take my calls." She sobbed loudly. "I need somebody to help me. I want some help, that's all I want."

"I'm going to have to give you something to calm you down, Mary. You are just—"

"No!" MaMary screamed. "I don't wanna be calmed down. I don't want to." She backed against the wall.

"I need some help in here," the attendant called. Another woman entered the room with a hypodermic needle. Together, they walked toward MaMary.

"No! Stop!" This time she screamed at the top of her lungs.

The other attendant grabbed MaMary's arm.

"I don't want no needle! I don't want none of that. I'll calm down. Please, I gotta talk to somebody."

The attendant injected MaMary and within seconds the drug entered her bloodstream. Subdued, she was assisted back to her room.

Sadness

It was just past dawn when Elsie entered Idella's room. Idella lay on her bed as her lifeless eyes lifted toward the maid's face.

"I thought I'd find you in here like this." Elsie's grip tightened on the maid's uniform she held. "Now look, girl, getting you up and to work isn't my job. But after the way you hit the floor last night, I knew you wouldn't be doing much better this morning." She sighed. "Now I got you in bed, but you gon' have to do for yourself. I got enough personal worries, and there's too much work in this Thorn household for me to do by myself."

She pulled Idella's bed covers down. "So get on up now. Get on up." She helped Idella sit up, but her body was limp. "If what we all found out last night is true"—Elsie shook her head—"then you've got to make things work here because you don't have no place else to go. And don't be thinking things couldn't be worse, because they could." She went inside the tiny bathroom, wet a washcloth and came back and wiped Idella's face.

Idella sat there inert.

"The way you approached Miss Thorn last night, she could have given you your walking papers, you know."

Slow tears appeared on Idella's cheeks.

"Like I said," Elsie repeated, "it's not my job to take care of you.
And I don't intend to. You've got your duties and I've got mine. I
brought you a fresh uniform." She placed it on the bed beside
Idella. "I want you to put it on and bring yourself on out there. Do
you hear me?"

Idella continued to look straight ahead.

"I know you hear me, Idella."

Slowly, Idella looked at Elsie.

"All right. I'm leaving now." Elsie walked over to the door, and
placed her hand on the knob. She turned and looked at Idella.
"Don't you let this world beat you down, girl. It-a-try. God knows,
it-a-try. It's up to us not to let it succeed." She closed the door behind her.

Idella continued to sit on the bed. She felt as if she had little
control of her body. She had heard everything Elsie said but it
seemed to come down a long tunnel. Or was it MaMary who said,
"Don't you let this world beat you down"? Idella couldn't tell the
difference.

Tears streamed down her face and a powerful sob heaved her
body so tough Idella felt she would throw up. *MaMary's gone!
MaMary's gone!* She laid on the bed and cried.

Afterwards, she felt exhausted. Sleep had evaded her all night
long. It was as if Idella hung between life and death herself. How
could it have happened without her knowing it? How could she
have left MaMary alone to face whatever had come when MaMary
had been there for her all of her life? What kind of world was this
to bring such pain?

Idella felt she had tried to be a good person. She had tried not to
hurt others, so to be saddled with this was beyond understanding.

An emptiness swept through her mind and her body. For a moment, Idella lost the ability to think. Nothing around her made
sense. All of a sudden, she saw MaMary's face as she was leaving:
the despair in her eyes, the fear. MaMary's eyes grew larger. They
blocked out everything in Idella's brain. Those eyes had brought
her comfort, given her love. And she was not there in the end
when MaMary had needed her. A waterfall of tears flowed. Idella
had no sense of time.

Her bedroom door opened again. Elsie stepped in and put her hands on her hips. "Are you still sitting there? Girl, look. If you gon' make it, you gotta do better than this. You can't start off like this, Idella." Elsie shook her head. "Look. You loved your grandmother. It's obvious. But I bet she didn't raise you to be like this. I bet she raised you to go on no matter what. She wouldn't want you to die because she's gone."

Silence filled the room.

"You wouldn't wanna hurt her, if she was here in the flesh or in heaven." Elsie made wide gestures. "But you do what you're doing now and your life is going to go down the tubes. It's going to go down the tubes real fast. So I'm telling you, you got five minutes to get out there." She held up five fingers. "Five minutes before Miss Thorn comes down here asking questions." Elsie disappeared again.

Idella's hands balled into fists and her body shook just a bit. Part of her knew that what Elsie said was true. MaMary would not want her to give up. MaMary never would have given up. *Or would she?* Idella questioned as she remembered MaMary's tears.

With feet like lead, Idella got up and walked over to the bathroom. She turned on the shower and washed in lukewarm water. The temperature made little difference to her body. It could have been as cold as ice and Idella didn't know if she would have felt it. When she was done, she managed to dry off, put on the maid's uniform and walk out to the kitchen. Elsie was nowhere to be seen, so Idella stood in front of the back door made of glass.

"You finally made it," Elsie said when she returned to the kitchen. "Good. Now I want you to take a little container of half-and-half up there for Mr. Thorn. Although the doctor say he doesn't need it, he's demanding it, so what can I do?" Elsie prepared a small pitcher as Idella continued to stare outside.

"Come on over here and get this pitcher, Idella. I want you to take it upstairs."

Idella turned and walked toward her. Elsie looked up. Idella's looks caught her off guard.

"Lord a-mighty! You can't go around looking like that. Did you even comb your hair? I don't know why I'm asking because I know you didn't." She turned Idella toward her bedroom. "You go back in your room and brush your hair, Idella. Put it in a ponytail or something. You can't go around looking like this. You look like you just came from death yourself." Elsie's eyes turned watery in spite of herself. "Go back in your room now. Hurry up. He's waiting on this half-and-half." Elsie turned away quickly as she swiped at a tear.

Idella picked up her brush and brushed her hair, but she didn't feel her hair or the brush. Out of a deep memory she stroked it several times, then gathered her hair at the base of her neck in an untidy ball. It was as if the light had gone out of Idella's eyes; the ability to see herself and others. What Idella saw and felt was death and disappointment. An instinct responded to the determination Elsie offered. It recognized a lifeline, however tenuous.

Finally, Idella took the tray with a small pitcher of half-and-half up the stairs to the Thorns' bedroom. She knocked, weakly, on their door.

"Come in," Mr. Thorn called.

With her head hanging and the tray in her hand, Idella entered the bedroom. She saw the tray Elsie had brought up. Silently, she went toward it. Idella nearly knocked it over when she added the pitcher beside the other breakfast articles.

"And good morning to you too," Mr. Thorn said sarcastically.

Idella managed to nod her head. Then she turned and headed toward the door.

Behind her Mr. Thorn said, "Janice, is this the kind of help we have nowadays? Each one is worse than the other. I don't need to pay someone who doesn't know how to speak to me."

"Give her a chance," Janice replied. "Things got a little rough last night. I've got to tell you about it."

Idella heard her name, but the rest of Janice's words faded as she closed the door.

Idella went through the entire day in a daze and the days that followed were very similar. She did what she was told to the best of her ability, but it was with a lifelessness. She barely spoke to anyone, not even Angela.

There was only one thing Idella did when she had an opportunity. She took out MaMary's beads and crafts. As time passed, Idella sorted them by color and the minutest similarities. The beads that MaMary made were very unique in character, and Idella felt closer to her by handling them. There were also seeds, nutshells with interesting shapes, seashells and bits of wood. There was copper, iron, bone, wooden and glass beads that MaMary had collected. To Idella, MaMary's world was before her, and she showed how she treasured it through her beading.

Sometimes Idella could hear MaMary's voice as she worked the flat beadwork panels long into the night. She felt that her hands were MaMary's hands, and the lessons and the stories about beading and their ancestors that MaMary told flowed in and out of her heart and her mind. Idella beaded until her fingertips were raw. In the end, the patterns she created on the purses she made were MaMary's stories filled with Idella's grief and pain.

Feminine Power

Three weeks later, Idella looked at the people who gathered in the large parking lot. She felt no desire to be at the crafts fair, but Angela had worn her down.

"You finally made it," Angela exclaimed when she saw Idella. "I knew you would. I knew you would. And I guess my auntie and her friend buying your purses helped to convince you too. I told you you could sell those things. I told you. You see, I carry mine all the time." Angela turned to the side. Idella's beaded purse hung by her hip. "Girl, I love it. I love it."

Idella almost smiled.

"So are you ready for the crafts fair this morning? How you doing?" Angela's exuberance never failed.

Idella nodded and simply said, "Fine."

"Well, that's better than you were a few weeks ago. Small steps at a time I say. One step at a time." She smiled. "You'll see that bringing some of your purses to sell in my booth is a good idea. They are going to love 'em." Angela picked up her box of handmade pottery—some ashtrays and other small containers. "You can put your purses in the wagon on top of my stuff."

Idella looked down at the little red wagon.

"If you pull it while I carry the box, I'll show you where we're going to be."

Idella did what she was told as Angela continued to talk.

"You just wait, they ain't never seen nothing like your purses here on Martha's Vineyard. Never. My aunt has showed her purse to everybody she knows. Then she got a little selfish because she wants to buy more for herself. Now she's afraid there won't be any left." Angela laughed while Idella walked in silence. "I told her there were plenty more. I don't know how you made those things so fast. Elsie says you hardly sleep. That's what she tells me. Either way, I'm glad you're steadily making them because I plan on buying me another one today. I want first pick of the litter. Has Elsie bought one yet?"

Idella shook her head.

"She's so stubborn. She knows she wants to. I see her eyeing mine." Angela paused. "But she's one of those folks that won't get on the bandwagon unless some of the other folks are buying 'em. If you know what I mean." She pointed her nose toward the sky, then shrugged. "But Elsie's all right. I'm not going to talk about her too bad. She's all right."

They stopped in front of an empty table.

"This is where we're going to set up, Idella."

Idella and Angela arranged their articles on the table as attractively as they possibly could. Angela's chatter never stopped. It didn't bother Idella. She didn't have much to say these days, not much to say at all. She spoke so little that her own voice sounded strange to her ears. There was so much in her heart and her mind that Idella felt her tongue was an insufficient tool.

She had come to accept that Miss Agnes had purposefully lied about her; that all the people in the Addisons' social circle thought she left because she was pregnant. At least, that's what Idella gleaned from what Elsie finally told her. Idella accepted that Gerald believed it too, and had probably dropped her with no intention of ever speaking to her again. After working on Martha's Vineyard and experiencing clearly the lines of who and what were acceptable to the black upper class, she figured that was true as well. The world that Idella thought she knew in Memphis seemed like a dream now. Idella accepted the truth that she was an outsider who would never be accepted inside the Addisons' world, but she could not accept MaMary's death. It was far too painful.

"There." Angela stood back and looked at the table. "I think we did pretty good." She tilted her head. "Your purses complement my pottery."

Idella just looked.

"Does that mean you agree with me?"

Idella nodded.

"Good. So we're almost ready," Angela said as she looked at Idella's hair. "But I've got to do something with that." She shook her head. "What happened to that woman I met at the market? Her hair was fried, dyed and laid to the side," Angela teased before her expression turned serious. "I'm sure one day she'll come back." She pulled a large-tooth Afro comb from her purse. "I don't have a brush or anything," she mumbled to herself. "Do you mind, Idella?"

Idella shook her head.

"I just want you to look as pretty as your purses. That's all." Angela looked up. "Oops. Better hurry up. I see folks are beginning to come in."

Quickly, she removed the rubber band from Idella's hair and combed through it. "Now we're going to put this rubber band back on here, like this." She talked as she created a smooth ponytail. "Just let it hang, Idella. Let it hang. Don't be balling it up like an old rat's nest. Nobody would have to tell me that if I had hair as long as yours."

Idella accepted Angela's ministrations with little reaction. Afterwards, she took a seat beside her on an old folding chair.

"Now more folks from my neighborhood will get to see your purses." Angela looked at their display with pride. "And they'll have no idea how hard it was for me to talk you into selling them. I don't know what in the world you were going to do with all of these purses stacked up like that in your room.

"Morning, Miss Patton. How ya doin'?" Angela smiled and waved at another woman. "I don't know why I waved over there at her," she said beneath her breath. "She's not gon' buy nothing like this. She's too cheap," she whispered.

Idella watched the crowd as Angela spoke to several more ladies before either one of them made a sale. One of Idella's purses sold for five dollars and Angela sold a piece of ceramic for two-fifty.

"They know they're getting away with murder buying these handmade products for this little bit of money," Angela complained. "But what can we do? We're what you call . . . new at this. Novices. I think that's the word. But give us some time." She surveyed her potential customers.

Idella listened to Angela's talk. People came and went and Idella sold two more bags. More often than not, Idella was more interested in the birds that flew overhead or the way the wind played with the tops of the trees. She could care less about what was happening with the people around her. Idella had finally agreed to sell the purses because Angela's insistence reminded her of a time when MaMary wondered if people would pay money for the beaded bags she made. Idella wasn't interested in life anymore. To her, one day simply folded into another; the day to serve the Thorns and the evening or night to create MaMary's memories.

"Look here." Angela pointed. "That woman right there that's coming. She's looking at the table with flowers on it. Her name is Miss Hill. Denise Hill. Now, she doesn't live in my neighborhood. She is an owner. She and her family have owned here on The Vineyard for a couple of generations, and I don't think I would have known who she was if it wasn't for her daughter dying in a car accident a year ago."

Idella looked at Denise Hill with a vague interest.

"Yeah, she's an owner, but she comes here during the summertime."

Angela hailed a passerby and began to talk about her pottery. She was still talking when Denise approached the table and began to examine Idella's purses.

"These are absolutely beautiful," she remarked. "Beautiful," she repeated. "Did you make them?"

Idella looked at her and nodded slowly.

"The handwork is amazing and they're all so different. I don't think I've seen beadwork like this before. The designs are absolutely exquisite." She smiled at Idella. "These are art. They are not just purses. They are works of art."

Idella watched Denise, but she made no effort to make a sale.

Finally, a questioning look crossed Denise's face.

"Good morning. Aren't you Miss Hill?" Angela jumped in.

"I am," Denise replied.

"Well, how you doin'? My name is Angela. I don't think I've ever introduced myself." She stuck out her hand and Denise shook it. "This is my friend, Idella. She's a worker here on The Vineyard like I am. Although, I'm a local."

"Oh," Denise said.

"Yes, ma'am, Idella did make these purses, but she's not much of a talker. That's my job." Angela smiled.

"Well, I really like your purses, Idella, and I'm definitely going to buy one. How much is this one?" She pointed to a purse shaped like a disk, with red clay beads accented by feathers.

"Five dollars," Idella said very softly.

"I beg your pardon?" Denise leaned in.

Idella held up her hand and showed her five fingers.

"Five dollars. You've got to be kidding."

"But Miss Hill, the purse is worth five dollars," Angela protested.

"It is definitely worth five dollars," Denise said. "I would pay twenty-five for this. You can't sell these purses for five dollars, dear. Not around here. This purse is worth every bit of twenty-five dollars and I'm going to pay you just that." She dug in her purse and took out the money. "So look now, don't sell anybody a purse like mine with this much beadwork on it for five dollars. I'd be too upset. You've got to up your prices if you're going to be a business-woman," she said to Idella. "You've got to know what your product is worth. And I'm telling you your purses are worth twenty-five dollars and more."

Angela's eyes grew big. "What about my ceramics? My pottery? Do you think I'm selling it too cheap? Like this." She held up an ashtray. "I'm selling it for two dollars and fifty cents."

"Well." Denise looked at it. "Actually, those are not bad prices for what you've got here. You could maybe go as high as three for this one. But I think you're in the right price range for what you have."

"All right." Angela frowned. "At least I know I'm not cheating myself."

Denise smiled. "It was nice meeting you, Idella and Angela." She looked from one to the other. "If by any chance I'm interested in buying more of your purses, or if some of my friends are, how can I get in contact with you?"

"I work for the Thorns," Idella replied.

"Janice and Thomas Thorn?"

Idella nodded.

"I know exactly where you work. Don't be surprised if I contact you."

Idella nodded again.

"You all have a good day," Denise said.

"Goodbye, Miss Hill," Angela piped up. She could barely wait for Denise to be out of earshot. "Twenty-five dollars. She paid you twenty-five dollars for one of your purses. And girl, you can believe she's going to show it to some of her friends. Idella, you are one lucky sistah. I just wish I knew how to bead. Oh well." Angela sat down, but stood up again as new prospects arrived. "Hello there. How ya doin'? Would you be interested in some pottery?"

Angela continued to entice people over to their table. Idella's purse sales were respectable, but Angela's pottery sales were lackluster. "I have talked until I'm blue in the face"—Angela fanned herself—"and now I am so thirsty. I'm gonna buy me something to drink. Do you want anything?"

Idella shrugged.

"Idella, it's hot out here. We need something to drink. I'll bring you something back, okay?"

"Okay," Idella replied.

Angela made her way through the crowd over to a lemonade stand that sat between two booths. One sold plates of food, and the other desserts. She was pleased to see Denise standing in the line ahead of her. "Here you are again, Miss Hill."

Denise turned around. "Angela. How are your sales going?"

She shrugged. "Pretty good."

"And your friend?"

"Idella? She's definitely doing well. And to think she wasn't going to come today but I convinced her to do it," Angela said. "Idella wasn't going to sell those purses at all. Can you believe that?"

"I can't," Denise replied. "They are extraordinary. I've seen beaded bags before, but what Idella does is very unique."

Angela wiped her brow. "I discovered her. I was the first person to buy one. Then I got my aunt and her friends to buy some and convinced Idella she needed to sell them. Now I'm glad I did." Angela looked down for a moment. "It's helped Idella out a lot."

"Do you mind if I ask you something?"

"No, ma'am."

"Idella . . . has she always been the way she is?" Denise paused. "I don't know how long you've know her, but—"

"I haven't known her that long. She's only been working on The Vineyard for about two and a half months." Angela waited for Denise to order her lemonade. "When I first met Idella she was as talkative as me." She thought a moment. "That might not be true. It takes a lot to talk as much as I do." Angela laughed and so did Denise. "But she definitely wasn't as quiet as she is now. You can barely get a word out of her."

"I noticed," Denise replied.

"And Miss Denise, the truth is since she's been here a lot of things have hit her. A lot of tragedy. Her grandmother died. She was the only relative Idella had, and when she died, Idella lost where she lived and everything. Now she really doesn't have any place to live besides the Thorns' house."

"Oh no." Denise appeared deeply touched.

"Yes, ma'am. It hit her hard. Real hard." Angela shook her head. "It took the life out of her."

"I know how that is." Denise paid for her drink and Angela ordered. "When somebody you love dies it changes everything. Somehow life doesn't seem real anymore." Denise looked in the direction where Idella sat. "And she's so young."

"I say Idella's about my age," Angela replied. "I'm twenty-five. I think she's probably 'bout twenty-five or twenty-four years old."

"Almost the same age as Nina."

"As who?"

"Nina, my daughter. I had a daughter who died in a car accident about a year ago."

"I believe I heard about your daughter. I'm so sorry," Angela replied.

Denise didn't seem to hear her. "I'm going to see what I can do to help Idella sell her purses. I'm definitely going to show mine to some of the ladies I know, and she'll be able to get a good price for her work."

"I'm sure she'll really appreciate whatever you do for her, Miss Denise. Lord knows, she could use some help at this time."

Anger

There'd been a constant flow of people at The Socialites' club-house. Idella was one of the servers at their fund-raising bar-becue for another island charity. It was an impressive gathering. There were people from all over the United States. Idella heard some say they were from Washington, D.C., New Jersey, Detroit, New York, Massachusetts, Philadelphia and even Los Angeles. Once again, she was amazed at how black folks with money from all around the country converged on Martha's Vineyard during the summer-time.

Idella offered drinks from her tray to whoever was interested. Some people took them without looking at her; others would take a glass, look and nod. No one actually spoke to her, but Idella had come to accept that was the way it was. The line between the haves and the have-nots was clearly drawn—as clearly as Angela had ex-plained to her the first time they met at the market.

At events as large as this one given by The Socialites, people tended to wear their very best. The women's clothes matched from head to toe, and the men dressed in the latest fashions. Even the children seemed to have walked out of catalogs. Idella appreciated the fashion show, but she had worked for six hours and her feet were telling her it would be a long evening.

"Shoot. I should have ate before I came here," Angela said. "These fund raisers can be brutal. I'm so hungry even the smell of the barbecue is beginning to make me feel sick. Just the smell." She held her stomach.

"I think we've got a couple more hours before the next crew comes aboard," Idella replied.

"If I can hang in there," Angela said. "If I can just," she sang in Idella's ear, " 'Hold on. I'm leaving. Hold on. I'm leaving.' " She changed the popular rhythm-and-blues song to fit her needs. "Come over here and help me put some of these drummette plates on a tray," Angela instructed. "Hold it still, now. I don't want to drop any of these."

Idella steadied the large tray.

"Okay. How many can we get on this tray? One, two, three, four, five," she counted. "Speaking of five, you said Miss Denise was going to get five more purses for some of her friends. Did she get 'em?"

Idella nodded.

Angela shifted a couple of plates. "My God, girl, you gon' be rich off of those bags. After a while, you won't have to carry any trays; you can open up your own shop right here on The Vineyard."

"No," Idella said. "I'll never do that. Once I get enough money to get my own place, I'm going to go back to Memphis. There's nothing here for me in this place."

Angela looked at Idella. "I guess we all see things a little differently. Of course, it's my home so I see my future here."

"I don't mean any harm, Angela," Idella said.

"Well, at least I know what to talk about in order to get you to say more than a word or two. I guess that's enough plates. And this is one big tray. Neither one of us can carry this by ourselves," she remarked. "Let's carry it together and let people choose what they want." Angela held the tray with Idella.

Idella shrugged. "It's fine with me."

They walked out into the crowd.

"I don't know how else they expected us to handle trays this big," Angela complained. "We're not elephants." She smiled as a gentleman took a small plate of drummettes and a napkin. A woman took another. "Hey. I think this is going to work pretty well. We'll just continue—"

Idella stopped suddenly. Her eyes fixed on something across the room.

"What is it?" Angela asked as Idella let go of the tray. All of the plates fell to the floor. "Idella," Angela gasped.

Idella didn't hear her or the crashing ceramics. All she could see was Rachel's smile as she talked to a man. Patricia and Gerald stood not far away. Their smiles were as bright as she remembered. It was obvious life had not been altered for them. MaMary's death and her being exiled on Martha's Vineyard had not affected their stride in the least. To Idella, it was as if they did not care or had never cared about her or her life. She was a forgotten commodity—someone who was easily discarded.

The weeks of near silence burned Idella's throat as she crossed the floor. How dare they be so happy in the face of her grief? How dare they abandon her to an unhappy fate they had helped create? The anger blistered Idella's eyes like pepper. She raced toward them.

When she spoke, it was a force unleashed. "How dare you not tell me about MaMary? How dare you not tell me MaMary died? What kind of people are you anyway? We trusted you. I looked up to you, Miss Rachel. And I opened my life to all of you. MaMary did too," she declared. "We did the best we could. We never knew people like you before in our lives. We thought we had come across something good. But here you are, some of the worst human beings I ever met. And I hope never to meet again."

By now, all the people at the barbecue had stopped and were listening in shocked silence. "You lied on me. You lied to these people here and told them I was pregnant. How did you put it? That I was 'in trouble'? And I'm sure you told half of Memphis the same thing."

Idella turned to Gerald. "And you." Gerald's face lost some of its color. "You willingly believed everything about me, didn't you? You believed it because I wasn't one of your kind of people. All of you could just throw me away because I wasn't a part of you. And you could just let my grandmother die without even trying to contact me. Without even allowing me to say goodbye. What kind of people are you?" Idella demanded again, "What kind?"

Patricia's hand covered her heart. Rachel's mouth stood open. "Idella," Rachel finally said. "I barely recognized you. You're so thin."

"Thin. Is that all you can say to me—how thin I look? I don't give a damn what I look like. I barely ate for weeks. I couldn't talk. So what I look like to you or anyone else around here makes no difference." Her eyes were like daggers. "I just have one question for you. Why didn't you tell me about my grandmother? Why didn't you tell me MaMary was dead?"

Embarrassed, Rachel looked around at the crowd. "I didn't tell you because she isn't," Rachel finally said. "She is in a mental institution."

Idella was stunned. "MaMary isn't dead?"

Patricia came and stood by her mother. "No, MaMary is not dead. My grandmother is the one who's fighting for her life. She was in the hospital for weeks, and she *made* us come here. Grandmother Agnes wasn't thinking about herself. She was thinking about us." She hit her breasts. "She tried to help MaMary. You know she did. It wasn't her fault MaMary had mental problems. And seeing how you're treating us, I think you need to find out if you've got some problems too."

There was a rush of talk around them.

"Come on, Mama." Patricia took Rachel's arm.

"I really can't appreciate your making a scene like this in front of everybody, Idella," Rachel said as Patricia led her away.

Idella did not back down. "You say MaMary's in a mental institution. What mental institution? Where?"

"We don't know," Rachel said angrily, as they continued to walk.

"You put her in there, didn't you?"

Rachel snatched around. "She committed herself."

"I don't believe you."

"We don't care what you believe." Patricia held Rachel's arm as they moved farther into the crowd.

"Idella, what is wrong with you?" Janice Thorn demanded. She looked at the Addisons, the spilled chicken and Idella again.

"We have never had this kind of thing happen at a Socialites' function," someone in the crowd commented.

"This is unacceptable," Janice said. "This is totally unacceptable behavior. I've tried to be patient with you, but this is the last straw. You've got to get your things and go."

Idella looked at the Addisons. She took off her apron. "It's fine with me. I've taken enough from you people." She threw it down and walked away.

"Rachel," Janice called.

Patricia and Rachel turned around.

"I'm so sorry this happened," she apologized. "This is simply awful. I don't know what to say."

"Don't worry about it, Janice." Rachel drew a deep breath. "There was no way for any of us to know that this would happen. I must say, I am shook up a bit."

"What's going on?" Roger returned from the bathroom. He had a drink in his hand.

"Dad, Idella's here." Patricia went to his side. "And you would not believe how she talked to us. She accused us of lying in front of everybody. She claimed MaMary was dead and that we hadn't told her." Patricia shook her head. "She was like a crazy woman. It was horrible."

"She laid it on pretty heavy, Mr. Addison." Gerald put his arm around Patricia. "Are you okay?"

She shook her head. "This is so-ooo bad."

"Where's Idella now?" Roger scanned the crowd.

"She left because I fired her," Janice replied. "I can't have someone in my employ acting like this, embarrassing me and disrespecting the guests. Even though I must admit, it's partially my fault. I thought my mother told me Idella's grandmother passed away. Please accept my apology. I've been so busy this season."

"People make mistakes," Rachel said. "But there is no excuse for the way Idella attacked us. It's not our fault that her grandmother committed herself to an institution. She needed help," Rachel defended herself while looking deep in Janice's eyes. "And if she chose not to tell Idella that, then it was not our responsibility to do so."

Roger took a swig of liquor and looked down.

"This is so embarrassing," Rachel repeated. "And it pains me. It truly pains me." Her face melted. "With all we tried to do for Idella and her grandmother and she does this to us."

Angela intercepted Idella at the door. "You've done it this time, Idella."

"I don't care." Defiantly, Idella looked into her eyes.

"Those were your friends from Memphis?"

"Friends?" Idella shook her head. "Those people were never my friends. I just didn't know it. MaMary and I are little pawns to people like them. To people like this. We don't count for anything."

"What are you going to do now?" Angela insisted.

"I'm going to go get my things and leave like Miss Thorn ordered me to."

"Then what?"

"I don't know." Idella threw up her hands. "I'll figure something out. Maybe I'll get a room at the Shearer's Cottage."

"It's not that easy to get a room there, first of all. And I'm quite sure it's full this time of year."

"I don't know," Idella repeated. "I'll come up with something. Don't you worry about me. I don't need nobody to worry about me." Idella left and headed for the street.

"Idella. Idella," someone called.

Idella turned and saw Denise Hill walking toward her. Idella wanted to keep going, but she made herself stand and wait.

"You really blew your top back there." Denise's face was grave. "I'm sorry things turned out the way they did."

"It's all right," Idella replied. "I don't need nobody's pity."

"I don't pity you. I just want to let you know I'm sorry for what has happened to you."

Idella looked at her with disbelief. "Well, you'll be one of the first."

"I am sorry, Idella." Denise looked straight into her eyes.

Idella looked away. Her mind raced. *MaMary is not dead. MaMary is alive and in a mental institution.* As horrible as that sounded, it brought life back to Idella's heart. MaMary was alive and Idella knew she would not rest until she found her grandmother.

"I also want to say, if you like, you can stay at my place tonight."

Idella pinned her with a stare. "And why would you do that?"

"Because you need a place to stay," Denise replied.

"Yeah, I do need a place to stay. But what are you going to get out of it? It seems everybody that I've met that's like you has some kind of hidden agenda."

"I don't have an agenda at all, Idella."

"Well, I don't believe you," Idella spat. "I'll never accept anything else from you people. I don't trust you."

Denise looked sad. "Are you going to turn bitter now that you've found out your grandmother isn't dead? You're too young to determine that being bitter is the right way to live your life. There is good and bad in all kinds of people, Idella. You should know that by now. Don't judge everybody by what you've experienced. Don't judge me."

Idella looked down.

"I'm offering you a place to stay because I want to . . . and you need it. There's no strings attached."

Idella felt that what Denise said made sense. She felt she had no right to hold what happened to her and MaMary against everybody in the black upper class. She surely had no right to be unkind to Denise, who had only supported her. "All right," she said. "I do need a place to stay."

Denise gave a relieved smile. "I could meet you with my car at the Thorns' house in about an hour?"

"I'd appreciate it," Idella said. "I'd appreciate that a lot."

Distrust

"I hope you slept well last night," Denise said to Idella when she walked in the kitchen.

"I slept some," Idella replied. "I would dream, then I'd wake up. Dream and wake up. It wasn't the best of dreams either."

"That is to be expected," Denise said. "Yesterday was some day for you. A lot went on."

"That's how life has been for me lately," Idella replied. "For a while it just sucked me in. It was like walking in a fog. I couldn't come out." Idella looked at Denise. "But now I know MaMary is still alive and I'm going to spend every moment I can trying to find her."

"I'm glad you're going to be able to look for your grandmother." Denise got up from the breakfast table. "Do you want something to eat?" She motioned toward a platter of bacon and toast.

Idella didn't answer. "None of this seems real." She looked out a window. "Every time I woke up last night, part of me was overjoyed MaMary was alive, but to think she's in a mental institution." She shook her head. "It just doesn't seem real to me."

"Give yourself time to digest it all, Idella. It's even more to handle than you realize. Once you're ready, make yourself a plan and execute it." Denise sat down again. "I'd give anything for Nina to be alive again. Mental institution or not."

Idella took some bacon and one piece of toast and sat down. "How long has she been dead?"

"One year. It'll be one year and two months tomorrow," Denise replied. "I was planning to tell her, even if she didn't have anyone else in the family behind her I was in her corner. She didn't have to be what the family was pushing her to be." Denise gave Idella a sad smile. "Everyone was determined she would be a lawyer. I wanted to tell Nina she didn't have to be a lawyer if she didn't want to. There were plenty of things that she could be." She paused. "I knew she had been under a lot of pressure. But I had no idea that it was as bad as it was. And although it was the car wreck that killed her, it was the pills that she had taken beforehand that made her pass out at the wheel."

Idella listened. She wanted to tell her that she was sorry about her daughter but the words stuck in her throat. "Well, I have no idea how my grandmother is doing. I don't know if the Addisons were telling me the truth or not. They lied before." She stared at her bacon. "The more I thought about everything last night, the more convinced I became that they misled us deliberately. They were looking out for themselves. Me and MaMary didn't matter."

"But isn't that what most people do, Idella? Look out for their families? If they care for them, that's what they do."

"Looking out for your family is one thing. But lying and hurting others is another. I believe Miss Agnes lied because she wanted me out of the way. I do." Idella crossed her arms. "I don't know how, but I swear I believe she was behind everything that happened to MaMary and to me."

"Hurting others," Denise agreed, "should never be done for any reason. But you've got to know holding anger against the Addisons isn't doing you any good."

"You expect me not to be angry." Idella squinted. "You think I should feel nothing after all that has happened to me. I feel like I was shipped away to be somebody's servant under false pretenses. My whole life was shaken upside down just because some rich folks felt I could be used. Is there some law that says poor folks aren't people too? I can't believe all the prejudice I have seen and experienced that involves only black people." She smacked her hands. "And I truly believe if my skin were darker, I would have been treated worse. You couldn't have paid me to believe this kind of thing goes on at this day in time. But I've lived it so I know it's true. We black folks don't know how to treat one another. If you're not the right color, if you don't have enough money, if you didn't go to the right schools . . . All that stuff we claim white folks have done to us, we do it to each other."

"Prejudice is an ugly fact of life." Denise sat back. "It doesn't matter who's doing it. But you have to understand that the world of the black elite came out of us trying to protect our own, that's all; trying to protect our own from racial abuse. We wanted to create an environment where we could see our worth, live it, experience it, and we wanted to keep anyone or anything out that might threaten it. That's all. It's called protecting your own."

"But don't you see that's just another form of racism?" Idella declared.

"You might see it that way." Denise shrugged. "But it's a way of life for my family, so I won't say that because I know that was not my or their intent. What I can say is, you're not going to change what generations of people have put into place, be they black or white, with anger. All you can do is work on yourself, Idella. And if you allow me to help you"—she looked down—"I'll feel like I'm giving my daughter another chance to live her life the way she wanted."

Idella placed her elbow on the table and leaned her face on her hand. "What I want to do is find my grandmother. I've got to find her."

"Can I suggest something?" Denise asked softly.

"What?" Idella closed her eyes.

"I'm going to be leaving here, going back to Nashville where I live. You could come back to Nashville with me and make that your home base until you can get on your feet."

"But I don't want to go to Nashville," Idella said. "I need to go to Memphis so I can see if MaMary is in some crazy house there." Hot tears dropped from her eyes.

"Well, go. Nothing's stopping you from going to Memphis. But from what I understand, you don't have a place to stay there anymore." Denise leaned in. "And Memphis isn't that far from Nashville. Use my telephone. Work smart, Idella. Even if you find your grandmother, what are you going to do? Do you have enough money saved up where you can rent a place for yourselves?"

"No. I don't."

"Well, come to Nashville with me and work from there. I'll help you in every way I can."

Idella looked at Denise. "I gotta find MaMary. That's all I know."

"And you have to take care of yourself. Never underestimate that. You've been through a lot emotionally. And sometimes that takes more out of us than we realize. You don't want to end up in a hospital yourself."

"I'm not going to end up in nobody's hospital." Idella shook her head. "If believing MaMary was dead didn't kill me, nothing will."

Denise sat back. "I believe you're right." She smiled a little. "You've got a lot to look forward to."

"How's that?" Idella asked.

"I'm thinking about your purses. There's a real business there, Idella. The possibilities are endless. And if you come back to Nashville with me, I can help you sell them through house parties, organizations I belong to. You name it."

Idella's tone softened. "MaMary was the one who taught me to bead."

"She did?"

"Yes. From the time I was a little-bitty girl she sat me down and she let me play with the beads and she talked to me about what they meant. What each color and design represented. She said they were messages. That if you knew the language of the beads, you would know what they were saying. She said her mama taught her that and her mama's mama before that. That it was a tribal way from my African ancestors. And right now, I don't care how light my skin is, I feel that connection deep in my bones."

"Your heritage and your grandmother sharing it with you could be your future."

A tiny spark of hope lit Idella's eyes.

"But I did say 'could,' " Denise said.

"Yes, ma'am. I heard you."

"Let me ask you something, Idella."

"Ma'am?"

"How far did you get in school?"

"I finished high school," Idella said. "I had a scholarship to Fisk University, but I never used it because I took care of my grandmother."

"Fisk is right there in Nashville."

"I know that," Idella replied.

"Who knows, maybe you'll end up going back to school if you come to Nashville."

Idella looked away. "Miss Hill, don't you try to carry me too fast. I'm gon' make my own decisions about my life. I had too many people already having me do things that I didn't want to do. I know you wanna help me, but don't you carry me too fast."

"I have no intention of doing that, Idella. Don't worry. I have no intention of doing that at all."

There was silence.

"But I got to think straight. That's the only way I'm going to help MaMary. So I accept your offer to help me, Miss Hill."

"Call me Denise, Idella. Denise."

"Denise." Idella sat back. "But once I'm able, I'm going to be on my own. I'm going to take care of myself and MaMary because I don't want anybody to ever feel we owe them anything."

The Path of the Ancestors
Is Difficult to Follow

"It doesn't make sense to me." Idella looked at Denise. "Why wouldn't MaMary commit herself somewhere right there in Memphis?" She sat down. "God knows I've learned more about mental institutions than I thought I'd ever have to know, and I'm so tired." She leaned against the back of the couch. "Residential institutions, state institutions, private institutions, small ones, big ones, you name it. It's not as simple as I thought it would be."

"Well, really you've just got started," Denise said.

"I know. I'm not ready to give up or anything . . . it's just crazy. What more can I do under these circumstances? From now on, I'm definitely going to use the telephone. It would make things so much easier."

"I told you that it would."

Idella looked down. "And I appreciate you letting me use your car."

"That car has been sitting for a while. I was still deciding what to do, and now you've found a use for it. I'm glad."

Idella yawned. "It was unbelievable. And I'm not just talking about the driving." She yawned again. "The first couple of places that I went in and told them that I was looking for my grand-

mother, they automatically started looking up names of white people. And then when I explained to them that my grandmother
wasn't white, I got these strange looks. They started looking at
each other funny. And at two places, there was a different set of
books for black people. I felt like I was back in the day of colored-
only fountains. You know what I mean? It was crazy, Denise. Crazy."

"By looking at you I can see how they could make that mistake."

"And I know that. I've been knowing it, and it hasn't been a
piece of cake. Going to public school and everything. . . ." She
made a face. "I can't tell you how many times when I was growing
up someone wanted to beat me up because I was too light. Calling
me 'White Mama' and all sorts of names. One year, these girls sur-
rounded me and wanted to cut off my hair. Oh my God. Having
long hair was just a curse. It was a curse." Idella shook her head. "If
I wasn't getting it from one side, I was getting it from another."

Denise simply nodded. "See. Those are the kinds of things that
my family and other black folks who looked a lot like you, but who
had money, knew, and we, me included, wanted to protect our kids
from that. So what did we do? We sent them to private schools.
And guess what? There were plenty of people who looked like
them and they didn't have to go through what you went through
just because of how you looked." Denise crossed her legs. "You
could be beat up because of the kind of clothes you wore, having
new shoes, a new car. I know I wanted to avoid that for my daughter and I did everything I could to make sure she didn't have to
deal with that. So what you're talking about right now, Idella, is
why a lot of things evolved the way they did. The 'black elite,' as
we've been called, dealt with those issues. Private schools, clubs
and organizations solved a lot of problems on both sides, from
white and black people."

"I guess so," Idella replied. "God, life is so crazy. You know what?
I can remember one year when I was in high school, I wanted to be
dark so bad. I wanted to be dark soooooo bad." She closed her
eyes. "I mean, the Ultra Sheen foundation that I was wearing was
so many shades darker than my skin. And I wanted to be dark because"—her fingers formed quotation marks—"'Black Is Beautiful.'
'Say It Loud, I'm Black and I'm Proud.' All that. James Brown was

right in my face and I felt like he was saying to me you aren't black enough. 'The blacker the berry, the sweeter the juice.' I wasn't nearly black enough in my mind. So I tried everything I could to fit that image. And to tell you the truth, it wasn't that long ago that I was still trying." Idella closed her eyes and for a moment it looked like she might cry. "In a way, it was MaMary who helped bring me to my senses. She said to me, no matter what color my skin was, the blood that ran deep in me was the blood of my ancestors. That I was still a child of the Motherland. And don't let anybody ever tell me that I wasn't. That was my MaMary."

Denise looked down. "You're always talking about MaMary, Idella, but you've never said anything about the other side of your family."

"That's because I really don't know that much about them," Idella replied. "I know that my mother was white. And that she didn't want me. She just left me on MaMary's porch because she was the daughter of an important white man and because of that my father was killed. He died in a fire that was started by my mother's people."

"Oh, Idella."

"Yeah. Sounds pretty bad, doesn't it? For some reason I don't feel much about it. I know people have gone through harsher things. Plus, I was a baby so I don't remember. All I know is MaMary saved me from that fire and she's been here for me all my life." Idella paused. "But one thing MaMary never did was instill anger in me about it. She wouldn't talk bad about my mother or my mother's people, or white people in general. She never would. MaMary wouldn't talk bad about anybody. And you know, even with her talking about my African ancestors, she told me I should still claim all of me. The white part as well. MaMary said that's what made me, me. It's not until now that I don't have her around that I remember these things so clearly." She rubbed the smooth material of the couch with her hand. Then she said softly, "She said God didn't make any mistakes. And if one of my parents was white and the other one was black that that is the way it's supposed to be. People could stick all the labels on me that they want, but I am who I am. And I need to be able to be proud of that."

"Amen," Denise replied.

Silence filled the room.

Then Idella giggled. "Lord, I must have looked mighty funny with my face all brown and my neck all white."

Denise laughed. "There you were trying to paint yourself brown when I know a lot of people who wouldn't dare go out into the sun without a huge sun hat to make sure they don't get one pinch browner."

They laughed some more.

Denise could barely talk. "I mean these ladies would wear hats and gloves, and whereever the sun was, they'd move out of it. Like dodge ball."

Idella rolled her eyes. "That sounds like something Miss Agnes would do."

"Rachel Addison's mother?"

"Yeah."

"You're absolutely right. Now she's a special case. She made sure folks in the community knew she put high stock in her fair skin."

"And I was out there trying every way I could to call the sun in." Idella shook her head. "You know what's even funnier?"

"What?" Denise wiped her eyes.

"I thought I was getting darker. I thought I was getting brown. You couldn't have told me I wasn't brown. And with that Ultra Sheen." She waved her hand. "But I was as pale as all get out."

They laughed and laughed and laughed.

"There was this girl that I use to see in the hallways. And I tell you I thought her skin was so beautiful. You know the velvet paintings you see sometimes that have Elvis Presley on 'em?"

Denise nodded.

"Her skin was as black and shiny as that velvet. And I thought she was so beautiful. So with my experience of being light skinned, I truly didn't and don't understand why some people think it's such a great thing." Idella looked puzzled. "The really wonderful things I know about life that MaMary told me came from my African ancestors. Maybe if I knew more about the other side of my family, I'd see it differently. But considering what happened to me when I was a baby." She looked at Denise. "It's like celebrating the ones who threw you away, or celebrating the ones who oppressed you by being proud about looking like them."

"I can see that," Denise said. "But did you know it was Africans who sold Africans into slavery in Africa in the first place?"

Idella shook her head again.

"It's true." Denise looked at her. "So it's not as clear cut as it may seem."

"No-o." Idella looked pensive. "I guess not."

"See there." Denise nodded.

"That gives me a whole different mindset to tackle and I've got enough with MaMary."

"You just keep looking for her."

"Yes, that's exactly what I'm going to do. But it's the strangest thing switching from her being dead to missing. It's like she just disappeared."

"You've got nothing but time, and I've set up a couple of house parties for you to show your purses. You know people do Tupperware parties."

Idella nodded.

"You can do house parties like that. The host could be entitled to a free purse," Denise said enthusiastically, then pulled back. "If you'd like to do it that way."

"It sounds like a good idea." Idella focused on her. "You're forever coming up with something, aren't you?"

"I try." She looked down.

"I don't know how in the world I'm going to thank you for all that you've done. You have put up with me and my anger about so many things."

Denise smiled at Idella. "Like I said, it's my pleasure. In a way I think God is giving me a second chance through you, Idella. He knew I'd probably go crazy if I didn't have you in my life right now to focus my energies on. So indulge me, please."

"Why not?" Idella gave a little smile. "It's not doing nothin' but helping me."

They looked at one another.

"So how do you like the car?"

"I like it," Idella replied. "Never thought my high-school driving classes would come in this handy. And I felt good driving up there on my own."

"Well, look." Denise leaned forward. "If you want to, we can work out a deal where it could be yours. You can pay me a little something whenever you get it, or you can pay a small"—she pressed her thumb and index finger together—"lump sum. We'll come up with whatever works for you."

"Oh no, Denise." Idella shook her head. "That's too much."

"No, it's not. Let me help you." Denise's eyes pleaded. "And you'll be helping me by taking it off my hands. I didn't know what I was going to do with it and I don't need that car."

"I don't know about this." Idella looked almost scared at the possibility of having her own vehicle.

"I do," Denise insisted. "We'll work out the details."

"All right. I've saved up some money from my purse sales. I can pay you out of that."

Denise smiled. "Sounds like a plan."

Idella took a deep breath. "And since my purses are selling pretty well, I thought about what you said about my possibly going to school here. Going back to school has been something I wanted to do, and I'm thinking about looking into how much it would cost me to go to the community college."

"I think that's an excellent idea, Idella."

"Yeah, I do too. With school and making the purses, it'll keep me sane while I'm looking for MaMary. And who knows? Soon, with your ideas and my working hard, I should be able to move out on my own. That's if the purses sell here anywhere near as well as they sold on Martha's Vineyard."

"I think you're going to be surprised." Denise winked. "I think you're really going to be surprised at how well you do here."

Idella's brow creased.

"What's wrong?"

"Do you think something else could have happened to MaMary? Maybe something really did happen to her. Like, maybe she did die."

"I don't know," Denise said. "But if it were my daughter, knowing what I know today, I wouldn't put any energy into that thought.

I would do just what you're doing. I would search until I couldn't search anymore."

"I'm sure there's some reason why she wasn't in one of the Memphis institutions." Idella looked puzzled.

"And I'm sure one day you'll know the answer. But until then, do not give up hope, Idella. Focus on getting yourself in order. Getting your life in order and when the time is right, I'm sure you'll find your grandmother."

"I hope so," Idella said. "If I don't, it won't be because I didn't try. Because she always wanted better for me. Even when I realized she was having some problems with her memory, MaMary was still a source of inspiration. No, I'll never give up on her. I never will."

Confrontation

"She's always pushing that young woman on us," Rochelle, a longtime member of The Friends social club, complained. "Just because Denise has attached herself to her doesn't mean we have to be obligated as well to promote her purses."

"I have to say, I agree," another woman said quietly. "But what can we do? Denise has been around for a long time. Her family has a lot of clout here."

"But so do we. We should have some say in this. Does this mean every time we find a new interest we can just force it on The Friends?" Rochelle looked disgusted. "I don't think so. I don't think it's fair. And we need to tell Denise that. Everybody here is either a member of The Friends, one of our daughters, or someone who was invited by the entire group. We built up this network to benefit ourselves." Rochelle crossed her arms. "I'm not like everyone else around here who's keeping their mouth shut. I'm speaking out because I am sick and tired of it."

"Well, I don't know why you're complaining to Jessica." Denise walked up behind them. "If you have something to say to me, Rochelle, you should say it."

"I do have something to say." She threw her head back. "It's not that I don't like Idella. The truth is I don't know enough about her to like or dislike her. What I do know is, she has been living with you for six or seven months now and it appears to me and quite a few others, who just don't want to say anything, that you are pushing her and her purses on us and . . . making her success our responsibility. Every time we have something, Denise, whether it's a fund-raiser, party, group sale or a get-together, some kind of way you make sure Idella is mentioned. She may be your personal crusade, but I don't think you should make her The Friends' crusade."

Rochelle placed her hand on her hip. "From what I've heard, her background simply doesn't measure up to our standards. First of all, she's half white. Secondly, she's illegitimate. But it doesn't stop there." She inhaled. "This grandmother of hers that she's looking for, from what I understand, is in a mental institution. And this is the type of young woman you want The Friends to support as if she's a mascot of ours? I just don't think it's right." The words tumbled out.

"Contrary to what you said, it sounds like you know a lot about Idella." Denise looked down. "I'm sorry if you feel that I've been pushing her on you and The Friends, Rochelle. But this is how I see it." Denise's voice turned low with a steely edge. "My daughter died a year ago. And I have done everything I can to stay on this side of sanity because of it. It was because of groups like this, with all our strict rules, that ended up being too much for my child, but I couldn't see it at the time. I couldn't support her in what she wanted to do because I was too busy supporting our causes and what we deemed socially right. She was a part of us, as you pointed out. But now she is dead, so that leaves a slot open that I feel I have the right to fill with whomever I please. And if I choose to push Idella, and it's not taking anything from anybody else, I don't think you have a right to tell me not to. Life is too short, Rochelle, and you don't want what happened to me to happen to you. If it did, if one of your children should die, you'd realize all this stuff that we're so busy acquiring and making sure we protect isn't worth a cent. All the money in the world won't feel like anything. Being a blood member of whatever family won't be worth a hill of beans because you know why? Death takes care of that. Just as all of us will be gone one day or another, somebody else will be standing in our places holding these charities, having these luncheons and making sure their pictures are in the society paper. So that's the way I see it."

"Well." Rochelle looked around, then walked away. "Some people."

"That was quite a speech, Auntie." Wesley stepped up behind Denise and gave her a kiss on the cheek.

"Wesley. What are you doing here?"

"Just thought I'd drop by and show my support."

"Right. I'm glad your mother told you that you had to come by and see me because I hadn't seen you in such a long time."

"That too." He smiled. "And talking about newspaper articles, I saw that little piece on your protégée in the paper. Her and her business of beaded purses seem to have swept Nashville's society by storm. Courtesy of you."

"Courtesy of Idella's beautiful purses," Denise said.

"Her purses were beautiful. She didn't look too bad either from the photograph."

"You can make up your own mind." Denise looked past him. "Idella, is everything ready?"

Calm and confident, Idella walked toward Denise and Wesley. "Yes, I packed up everything. Putting out samples and taking custom orders really worked. The demand for custom bags has really shot up since that article appeared in the paper."

"I know," Denise said. "Isn't it great?"

"Yes, isn't it?" Wesley jumped in.

Idella looked at him.

"Oh. Idella, I want to introduce you to my nephew, Wesley Saxon."

"Hello, Idella. I've heard so much about you from my mom, who's heard so much about you from my auntie."

"Hi," Idella said. "Denise is one of my biggest fans, that's for certain. I owe her a lot. You're very lucky to have an aunt like this."

"I know it." Wesley kissed Denise again on the cheek. "I understand you've been in Nashville for about six months now," Wesley commented.

"Yes, I have," Idella replied. "And it's a shame this is the first time I am meeting Denise's one and only nephew."

"Well." He hung his head in mock remorse. "I guess that is pretty bad. But I'm a busy man. Really I am. I'm busy helping my father out with bank business; we own one of the local banks." Wesley threw in for good measure: "I'm also an attorney with political aspirations."

Idella lifted an eyebrow. "It's a wonder you have time to breathe, let alone come see your one and only aunt."

"You're not going to let that pass, are you?"

Idella smiled. "No. She's too much of a sweetheart."

"I totally agree." He looked at Denise. "That's why I dropped by to see you, Auntie. So help me out. Let her know I'm not such a bad guy."

"Wesley is my only nephew and he's my favorite," Denise replied innocently.

"See there? I'm her favorite nephew."

"You're her *only* nephew," Idella replied.

"The lawyer in me says that's immaterial." Wesley paused. "Now let's talk about you. I'm going to a party tonight. What have you been doing since you've been in Nashville? Hanging out with my aunt? Or have you gotten to meet people your own age?"

"That's not important to me," Idella replied. "I've got other things on my plate."

"Now see, I can understand that. And I'm not going to give you a hard time like you gave me."

Idella smiled.

"But"—Wesley waved his finger—"if I can break my routine, then you should break yours. Why don't you come to the party with me tonight?"

Idella looked at him. "I don't know about all that."

"Why not? What else do you have going this evening?"

"Actually, Denise and I were going to have dinner at home tonight."

"Look, Idella," Denise said, "you should go with Wesley. Go to the party. Meet some other young people. I'm glad he said that. I'm so busy helping you with your business I haven't thought about your social life. Wesley will be an excellent person to introduce you to some nice people here in Nashville."

Idella hesitated. "I really don't know if I'm up to that."

"What is there to be up to?" Wesley asked. "You go. You eat. You drink a little bit. Whatever you want. You talk to people if you want to, or you stand up against the wall and be a wallflower." He teased, "If you choose to be a wallflower, I'll stand around and help you hold the wall up."

"Go," Denise encouraged.

"Well . . . Do I need to go home and change?"

Wesley looked at her jumpsuit and bolero jacket. "No, you're fine just as you are."

"Okay," Idella agreed. "I won't be too late, Denise."

"Don't worry about it. Come in when you're ready." She gave her nephew a look. "Wesley, you take good care of my girl."

"You know I will." He flashed a set of perfect teeth.

Idella and Wesley shared a comfortable conversation on the way to a club that had been privately rented for the night. Expensive cars filled the parking lot behind the building and lined the street in front of it.

Idella simply made a mental note of it all. Since Denise had taken her under her wing, she had come to know many of the black elite, and had come to accept, as Denise had said many months ago, that there was good and bad in all people. But still, Idella felt her wavy hair, light skin and sharp features helped them to embrace her more easily. She had concluded that the black upper crust was totally obsessed with skin color. Yet, Idella had to admit, she had sharpened her social and business skills by being in their company.

Wesley opened Idella's car door.

"Aren't you the gentleman?" she quipped.

"As always."

"Thanks," she added sincerely.

Wesley placed his hand gently on the small of her back. Together, they walked rapidly toward the front door, where a door handler stood just inside to keep the riffraff out.

"Hello, Wesley. How ya doin', man?"

"Doing just great," Wesley replied.

They entered without a hitch. Inside, the lobby was crowded with well-dressed young people. Most of them passed the brown-paper-bag test by leaps and bounds.

"Idella. How good to see you." Gerald Campbell reached out and hugged her before she knew it. "It is so good to see you again." He smiled. "Aren't you looking wonderful."

Idella was too stunned to speak.

"And Wesley, how you doin'?"

"I'm doing pretty good, and your name again?" Wesley checked him out.

"My name is Gerald Campbell." Gerald shook Wesley's hand enthusiastically. "We've met before at a couple of parties." He glanced at Idella. "Your bank loaned my father and me the money for the renovations on our new dentist office."

"Oh I see," Wesley said. "I'm so glad that we were able to help you out."

"Yes. We really did appreciate it," Gerald replied. "And here you are with Idella. I must say you've got good taste. Idella and I are old friends."

For a moment, Idella could not believe what Gerald said. But it didn't take her long to find her tongue. "So how's Patricia?"

Gerald looked down, then up again. "Haven't you heard? Patricia's not doing very well. She had a seizure not too long ago and I haven't seen her recently. The word is she has epilepsy."

Idella eyed him. "So she's ineligible now too?"

Gerald started to speak, but Idella cut him off.

"I can't believe you had the nerve to speak to me. The last time I saw you, you looked at me like I was something that had crawled from underneath a rock."

Gerald looked at Wesley, then at Idella. "Idella, I'm sorry."

"Yes, you are sorry. You are one sorry son-of-a-bitch."

Gerald's mouth tightened.

"When I was first sent to Martha's Vineyard, I wanted to let you know what happened to me. I mean, I would have wondered where you were if you just up and disappeared. So I assumed you wanted to know. I found a pay phone and called your house, long distance. I left a message with your grandmother, to let you know where I was staying and that I had called. But you never got in contact with me and I couldn't understand it. Then, when I realized what lies had been told about me being pregnant by some other man, it hit me." She faked a smile. "Poor Gerald. He dropped me, the pregnant maid, like a hot potato. Being Gerald Campbell, heir to a dentist dynasty, he couldn't be involved with someone like that."

Gerald looked around uncomfortably.

"But what bothered me was you never had the guts to tell me so." Her eyes bored into his. "I wasn't worth your talking to. I wasn't worth an explanation. So"—she lifted her chin—"you can believe you are not worth my talking to either." Idella turned her head.

Wesley's eyebrows went up.

Gerald's chin went down. "Well, I guess that's that," he said before he disappeared in the crowd.

Idella glanced at Wesley, then looked straight ahead.

"You're full of fire, aren't you?"

"He had it coming," Idella replied.

"Even if he didn't, he got it from you."

"Believe me, he did," she said. "But I'm sorry if I embarrassed you." She looked down.

"No, I can take it," Wesley replied. "I like a woman with some backbone."

Idella smiled a little. "After you've been through what I've been through, you develop quite a bit of that."

"Is that right?" Wesley locked eyes with her.

"Yes," Idella replied without hesitation.

Wesley smiled. "Strangely enough, all I know is I find myself looking forward to knowing more."

Worldly Goods

Wesley kissed Idella again as they lay on the carpet. It was good. *We go good together,* Idella thought. *Real good.* "I have never done anything like this in my life," she said when their lips parted.

"Well, I can't say that." Wesley's eyes sparkled.

"You mean to tell me you go around christening empty houses all the time?"

He laughed. "Of course not. I was just messing with you. I've never done this before either."

"Yeah right." Idella looked at him suspiciously.

"Even though I got a carpet burn or two to prove otherwise," Wesley taunted.

"You get away from me." She pushed him, gently.

"Oh, the deed is done now," Wesley replied.

"The deed's been done quite a few times. I can't believe how quickly you were able to get me to forget Denise's advice about you."

"Oh, my auntie loves me."

"Yeah. That's why I should have listened to her, because she loves you. And that's what she said: That she loves you but I needed to be careful when it came to you."

Wesley drew Idella back into his arms. "She only said that because she knew I'd be irresistible."

"That you are." Idella pecked him on the mouth.

Afterwards, she went in the bathroom and freshened up. Idella admired the bathroom again as she dried her hands from a roll of paper towels that sat on the empty counter. When she was done, Idella found Wesley in the kitchen. She sprang up on the counter and sat down. "I can't believe this is mine." Idella looked around. "I've got a house."

"Yes, you do." He leaned against the counter between her legs.

"And with your expert help, after a year of renting, if I want to, I can buy it."

"I'm good for many things, aren't I?" His eyebrow went up seductively.

"You are." Idella chuckled softly.

"And you should really look at buying this place. I hope you know that."

"I do know it," Idella replied. "It's so perfect. I've got my own bedroom, and there's a room for MaMary, when I find her."

Wesley looked down.

"The third bedroom will be the office–purse-making space. I can run the business out of there. And once MaMary is back with me, we can both make the purses, and I can continue to go to school without any problem."

"Idella," Wesley said gently.

"Huh?"

"Do you still think you're going to find your grandmother?"

"Of course, I'm going to find her," Idella said too quickly.

"You've called and been to almost every institution here in Tennessee. You've been to all the institutions in and around Memphis, and like you said, it doesn't make sense that a woman her age would have gone so far away from home."

"So what are you saying, Wesley?"

"I'm simply saying you must look at the facts." He paused. "It's a possibility that you may not find her."

Idella moved him away and jumped off the counter. "Well, that's one possibility I am not willing to accept." She walked toward the rear of the house and went out on the deck.

Wesley followed. "I don't mean to discourage you, baby." From the back, he put his arms around her and kissed her on the neck.

"Well, that's exactly what you're doing." Idella looked out into the yard. "I hope you know that."

"No. Don't take it that way." He squeezed her. "We've been going together now for three months and we've never had a quarrel. I think this is our first one, don't you?"

"I'm not quarreling. I'm just stating how I feel," Idella replied.

"And I just don't want my favorite woman to get hurt, that's all. I want her to consider she may have to look at a different kind of future. One that, I might add, will still be bright factoring in what's on the horizon for her. A college degree is in her future. An increase in sales for her business. And the best-looking, rich, black attorney at her side. What more could a woman want?" Wesley whispered near Idella's ear.

Idella's eyes were full. "To find my grandmother."

They both looked next door when a sliding-glass door opened. A young, black man stepped out onto the deck.

"Oh, excuse me," he said when he saw Idella and Wesley. "Didn't mean to interrupt a private moment."

"That's all right." Idella moved away.

"I've got plans for building a privacy fence one day so these kinds of things won't happen."

"Really? So you own that house?" Idella asked.

"Yes, I do," he replied.

"I just rented this one"—she thumbed behind her—"and I've got an option to buy in a year."

"Good for you. You're going to love this neighborhood. It's quiet, and we're right here in the cul-de-sac. And, as you can see, the backyards are great. My name is Brandon Jacobs, by the way." He waved.

"I'm Idella Baxter and this is my friend, Wesley Saxon."

"How ya doin'?" Wesley said.

"Good and yourself?"

Wesley nodded.

Excited, Idella asked, "And so, do you live alone?"

"I sure do." Brandon smiled. "I've been in this neighborhood now for over a year. And it's so-o quiet. I work from home sometimes and it's just been excellent for me. I can come out here on my deck and work and not worry about noise. It's great."

"I can't wait," Idella replied. "Are you from around here?" Wesley touched her arm as if he wanted to go inside.

"Actually, I grew up in Atlanta. I came here to Tennessee State for school and ended up staying. And you?"

"No. I'm not. I grew up in Memphis."

Brandon looked at Wesley and nodded. "Well, it was good to meet you, Idella."

"You too, Brandon."

"You as well, Wesley."

"Same here," Wesley replied rather curtly.

"It's always good to know who your neighbors are," Brandon said before he opened his sliding-glass door.

"It sure is," Idella smiled before Brandon closed the door.

Idella and Wesley went back inside the house. "He seems like a pretty nice guy," Idella remarked, then locked the door that led out to the deck.

"Yeah, too nice." Wesley gave her the eye. "I don't know what I think about a single man living next door to my woman. But then again, because he lives there by himself doesn't mean that he's really single. He could have a wife tucked up in the attic or a girlfriend living in his car for all we know. As long as he keeps his eyes off of what's happening over here, it doesn't matter to me."

"Wait a minute." Idella put her hands on her hips. "This is my house, not yours, last time I checked."

"I know that." Wesley looked rather hurt.

Her tone softened. "And you know you don't have to worry about me, Wesley."

"I don't?" He looked in her eyes.

"No." Idella kissed him.

"I know I don't," Wesley replied. "You'd be a fool to let me go for a fellow like that."

Idella looked at him, and thought about what he said. It was moments like this she didn't like. Wesley's confidence oozed the arrogance of the black elite. But Idella liked Wesley, so she figured she'd learn to deal with it.

Thirst

"It seems that we have the same schedule for our Saturday morning coffee breaks," Brandon said from the deck next door.

"It's a good time for coffee," Idella replied. "More birds tend to come out early."

"I've noticed that," Brandon said.

"You know, I never thought I'd actually live in a place like this," Idella said. "I dreamed of it and I know my MaMary dreamed of it, but I never thought I would be here."

"What did you say?" Brandon asked.

"I said," Idella spoke up, "this is like a dream come true for me. Sitting out on a deck overlooking a backyard, sipping on a cup of coffee in a house that I'm renting and might own as soon as next year."

"This is the first house I've owned. And I'm glad I chose this one."

"Is it really that different? Owning a house versus renting?"

"Yes, it is," Brandon replied. "You have to fix everything yourself when you own it. You can't call in Mr. Jones and say"—he changed his voice—"'Hey! My water pipe is busted.'"

They laughed.

Brandon took a sip of coffee. "It also helps that I'm a pretty good handyman."

"What did you say?" Idella leaned over. "I couldn't hear you."

"I said, it's good that I can basically fix anything," he raised his voice. "You know what? It's kinda crazy talking to each other with you sitting on your deck over there and me sitting on mine. Why don't you come over and let me fix you a cup of my coffee? It's the third time we've seen each other like this. We might as well share some coffee."

Idella looked unconvinced.

"Come on," Brandon insisted. "I make a mean cup of coffee."

"I got a fresh pot that I made sitting inside," Idella replied.

"I bet you don't have homemade cinnamon rolls."

"Homemade cinnamon rolls?" She looked at him.

Brandon nodded.

"You made cinnamon rolls this morning?"

"Naa." Brandon smiled. "My mom made some yesterday and brought them to me last night."

"I was about to say." Idella moved to the edge of her chair. "But I can't pass up homemade cinnamon rolls." She stood up. "I'll be right over."

Idella went inside. She washed her face, brushed her teeth, made a ponytail and ran next door. She reached for the doorbell but Brandon opened the door before she could press the button. "Come on in, neighbor."

Idella walked in and glanced around Brandon's living room. It was a man's house with little to no frills, but it was neat. "This is nice," Idella said.

"I try," Brandon replied. "Come this way. I think our houses are pretty much made the same." His eyes took in her face.

"Looks like it." Idella looked away. "Except my kitchen is over there and yours is on this side."

"Is that right?"

"Yeah. Other than that, it looks the same."

They reached the kitchen.

"Here. I already put the cinnamon roll on a plate. Now I'll pour you a cup of coffee." Idella leaned against the counter and watched. "How do you like it?"

"With a little cream."

"A little cream." Brandon shook his head. "Look. Let me do this. Okay, let's put in a dash of cinnamon, some brown sugar and the cream you wanted." He stirred the coffee. "Now see, that's just the right color. I think you're going to like this." Brandon passed her the cup.

"Looks good," Idella said as they walked out onto the deck. She sat where Brandon indicated and took her first sip. "Ummmmmm, this is nice."

"Now wait till you take a bite of your cinnamon roll and put it together. The flavor is going to kind of burst in your mouth."

"It's gonna burst in my mouth." Idella laughed. "Maybe you should have been a cook instead of a . . . What do you do?"

"I'm an accountant."

"Instead of an accountant," she said.

"I agree. Cooking may sound exciting compared to accounting, but accounting pays me much better than cooking ever could. Unless I was going to be one of those high-priced chefs. But I'm not going back to school for nothing like that."

"I'm in school right now," Idella said.

"What are you going for? Your master's?"

"Master's? No. I'm just starting college, really. I wanted to go when I was younger, but I took care of my grandmother instead." She heaved a sigh. "So with a little bit of encouragement from some friends, I'm trying it again."

"Well, it's good you're able to do that. Must be pretty hard juggling a job and going to school."

Idella took another sip of coffee.

Brandon continued. "I'm assuming you work and you're not the wealthy daughter of a king or something of that sort."

Idella laughed. "I work, but I don't go off to a job. I make beaded purses that I've been selling for almost a year. It's amazing how they've taken off."

"Wow. So an independent businesswoman."

"You can say that," Idella replied.

"Well, your grandmother must feel good that your life has gone as well as it has, knowing how mothers and grandmothers are. They can feel guilty just about anything. At least my mother can. They don't want to hold us back in any kind of way."

"The whole thing with my grandmother is kind of complicated." She looked into his eyes.

Brandon looked serious. "In what way?"

"I've been looking for her for a while now." Idella looked down. "The last year of my life sounds like something someone could have made up, but I won't bore you with the details."

"Doesn't sound like I'd be bored at all."

Idella sighed. "Let's say I don't want to share the details with you at this time."

"That's all right. That's cool," Brandon said.

"But I'm looking for my grandmother." Idella took a sip of coffee. "I'm hoping that I'll find her real soon."

"I hope you do too," Brandon said sincerely.

"Thanks."

"Now there's something that I must ask you." His eyes brightened.

"Yes?"

"I've noticed you got this habit of dancing in your living room. You see, I can see you from that window, right there." He pointed. "And you're always playing the same Miriam Makeba album."

Idella's jaw dropped.

Brandon held back a smile. "You must love that album. As much as you play it, I wonder if you've got anything else."

"You've been watching me inside my house."

"Doesn't take much. You don't have any curtains in the living room and I live right next door. Plus you're so animated." He flung his arms up. "Your arms are flying and you're jumping around."

"I guess I am." Idella laughed, then she turned serious. "I don't play music that often. But that one album has special meaning for me, so I play Miriam when I need to."

The deck went silent.

"How's that cinnamon roll?" Brandon changed the conversation.

"If I had cinnamon rolls like this around me all the time I'd be as fat as this house," Idella replied.

"It would take a lot of those to make you fat."

"What are you trying to say? That I'm skinny?"

"No, I'm not saying that. I've checked you out." His eyes darkened. "You're doing real well right where you are. But a few more pounds wouldn't hurt you."

"Really?" Idella shifted in her chair. "I see you don't mind sharing your opinion."

"Sometimes," Brandon replied.

"Now, let me see, what I can say about you?"

He leaned back in a sexy manner. "What can you say about me?"

Idella took another sip of coffee. "Just give me a little time, I'll think of something." She looked him up and down. "I have a question instead."

"Shoot," Brandon replied.

"Do you have a girlfriend?" Idella didn't know why she asked.

"Not right now. I'm in-between heartaches."

"Come on now. Why do you have to say it like that?"

"That's just what it's been for me."

"You're a good-looking guy. I don't know why it should."

"Good-looking guys get hurt too. Especially when you're simple like I am. Not very flashy. I am exactly what you see and what you see is what you get. Sometimes I think women want more. They want a little drama now and then."

Idella thought about how she and Wesley had christened her house. "Of course, we want a little excitement." Their gazes met before Idella looked down. "Life would be nothing without it."

"Now, I'm not saying I can't provide excitement in the way only a man can."

"Oh." Idella looked directly at him. "I heard that."

His eyes held hers. "I'm just telling the truth."

"Okay." Idella laughed. "I think I'll just leave that alone."

"I think you better," Brandon replied.

Idella stared into her coffee cup.

"So how's your friend, Wesley?"

"He's doing okay. Stays pretty busy. He's an attorney."

"Yeah, from that Mercedes he's driving I'd say he's doing pretty well."

"He does well." Idella nodded. "His family in general does." She added, almost under her breath, "They own the Nashville Trust Bank."

"His family owns the bank?"

Idella nodded.

Brandon rubbed his cheek. "That's some family."

Idella took another bite of cinnamon roll.

"People like that intrigue me," Brandon said. "I'm sure they've worked for whatever they have, but that's generations of money when it comes to owning banks. And here I am, I'll be the first person in my family to graduate from college . . . to have my own business. I'm not rolling in dough by any stretch of the imagination, but I'm comfortable." He looked out over his yard. "My life's simple, and I can sleep at night. One thing I decided early on was I didn't want success or the desire for success to own me."

"I've never heard it said like that." Idella glanced at him. " 'The desire for success to own you.' "

"Yeah. It means I don't want to be a slave to my money. Not that I don't want a good life. I do."

"I understand exactly where you're coming from," Idella replied.

They smiled at each other.

"But I've got to go." Idella drained her cup. "I've got an appointment this morning. But next Saturday if we're going to do coffee breaks, I owe you a cup of coffee."

Brandon nodded. "Sounds like a deal to me."

Breakthrough

"Why do you insist on coming to these things?" Wesley looked at the people in the strip mall with detachment. "Bad enough you do this in Nashville, but when you come all the way to Memphis." He crossed his arms. "Get three of Aunt Denise's associates to buy a custom-designed purse and you would make more money than you make coming here."

"It's not about money all the time, Wesley." Idella rearranged a couple of the coin purses. "It's about sharing with the ordinary woman. You don't know anything about that, but I do," Idella remarked. "She is me." She pointed to her chest. "Coming to these places—Baptist conventions, Methodist Church conventions—keeps me grounded. It reminds me there's a world outside your world."

"*Our* world, Idella. It's your world as well as mine now."

"That remains to be seen," Idella replied.

Wesley sighed. "How much longer do we have?"

"It will be over in half an hour. Don't worry."

"Then we have to drive all the way back, and it's already late." He looked at his watch.

Idella looked at hers. "It's a quarter to nine."

"I'm going to get something to drink. Do you want anything?"

"No," Idella replied before Wesley walked away.

She looked at the remaining coin purses. Idella had sold quite a few. The five-dollar price tag for the smaller pieces was a different ball game from the seventy-five-dollar, custom-made purses she sold.

"Idella? Idella Baxter?" Idella looked up.

"Idella. I can't believe it's you." Savannah herded her children to the table.

"Savannah!" Idella said. "Oh, my goodness, Savannah." Idella got up and hugged her. "It's so good to see you. I've been back to Memphis several times. I went to my old house, but nobody was living there and I've knocked on your door on more than one occasion." Idella looked deep into her eyes. "I was here not too long ago. My old house was still empty and you had moved."

Savannah nodded. "Yeah, I have moved."

"I am looking for MaMary, Savannah. I have not seen her since the day I left for Martha's Vineyard."

"You haven't?" Savannah covered her mouth. "Oh, Lord. And I feel so responsible, Dee. Especially since you told me to look after her. But the next thing I knew she was gone. It was like she just up and disappeared."

A man in a gray suit and a bowtie came and took a military at-ease pose not far away.

"Dee, you remember Ricky, don't you?" Savannah rolled her eyes. "I mean, Richard."

"Ricky-y," Idella said as recognition dawned.

"*As-Salaam-Walaikum,* Sister."

Idella didn't know what to say.

"You're s'pose to say '*Walaikum-As-Salaam,*' Idella," Savannah said.

"*Walaikum-As-Salaam,*" Idella replied.

"When Ricky became a Muslim, his name was changed to Richard 2X," Savannah explained.

"Wow." Idella looked at him again. "So many things have happened over the last year, huh?"

"No doubt about that," Savannah said as Richard 2X walked to another booth. "And Lord knows, Idella, he wants me to become one too. But I just don't know if I can. I don't wanna cover my head and wear dresses down to my feet." Savannah put a hand on her ample hip. "Can you see me covering up all this for any man?"

Idella laughed.

"I had heard you had your own business. You was even in the black newspapers here."

"I know," Idella said.

"Girrrl"—Savannah shook her head—"you've come a long way in a short amount of time. Would you ever have believed you'd be so successful?"

"I wouldn't have dreamed it back then. No," Idella replied. "At least not in this way. But Savannah, I have not been able to find MaMary. Even with all of this success, as you call it, there's a hole in my life."

Richard 2X returned to the table.

"I know it's gotta be, Dee. It's gotta be. There you all were, so happy. You working for Addison Catering and MaMary was working for the Addisons. Then the next thing I know, things went crazy and you had gone to Massachusetts."

"Yes." Idella looked down

"And MaMary just"—Savannah shook her head again. "I tell you."

"It's just the devil's world. That's what's wrong," Richard 2X said.

"Beg your pardon?" Idella said.

"The devil. The white man. It's his world. Even a brother like Brother Addison who has a strong business in this community is a slave to it. You would think, by face value, that he was a straight-up man. The kind of brother we would love to have as an F.O.I. for Muhammad. A Fruit of Islam for The Nation, but before I got my life straight that brother was going downhill and going downhill fast."

"How do you know that, Richard?" Savannah looked at him.

"I know it, Savannah. I know." He straightened his bowtie. "I know what I was doing and where I was going. And that brother was showing up in similar places. And you know how I know it was him? I came to see you one night and he saw me. He recognized me from the places where we had been gambling, among other things. He asked me if I would help make some funny business around a card game that was gon' be coming up."

"Say what?" Savannah looked at Idella, then back at Richard. "Help him cheat?"

"That's right. And I told him, no, brother, I'm not gon' do all that. Them folks that we were messin' around with at that time were mighty rough. And even though I mighta been out there in them streets, I wasn't crazy."

"You would see Mr. Addison at the places where you gambled?" Idella asked.

"I definitely would."

"And you saw him when you came to see Savannah one night?"

"Yes, I did. As a matter of fact, I did. And right after that, I guess it was your grandmother I saw come out of your house. She had a little bag with her, a little suitcase-type situation, and she got into the car beside him. The next thing I knew they had driven off down the street."

Idella looked at Savannah, then back at Richard 2X. "You saw my MaMary getting in the car with Mr. Addison in the middle of the night?"

"Definitely I did." Richard 2X went into at-ease again. "That brother was going down fast. If he was to come to The Honorable Elijah Muhammad, The Messenger of God, he could straighten his life out and come to realize who he is. The black man is the cream of the planet earth. We just don't know who we are. We're lost in this wilderness. You see, the devil used his tricknology on us. And he got us blind. That brother is asleep like so many others and he needs to wake up like I did."

"Mr. Addison might have been the last person to see MaMary," Idella said to Savannah.

Savannah's eyes were big. "Girl, I don't know. This is the first time Richard ever told me anything about this. Why didn't you tell me about this?"

"You never asked, Savannah. You never asked. And you don't listen to me. If you listened to me more often, I'd be able to protect you from this world. But you're hardheaded, Savannah. One day you gon' realize joining the Muslim Girls' Training is the best thing you can do. If you become a M.G.T. for The Nation, your life would be so much easier."

Idella hugged Savannah. "This is unbelievable. I finally got a solid lead on MaMary." Her brow creased. "And it involves the Addisons." She hugged Savannah again. "It was so good to see you, Savannah, but I got to go look into this. I got to see what Mr. Addison knows."

"It seems like he knows something." Savannah glanced at Richard 2X.

Idella started packing up the coin purses.

"We better let you go, Idella." Savannah held two of the children's hands. Richard 2X took the smallest one into his arms. "When you come back to Memphis, look me up. Richard and I live in Mrs. White's old house on the corner."

"I'll remember," Idella said, but she was focused on getting out of there.

Wesley returned to the table. "What's going on?" He watched Savannah, Richard 2X and the children walk away. "You know those people?"

Idella ignored his question. "Please, Wesley, help me pack. We've got to go by the Addisons' house."

"Tonight?" He looked at his watch again. "It's after nine o'clock. Do they know you're coming?"

"No, they don't, but I don't care." Idella's eyes dared him to dispute her. "We've got to go tonight because I'm going to find out once and for all what they know about my grandmother." She almost threw the purses in the boxes.

Unusually silent, Wesley helped Idella put the merchandise in the trunk of the car. Finally, he said, "Idella, I think you need to think about what you're about to do."

"No, Wesley. I am going by their house and I'm going by there tonight. Now are you going to drive me or not?"

He looked off, disgusted. "Well, I'm not going to let you go there by yourself. What am I supposed to do? Just leave you here in the middle of the parking lot?"

Idella went to the passenger door and opened it. "Please, Wesley."

They got in the car.

"Mr. Addison knows something about my grandmother. Ricky, the man who was at my table, saw her with him in the middle of the night. She had a suitcase in her hand."

"Look"—Wesley put his hands on the steering wheel—"you may trust what that man said. I don't trust anybody who goes around wearing bowties and dark sunglasses inside a building. Them Negroes who call themselves Muslims aren't doing anything but creating problems for all of us."

"Wesley, I don't want to hear what you think about Ricky right now. Are you going to drive me or not?"

He started the car. "I don't think this is a good idea, Idella. What kind of manners is it to go knocking on somebody's door in the middle of the night? The Addisons are well-respected people in my community. They've had their catering business for years."

Idella closed her eyes. "I don't care what they had. They could have owned all of Memphis for years, but I'm going to find out tonight what he knows about my grandmother. Turn here," she directed.

They drove in an energy-charged silence. Finally, Idella said, "Make a right. That's their house right there."

Wesley slowed down.

"Pull into the driveway."

"I am not."

Idella looked at him. "All right." As soon as the car stopped, she opened the door and ran up the walk. Wesley was not far behind.

Retribution

"**Y**ou could at least have some decorum."

"Wesley, you're beginning to get on my nerves. I could care less about decorum. Nothing. Do you hear me?" Her mouth tightened.

Idella reached the Addisons' door. She laid into the doorbell before she banged on the door. Idella heard "Who in the world could it be?" after she rang the doorbell several more times.

"I've got it, Rachel," Roger Addison's slurred voice came through as he cracked the door open. "Who is it?"

"It's Idella. Idella Baxter. I want to speak to you."

"We don't have anything to say to you," Roger said through the opening. "We've had enough trouble because of you. Get away from my house." He closed the door and Idella laid into the doorbell again.

"Idella. Please," Wesley said. "You need to get back in the car. He sounds like he's drunk."

"I am not leaving." Idella pushed the doorbell again. She could hear the tones ringing over and over and over in the house.

"Have you lost your mind?" Roger snatched the door open.

"No, I haven't. I want you to answer some questions. And if you don't, I'm going to ring this doorbell all night long."

"Roger, let her in," Rachel said. "Mother can't take this noise. Let her in, but you can be sure I'm going to call the police."

Roger opened the door. Idella and Wesley stepped inside.

"I'm sorry, Mr. Addison, for us barging in like this. I've met you under more pleasant circumstances, but Idella—"

She shut him up. "I don't need you to apologize for me, Wesley." Idella looked at Roger. "What I need is for you, Mr. Addison, to tell me where my grandmother is. I was told you picked her up in the middle of the night and she had a suitcase." Idella challenged, "You know where my grandmother is, and you better tell me or I'm going to the police."

"Don't you threaten me," Roger warned.

"What are you talking about?" Rachel held the telephone in her hand. "We don't have any idea where MaMary is. You've got some nerve coming here! You've done enough to ruin us as it is. From the things you said on Martha's Vineyard, the rumors have never stopped flying. You have club members that we've known for years wondering if we did something wrong to you and your grandmother." She slammed the phone down. "My mother is nearly an invalid because of your grandmother, and Patricia's seizures have come back under all this stress. That's how you have repaid our kindness."

"What's going on?" Patricia came down the stairs.

"Patricia, you don't need to be here, honey. You've had a bad day today." Rachel's gown floated as she met her daughter. "Go back to bed. Let us handle this."

"I want to know—where is MaMary?" Idella insisted.

"We don't know where MaMary is," Patricia retorted. "You've ruined everything with your lies. I mean everything. Now nobody wants to invite me anywhere and with these seizures, I'm not included in anything." Patricia trembled. "And it's all because of you. Grandmother Agnes said we should have never let you in this house. She said people like you and MaMary could never be helped. She was right."

Idella's teeth clenched. "Your grandmother is a self-centered, prejudiced old lady. She could barely accept her own granddaughter because she wasn't the right skin color. So don't you start idolizing her because she's old. She is no angel"—she drew a deep breath— "and it's obvious she wanted me out of the way."

Patricia's mouth opened, then closed as if she didn't know what to say.

"I was spoiling her plans to get you and Gerald together." Idella's eyes bored into Patricia's. "Miss Agnes didn't believe *you*, Patricia, her *own* granddaughter, could get the right man. In her mind, your skin was too dark."

"Don't you dare say that to me!" Patricia spat.

The guest bedroom door opened, slowly. Agnes, leaning on a cane, stepped into the room. "What's happening out here?" Her robe hung loosely on her too thin frame as she hobbled forward.

"Now, Mother, I know you don't need to be out here," Rachel reprimanded. "How did you manage to get out of bed?"

Agnes ignored her as she moved forward. She peered at Idella. "It's you." She looked Idella up and down. At first her face softened with recognition. "Jo . . ." His name melted into a scowl. "What are you doing back here? You get out of our house. Get out!" Her voice cracked.

Idella stepped back. "I'm not leaving until someone tells me where MaMary is."

Agnes drew her frail body up. "You half-white bas—"

Idella was shocked, but she refused to let Agnes say it. "If I leave here now, I'm going to report you to the police. Anything illegal that you have done, I'm going to make sure they find it. I'm going to put the authorities on all of you unless you tell me about my grandmother."

"Who do you think you are?" Agnes attempted to move closer to Idella, but nearly stumbled. "You can't help anybody do anything. Mary's granddaughter can't help anybody do anything because she's just a stupid—"

"Mother." Rachel tried to lead her back to her room. She looked at Wesley. "This is too much for her. She's taking a lot of medication and sometimes it has side effects."

Agnes pulled away. She looked at Roger. "This is your fault. If Patricia wasn't so dark, she would have been married before now. It's your fault Patricia can't find a decent husband."

Roger shook his head. "No matter what, you still blame me for everything that goes wrong. This is Roger's fault. Roger's the problem. But I told you I wasn't going to do it no more." He squinted at Agnes. "And I'm not."

"Roger, what are you talking about?" Rachel said.

"Your mother knows. She knows plenty, even though she seems to have selective memory." He paused. "She knows where Mary is and so do I."

Idella's eyes widened.

"What?" Rachel was obviously stunned.

"I know and your mother knows." Roger gave a drunken, satisfied smile. "She made all the arrangements."

Agnes gawked at him.

"I don't believe you," Rachel said. "You can't be telling the truth."

"I am telling the truth," Roger said. "I'm not going to lie anymore. There's been too much lying and deceit in this house and it's got to end. And that includes your telling Patricia who her real father is." Roger's eyes locked on Rachel's face.

"My real father?" Patricia said.

Roger's eyes turned soft. "Yes, your real father, baby. Maybe from that the doctors will be able to find out more and get you some real medical help."

"Mama?" Patricia turned to Rachel.

"Don't listen to these lies," Agnes said.

"Call me a liar if you want." Roger headed for the stairs. "But I'll be back with the admissions papers that prove what I've said about Mary is true."

Agnes's face turned ashen.

Idella looked at Wesley. Out of the corner of her eye, she saw Rachel sit on the marble floor. She began to cry.

"Mama?" Patricia knelt beside her. "What is Dad talking about?"

All eyes were on Roger as he descended the stairs. He walked up to Idella. "Here it is. She's in The Lilac Home near Clarksville. It's a private, residential institution. It would have been difficult if not impossible to find."

Idella took the paper. She saw MaMary's name at the top. She knew it was authentic, but suddenly, the reality of it all was too much. None of it made sense. She looked at Roger with her eyes full of tears. "But why? Why?"

Roger looked at Agnes. "I would have never known if it wasn't for a letter Mother Agnes had me hand deliver to a Joseph Wyndham. She told me not to read it"—his jaw went hard—"but only hell would have kept me from doing that."

Idella was stunned. "Joseph Wyndham, my grandfather?"

Roger nodded. "Mother Agnes had been blackmailing him for years. I gave Mr. Wyndham a copy of an old letter written by Mother Agnes when she was young. She wrote him because she thought he was going to marry her. In the letter she confronted him about deceiving her. You see, he was already married. And do you know how he answered her?"

Agnes covered her ears. "I don't want to hear it. I don't want to hear it."

But Roger continued. "He scrawled his message on her letter. It seems she had been passing for white and he'd found out the truth. He called her a nigger and said she would never be his wife."

Agnes's face crumpled. "I told you I didn't want to hear that." Her words caught in her throat as she began to cry.

Roger's red eyes stared into space. "There was a note with the letter. It indicated Wyndham must have said if he wanted a black woman he would prefer your grandmother to Mother Agnes." He shook his head. "And she just couldn't take that. Even after all these years, she's fixated on your grandmother." Roger looked at Idella. "And it appears the way Mr. Wyndham's family dealt with your birth was what Mother Agnes needed to punish him further." He looked at Agnes. "Yes, you felt there was an old bone to pick with Mary over some white man who preferred her to you."

Agnes's knees buckled.

"Mother." Rachel went to her aid.

"Your grandmother never gave Mother Agnes too much medication, Idella," Roger said. "She took it so she could blame her."

Idella's gaze fell on Agnes. "All this because you felt you were better than MaMary. Because you didn't want to be considered the same."

Agnes inhaled a loud sob, then immediately clutched at her chest.

"Mother!" Rachel tried to hold her up, but she slumped in her arms.

"Oh my God!" Patricia screamed.

Roger stood and watched as if he were in a drunken haze.

Rachel put her hand on her mother's chest, then frantically checked her pulse. She looked up with fear. "I think she had a heart attack." Slowly, she looked down at her mother. "Oh no, Mother. Oh no."

Idella just stood there, trying to accept the ugly human drama that had unfolded.

"Somebody needs to call an ambulance," Wesley said. He walked toward the telephone.

"No." Tears filled Roger's eyes. "I want you two to leave. Now. This is my family. What happened here is our concern."

Wesley nodded. He retraced his steps and took Idella by the hand. He guided her toward the door, but Idella's eyes remained on Agnes. "I think she's dead," she said softly.

"You think so?" Wesley closed the door behind them. "There was enough going on in there to give me a heart attack. Damn, Idella."

They walked toward the car.

"Wesley!" Idella stopped abruptly. "I found MaMary." She looked in his eyes. "I found her."

"I'm glad for you, Idella. I really am." He continued to walk before he looked back to where she stood. "But don't you ever bring me into something like this again. Blackmail and having people wrongly committed to mental institutions. That woman died right in front of us. I've got a political future to look after and I don't need this kind of thing."

"This could never happen again, Wesley." Idella wouldn't let his attitude dampen her spirits. Her mind was on MaMary. "We'll get a hotel room tonight and tomorrow we'll go get her."

"I'm not staying in a hotel," Wesley said. "I've got to get back to Nashville tonight. I've got court cases tomorrow that I can't miss."

They got in the car.

"We are going back to Nashville tonight, Idella. This has been a long journey for you. A day or two more won't make that big of a difference." He drove off as a siren sounded in the distance.

Kindling Emotions

Idella got out of Wesley's car. She walked up to her door, unlocked it and went inside. There was a nervous energy inside of her. Much of it was due to the concrete information about MaMary. The remainder was her dissatisfaction with Wesley. Idella's euphoria wore off as they drove in silence. Her mind kept replaying Wesley's conclusion that a day or two made no difference in going to get MaMary. It stuck deep in Idella's craw. Wesley seemed more concerned about appearances: how they looked in front of the Addisons, what people would say about his involvement, rather than the fact that the Addisons had been a key part of MaMary's disappearance. Finally, in the car, Idella told him how she felt about it and the outcome wasn't very pretty.

Through a window, she watched the light come on in Brandon's kitchen. Idella could see his outline move past the curtains. She continued to watch as that light went off and another came on in his living room at the front of the house. The Saturday morning coffee meetings were a regular occurrence now. Idella and Brandon had become friends and they talked about many things. She felt Brandon was a good man. She even met his mother one Friday afternoon when she brought Brandon spaghetti and fried fish.

Idella walked from the front of her house to the back and to the front again. So much had happened in Memphis and Idella yearned to talk about it. After a moment's hesitation, she picked up her keys and headed out the front door. Idella ran across their damp front yards and rang Brandon's doorbell. She regretted it when Brandon opened the door wearing only his sweatpants. Suddenly, it hit her. It was very late. Perhaps Brandon had company, although as far as she knew there was still no girlfriend in his life. But Idella also knew a man not having a girlfriend never cancelled out late-night calls. "I shouldn't have done this. I'm sorry, Brandon." She concentrated on his face. "If you've got company or something I can just—"

"Oh no. I don't have company. Come on in." He opened the door.

"Are you sure?" Her gaze ran over his chest.

"Yes," Brandon replied.

"I just needed to talk to somebody," Idella continued to explain. "I'm so excited."

"Come on in, Idella." Brandon stepped back. "Come on."

She eased past him into the living room.

He closed the door. "Do you want something to drink?"

"Like what?" Idella replied.

"Coke. Water. Wine. I've got some white wine. I don't know if you like white wine."

"It doesn't matter. I'll take a glass of wine. Whatever you have."

"Sit down and relax." His eyes were comforting. "I'll be right back."

Brandon returned wearing a shirt. He had a glass of wine in his hand. He gave it to Idella, then sat down in a stuffed chair far away. "What's going on?"

"I found my grandmother."

His smile was instant. "You did? Wonderful."

Idella scooted to the edge of her seat. "At least, I think I have." She took a sip of wine. "I'm so excited I don't know what to do."

"You should be excited," Brandon replied. "You've been looking for her for a long time. I'm glad for you, Idella."

She sat back. "Still, I don't want to put the cart before the horse."

"Now that's true." Brandon nodded. "You don't want to get too excited until you absolutely know that you've found her."

Idella stood and walked across the room. "I never told you exactly what happened with my grandmother. It almost sounds too bizarre to tell somebody, especially when you first meet them."

"Okay." Brandon leaned on the chair arm. "So are you ready to tell me now? Is that what you're saying?"

"I think so," Idella replied. She took another sip of wine and sat down again. "Basically, it went like this. When I was still living in Memphis almost a year and a half ago, I got involved with a family of wealthy black people. Their last name is Addison. I helped their daughter and as a result of that MaMary, my grandmother, started working for them in their house. Things seemed to be going fine. Patricia, the daughter, and I became friends. And what could have been a good friendship and a nice job for MaMary turned into something crazy." Idella paused. "A young man that Patricia's grandmother was particularly interested in her having a relationship with ended up being interested in me. Because, with those kind of people, I've come to know they are into matching each other up within their group."

"What are you talking about?" Brandon said. "What are you talking about, 'group'?"

"Well, it's like the black elite, the black upper class."

"Folks like your boyfriend, Wesley."

Idella looked down at her glass. "Yes, people like Wesley, who come from generations of money. They tend to know each other and they go to the same places. Their children go to Tots and Teens, Jack and Jill."

"Wow. I never heard of any of these things."

"Lots of people haven't, but it's a whole world out there that they've been able to create because of their money and their status. And the truth is," Idella sought to explain, "I've come to know the intention wasn't bad, but it ended up being an environment that separates us. They work together to benefit themselves, but it's a kind of segregation because it keeps people out who they don't want in." She drew a deep breath. "Anyway, I got involved with the guy and the next thing I knew I lost my job. I was working for a company that was owned by that family, the Addisons. And MaMary lost her job at the house because she made a mistake." Idella shook her head and looked down. "But even that isn't true. Although I'm sure MaMary believes it till this day." She looked at Brandon. "It was all a setup, Brandon. A strange, crazy setup to get me, I believe, out of the way."

"What do you mean"—he leaned forward—"get you out of the way?"

"I mean totally move me out. We both lost our jobs. We were behind in our bills. And in order for us to survive, I went to work as a maid on Martha's Vineyard because I believed we didn't have any choice."

"Who sent you there?"

"Miss Agnes did. Patricia's grandmother."

"The grandmother who was trying to make this relationship."

"Yes."

"And so she sent you to work like an indentured servant for some white people?"

"No. The people I worked for were black. All these people were black. And in the house where I worked I was the second maid. There was a butler. There was a gardener."

"I've never heard of such."

"Well, I'm telling you I lived it." Idella's gaze bore into him. "I know. Anyway, so while I was away, Miss Agnes basically told the people I worked for that MaMary, my grandmother, was dead."

"Oh no, Idella." Brandon came and sat on the couch beside her. "That's horrible. That's crazy."

"It was so horrible. It was so horrible for me, Brandon. You can't imagine. It was like reality shifted to a gray place. I couldn't talk. I didn't care what I looked like. And the only thing I had that kept me going was what MaMary taught me, the beading."

"The purses that you've turned into a business."

"Yes. That's what kept me going. My grandmother taught me how to do that." She shut her eyes. "And because I believed, with my grandmother dead, I couldn't go back to Memphis, I didn't have any place to go."

"Whoa-a, this is deep," Brandon said.

"Yeah, but then it gets even deeper. That family, the Addisons, came to Martha's Vineyard, and there I am in a maid's uniform serving people and I see them. The anger that roared up inside of me could have burned that entire place down. I was so angry because they said they were going to look after my grandmother and that was so far from the truth. And in my mind I'm thinking they didn't even tell me she was dead. So when I told them that in front of all those people, how I felt, they ended up saying that my grandmother wasn't dead. That MaMary was not dead. That she was in a mental institution. In other words, she was crazy and here I am screaming loud and looking like a crazy woman myself."

Brandon sat back.

Idella made a sound that could have been laughter or crying. "Because of that I lost my job at that house." She paused. "But there was a very kind woman. Her name is Denise Hill and she lives here in Nashville, who was vacationing there. She took me in. Her daughter died about a year ago and I could tell she was pouring on me the love she wished she could give her. And that's how I met Wesley. She's his aunt."

"I see," Brandon said.

"So, since that happened, I've been in Nashville. It's been a little bit over a year that I've been trying to find MaMary. And it just so happens when I was in Memphis earlier today at a show selling some of my purses, somebody who I knew saw my grandmother get in a car with Mr. Addison. She had a suitcase with her."

"No," Brandon replied with disbelief.

"Yes. Yes." Idella got excited again. "Wesley was with me and I demanded that he take me to the Addisons' house. I didn't care how late it was. And when I got there, Mr. Addison finally told the truth. That he and Miss Agnes knew where MaMary was. Although I could tell neither Rachel nor Patricia knew. And my God, Miss Agnes!" Idella shook her head. "What happened." Idella paused. "I knew she had been sick for a while, but when I saw her she looked so bad. And the things that came out of her mouth. The prejudiced things. Miss Rachel blamed it on the medication, but what came out of her was what she believed."

"She was a piece of work, huh?"

"Yes, she was." Idella nodded. "And she got so upset when Mr. Addison started telling the truth about things." Idella looked as if she could see it all again. "She got so upset that it looked like she had a heart attack!"

"No way." Brandon's eyes widened.

"Yes," Idella replied.

"Did the paramedics come?"

"Mr. Addison made us leave so I don't know."

"Wow." Brandon sat back again.

"But before that happened, he gave me a piece of paper." Idella had it in her hand. "I told Wesley when we got outside that we had to go get MaMary. But he seemed more upset with me because of how I acted in front of everybody. You know"—she looked at Brandon—"he is obsessed with his reputation and how things look. He wasn't concerned at all about what they'd done to me or that I wanted to be with my grandmother. I wanted to go get her in the morning. She's right there in Clarksville, Tennessee. But he refused. And told me, basically, I had waited that long to see her, I could wait another day or so."

Brandon just looked at her.

"A few minutes ago he dropped me off in front of the house. I saw your light on and I just came over."

"I'm glad you did."

"I'm going to get her tomorrow, Brandon," Idella said with determination. "I am not waiting on Wesley."

"Do you want me to go with you? I don't mind driving."

Idella looked deep into his eyes. "Do you want to?"

"Hey, at a time like this you need somebody with you. This is some heavy-duty stuff, Idella."

"It is." She nodded, then said, "I'd love for you to go with me."

"Well, I'll go then."

They studied each other.

Finally, Brandon said, "So exactly where is she?"

Idella looked at the paper. "It's called The Lilac Home and it's outside of Clarksville."

"We'll find it," Brandon said. "We'll go first thing in the morning and get your grandmother."

"Thank you." Idella put her arms around his neck and hugged him. He held her for a while as Idella released unshed tears.

"I always believed that I'd see this day, but I wasn't sure I'd make it," Idella said softly. "I'm going to get MaMary. I'm finally going to get her."

Love . . . Life Force

Idella finished her beading in the wee hours of the morning, then slept for a few hours more. When Brandon knocked on her door, she was more than ready to go. He kept a light conversation going the entire hour it took to reach Clarksville. There, they asked for directions, and in short order they arrived at the driveway of The Lilac Home.

Idella looked at the old, isolated plantation-style house. There was an air of emptiness about it, although the landscape looked well kept. Slowly, a funny feeling moved in the pit of her stomach. She looked at Brandon.

"Are you ready?"

"I'm ready." Idella made herself open the car door.

They walked up the walkway together. Idella took control of her nerves by the time she opened the front door. A bell rang over the door as they stepped inside what used to be a foyer, but now served as a reception area. A woman in an extremely starched gray dress entered the room from a side entrance.

"Hello. May I help you?"

"Yes, you can," Idella said. "My name is Idella Baxter and I've come to get my grandmother. Her name is Mary Baxter. I understand she is a patient in this institution."

"You *understand* she is a patient in this institution," the woman said.

"Yes. I was told that she was," Idella replied.

"I see." Her hand circled the base of her neck. "So you didn't have anything to do with her coming here."

"I did not. But I am her next of kin and I am in a position to take good care of her. And that's what I plan to do."

"Well, we'll have to see what her records say."

"Ma'am." Idella's heart beat faster. "To be honest with you, I don't care what her records say." Brandon touched her arm. "Here is the paper that was signed when she was put in here." Idella offered the paper Roger Addison had given her. "And what I want you to do is look in your records and tell me that she is here. From there, I will be taking her home."

"Ma'am, there's no need for you to start off with an attitude."

"And I don't want to," Idella said. "That is not my intention. So please, can you just confirm for me that my grandmother"—Idella pushed the paper toward her—"is in this institution."

The woman picked up the paper and looked at it. "Yes, this is one of our forms." She hesitated, then said, "Let me see."

She opened a file cabinet, thumbed through it and pulled out a somewhat new-looking manila folder. "Yes, I can tell that Mary Baxter has been here for little over a year now."

Tears, like water from a tap, ran down Idella's face. She wiped them away. "Is she all right? Can I see her?"

"Well, ma'am, just because you say that you are her relative"— the woman looked uncomfortable—"I don't know if I've got the right person. The woman we have here is black."

"I know what color my grandmother is," Idella replied. "What I need to know is, can I take her home?"

The woman cleared her throat. "First of all, we'll need proof that you are who you say you are. Then—"

"Here are all the records I could get. I know they're only school records, but you can see they were signed by my grandmother. The rest got thrown away and I never had an official birth record."

The employee shook her head. "To be honest with you, school records aren't going to be sufficient for you to take someone out of this institution."

Idella closed her eyes.

"She's told you she doesn't have anything else," Brandon jumped in. "What should she do? I can't imagine that strangers come to mental institutions and out of the clear blue decide they want to take one of your patients off of your hands for no reason."

"Believe me, sir, I am more of an expert about imagination than you can ever be," she replied.

"You're going to do something." Idella's voice cut the air. "My grandmother was put in here after Mr. Joseph Wyndham asked that she be admitted."

The woman looked surprised.

"Yes, Mr. Wyndham, who is my grandfather." Idella paused dramatically. "Now, if I have to come back to this place with a story that involves Mr. Wyndham that I am quite certain he doesn't want the public to know"—Idella's gaze cut into her—"seeing that he's an important man around here and his family's reputation means a lot, you and everybody else who was involved in this are going to wish you had allowed me to take her away quietly."

The woman looked down at the file again. She rummaged through it and picked up what appeared to be a letter. After she read it, she looked as if she were attempting to make up her mind.

"If you want everybody to know that Mr. Wyndham has a secret, half-black granddaughter, then you stand in the way of me taking my grandmother home," Idella threatened.

The woman stuck the letter back in the file. "Wait right here. I'll go get her."

Idella took hold of Brandon's hand. She squeezed it before she walked over to the window, then back to the middle of the office and back to the window again. It took about ten minutes for the woman to return. She walked through the door and MaMary, thinner than she'd ever been, walked behind her.

When MaMary saw Idella, a light appeared in her eyes that lit her entire face. "Dee."

"MaMary." Idella ran to her grandmother and wrapped her

small body in her arms. "I'm so glad I found you." Idella continued to hold her. "So glad." They stood like that for a moment before Idella backed away. "How are you?"

"I'm doing fine now, baby. Just fine," MaMary replied.

"Did they treat you okay?" Idella was afraid to ask.

MaMary looked down. "Life coulda been better." She touched Idella's face. "I had a dream one night, and from that I knew as long as I was strong that you'd be able to be strong. And that one day I'd see you again. That gave me the strength to hold on, Idella. Knowing I'd see you again gave me the strength I needed."

They hugged and cried while Brandon and the employee watched in silence.

MaMary finally pulled away and wiped Idella's face with her hand.

"I want to show you something," Idella said. She reached inside her purse and took out a beaded bag. "This is for you, MaMary."

MaMary's face was a mirror of surprise. "For me?"

Idella nodded.

Gently, MaMary took the purse from Idella's hands. With focused intent, she examined the colors and the pattern. It was a white bird with its neck and head bent backwards so that its beak touched the top of its back. "Sankofa," MaMary said softly.

"Never forget where you come from," Idella said. "I never forgot, MaMary. What you taught me never allowed me to forget. It was my strength at a time when I needed it most."

Tears streamed from MaMary's eyes as she stroked the pattern. "Learn from the past," she said softly. "Never forget."

Idella touched her hand. "Are you ready to go home now?"

"Home?" A rather blank look entered her eyes.

Fear touched Idella's heart. "Yes, home. Yours and mine." She settled MaMary's purse on her shoulder.

Light entered MaMary's eyes again. "Home."

"Yes." Idella smiled.

Spiritual Purity

That evening, Idella watched MaMary as she napped in the easy chair. Even when the front doorbell rang MaMary didn't budge. Quietly, Idella answered it. Wesley greeted her with a peck on her lips.

"Hey, baby." He stepped inside. "Today was such a busy day. I had several cases, and I tell you, some of these people." He shook his head. "But I think I was able to get one man off scot-free. We shall see what the judge decides." He kissed her again. "I'm sorry I wasn't very pleasant last night. I was tired and so were you. Do you want to go pick up your grandmother tomorrow?"

"MaMary is already here," Idella replied.

"Oh." Wesley looked surprised. "She is?"

"Um-hmm. I've got to call Denise and tell her."

"Wow." His eyebrow went up. "Well, can I meet her?"

Idella started toward the den. "She was looking at television a few minutes ago. Then she dozed off. But come on back." They walked to the back room. MaMary's head hung to the side as she slept in a large chair.

Idella smiled. "She's still sleep." She turned to Wesley.

"Yeah." He looked MaMary over and turned away. "Yeah, she is. So let's not bother her."

They returned to the living room.

"Well, I'm so proud of you," Wesley remarked. "You went to get her on your own."

Idella tried not to make a face. "She was only an hour away, and I've driven further than that by myself before I met you."

"I know. But I'm still proud that you would go do that alone." He touched her hair. "No matter what you might think, I wanted to be with you."

"Actually"—Idella looked at him—"I didn't go alone."

"You didn't?" Wesley's brows lowered.

"No. Brandon offered to go with me."

"Brandon who? That man next door?"

"Yes," Idella replied.

"What were you doing letting that nigger take you out there?" Wesley's anger exploded.

"What?" Idella said.

"You heard me."

Idella crossed her arms. "What makes him a 'nigger' and you not one?" she challenged.

"All you gotta do is look at him."

"Oh, I see." Idella's eyes narrowed.

"And he barely made it out of high school. You can tell he don't have no money."

"He's doing all right to me," Idella replied. "I think he and I are probably about the same."

"See," Wesley pointed out, "this is the type of thing, Idella, you cannot do. You can't just pop up and do things like this. I've got a reputation to protect, and what you do and say as my woman reflects heavily on me."

Idella looked at him. "Exactly what did I do, Wesley?"

"You have to be careful about who you associate with, where you go. My life has been a class act and I intend for that to continue." His brown eyes narrowed. "And that's something that you're going to have to start realizing."

"You're right, Wesley." Idella shook her head. "A class act. And I don't mean a person who knows how to conduct themselves. But class, meaning you dividing everybody up into compartments. Who's right and who's wrong. Who's a nigger and who's not." She counted off on her fingers. "I tell you what, if you can stand here in my house and call Brandon a nigger just because of what he looks like, because of the color of his skin, because you don't know anything else about him, what did you think when you saw my grandmother?"

Wesley looked down, then up at Idella.

"Don't answer it, Wesley. Don't answer it." She showed him her palm. "Your aunt warned me against you. I should have listened. But it's never too late. So I think you just need to get out of my house. Because I don't need anybody like you in my life."

"Are you breaking up with me?" He couldn't believe it.

Idella couldn't believe him. "Yes, that's exactly what I'm doing."

"I see." Wesley walked over to the door. "You just made one of the biggest mistakes you are ever going to make in your life."

"Let me be the judge of that." Idella opened the door.

Wesley walked out the door and Idella shut it behind him. She returned to the den and lowered the volume on the television. From time to time, she looked at the screen, but the majority of the time she watched her grandmother's sleeping face.

Later, MaMary opened her eyes.

"You needed that, didn't you?" Idella said.

MaMary smiled. "I sure did."

"Are you hungry?"

MaMary shook her head. "Although I took that nap, I still feel tired."

"Why don't you go and lay down on your bed? It's got to be more comfortable than that chair."

"Are you going to be all right in here by yourself?" MaMary asked.

"Yes, MaMary." Idella smiled. "Don't mind me. You get all the rest you need."

"Hearing the truth about things has worn me out." MaMary got up. "My goodness, Miss Agnes carried some vengeance in her heart for a long time. It's a wonder that it didn't kill her earlier than it did. But I have to say, even though what she did was horrible, she and I were more alike than she ever realized." She kissed Idella's cheek. "Miss Agnes loved her granddaughter and wanted what was best for her future. Just as I love you, and I thought I was doing what was best for yours."

Idella sighed. "How will we ever forget this?"

"I believe harsh feelings like these become less with time," MaMary said. "God doesn't send you through these types of changes without you benefiting some kind of way. Look at you." MaMary smiled. "You've grown into a beautiful, confident young woman with a life"—MaMary looked at the room—"that is worthy of you. I don't know if you coulda made such change so fast without there being some major upheaval in your life."

"I probably wouldn't have," Idella said.

She heard Brandon's sliding-glass door open. Idella watched him walk out on his deck, remove something from a table, then go back inside. "You're right, MaMary. And now I owe it to myself and to you not to be bitter about it."

MaMary patted her hand and left the den.

Later that night, Idella heard a noise. It woke her out of her sleep. "MaMary? Is that you?"

"It's me. I bumped into the chair here in my room. I got to get used to the house, that's all."

Idella got up and went to MaMary's room. She switched on the night light. "You didn't hurt yourself, did you?"

"No." MaMary looked at her. "I had a dream that woke me up. So I went to get some water."

"What kind of dream?" Idella sat on MaMary's bed.

MaMary seemed to collect her thoughts. "I was in the institution and a bunch of us women, all colors, were in a circle holding hands and we were all shouting, 'I want to go home. I want to go home.' "

Idella touched MaMary's hand.

"But we stood there all together doing it," MaMary continued. "The differences didn't matter."

"What do you think it means?"

"I think it means we got to learn to join together to make things work. The ancestors said we've got to if we're going to survive."

"MaMary"—Idella pressed her hands, which were in a prayer position, against her lips—"why does it seem like the darkest people are at the bottom everywhere you go?"

MaMary thought a moment. "My mama said the ancestors said everybody came from the same seed." She spoke into the near darkness. "But that people like the ancestors focused on the spiritual laws. They wouldn't go against them, no matter what, while others focused on the physical." MaMary paused. "This is the physical world; what people call progress grew out of that. But in the end, Idella, all things go back to the spiritual. That's why there's got to be a balance."

"Do you think there ever will be?" Idella asked.

MaMary didn't answer.

"MaMary?" Idella touched her grandmother's arm.

MaMary looked around. "Where am I?"

"You're home, MaMary." Idella's voice shook. "You're home." And she held MaMary's hand.

African tribal beading is considered to be a craft by some and an art by others, but it is also a means of communicating for those who understand the symbology. It is a symbology that involves geometric patterns, symbols specific to the tribes, and color codes with positive and negative aspects. These beautiful silent messages express feelings, ideas and facts.

To reflect the chapter content, liberties have been taken and materials included.

Unexpected
Bead Color: Black   Material: Clay

Request
Bead Color: Blue   Material: Seed

Possibilities
Bead Color: Pink   Material: Glass

The Decision
Bead Color: Brown   Material: Clay

High Status
Bead Color: Pink   Material: Glass

Endings & Beginnings
Bead Colors: Black & Green   Material: Seeds
Heartache
Bead Color: Red   Material: Bone
Contentment
Bead Color: Green   Material: Glass
Suspicion
Bead Color: Yellow   Material: Shell
Discovery
Bead Color: Yellow   Material: Nutshell
Attraction
Bead Color: Bright Red   Material: Glass
Hostility
Bead Color: Blue   Material: Iron
Withering
Bead Color: Yellow   Material: Wood
Blame
Bead Color: Green   Material: Clay
Sadness
Bead Color: Black   Material: Charcoal
Ill Will
Bead Color: Dark Green   Material: Seed
Deceit
Bead Color: Yellow   Material: Shell
Discovery
Bead Color: Blue   Material: Clay
Jealousy
Bead Color: Yellow   Material: Seed
Confusion
Bead Color: Red   Material: Copper
Fear
Bead Color: Red   Material: Glass
Sadness
Bead Color: Black   Material: Clay
Feminine Power
Bead Color: White   Material: Cowrie Shell

Anger
Bead Color: Red   Material: Brass
Distrust
Bead Color: Green   Material: Nutshell
The Path of the Ancestors Is Difficult to Follow
Bead Colors: Black & White   Material: Clay   Pattern: Diagonal
Confrontation
Bead Color: Green   Material: Wood
Worldly Goods
Bead Color: Yellow   Material: Glass
Thirst
Bead Color: Yellow   Material: Clay
Breakthrough
Bead Color: Green   Material: Glass
Retribution
Bead Color: Brown   Material: Wood
Kindling Emotions
Bead Color: Pink   Material: Shell
Love . . . Life Force
Bead Color: Red   Material: Seed
Spiritual Purity
Bead Color: White   Material: Bone

SOMETHING DEEP IN MY BONES

Eboni Snoe

ABOUT THIS GUIDE

The suggested questions are intended to enhance your
group's reading of Eboni Snoe's
SOMETHING DEEP IN MY BONES.

DISCUSSION QUESTIONS

1. At the beginning of the novel Idella admonishes one of her co-workers at Addison Catering and Restaurant for being late. The co-worker retaliates with a comment about her skin color. Why do people attack others based on physical appearances? Is it out of their own hidden pain? Out of fear?

2. Idella is amazed at how the wealthy Addisons live. What are some of the problems, real and perceived, a person might face when they quickly go from financial struggle to financial abundance?

3. MaMary is having problems with her memory. How difficult is it to face our loved ones' mental challenges? What about our own?

4. Idella is certain of her "blackness" although she is a child of mixed parentage. Should a child be forced to choose one race when her parents are of two different races?

5. Grandmother Agnes is very "color conscious" and sees her fair skin as an asset. Does that mindset still exist today?

6. Despite their financial condition, MaMary feels the love she shares with Idella is more important than money. Explore real life examples or the lack thereof.

7. The haves and the have-nots are very present in *Something Deep in My Bones.* Can a person who has known wealth all her life, or vice versa, truly understand the mindset of a poor/wealthy person?

8. Grandmother Agnes nearly killed herself setting a trap for MaMary. What was the strongest catalyst for her need for revenge? Jealousy? Prejudice? Etc.?

9. Both Patricia and Rachel seem to pale in Grandmother Agnes's strong matriarchal light. Can a very strong female in the family be a detriment for younger females blossoming in their own right?

10. Are groups who reject others based on looks, finances, etc., exhibiting a form of prejudice, as Idella concluded about the black elite? Or are they protecting their right to define themselves?

11. The African tribal beading taught to Idella by MaMary was her lifeline. Is there strength in connecting to your ancestors' tribal/ancient ways?

12. MaMary considered her dreams to be very meaningful. Can dreams hold messages?

13. Why are people like MaMary, who possess tribal/indigenous wisdom, not valued by the mainstream?

14. At the end of the novel Idella asks MaMary, "Why does it seem
    like the darkest people are at the bottom everywhere you go?"
    Discuss the question and the answer.

35674039890232